Books by

Criss Cross
Winter Memorial
Cross Fire
Crossed Off

INJUSTICE FOR ALL

A Seeking Justice Novel

C.C. Warrens

Injustice for All is the first book in the Seeking Justice series. This series ties in with the Holly Novels. To see where it all began, check out *Criss Cross: A Holly Novel*.

Prologue

He slid down the wall to the floor and stared at his bloody hands, horrified by what he had done. There hadn't been any other way, and he knew that, but the terrified look in the man's eyes was an image he would never be able to purge from his mind.

He swiped at his face with the sleeve of his shirt and let out a heavy breath.

The doctor had paved his own path, and he had only done what needed to be done. He grabbed the spiral notebook from the desk beside him and drew a line through the man's name.

He tossed the notebook and pen aside and fished his phone from his jacket. He clicked on the first contact and waited as the call rolled over to voice mail.

"Hey, looks like you just missed me. I'm probably doing something super important, but if I like you, I promise I'll get back to you!"

The sound of her sweet voice made his heart ache, and he wished he could see her face-to-face. He ended the call and whispered, "I really need to talk to you."

He called the number again and the call went straight to voice mail. "Hey, looks like you just missed me . . ."

He closed his eyes against a surge of tears and let the voice mail play out, wishing she would pick up the phone and tell him it was all just a terrible dream.

1

*I*t was like staring at an insect display—pinned in place with arms and legs outstretched and labeled for all to examine—only this *display* featured a man pinned in place by scalpels that had been driven through his hands into the tile of his kitchen floor.

Detective Richard Marx crouched alongside the body with a thoughtful expression. In his twenty-six years as a cop with the NYPD, he'd seen more than his fair share of gunshots and stabbings, but this made the short list of *unusual* murders.

His victim was a man in his late thirties, with russet features that placed his ancestry somewhere in the Middle East.

The pattern of previous cases tempted him to consider this a hate crime, but there was nothing to indicate that the victim had been a believer in Islam. And the handwritten note pinned to his chest with a scalpel didn't have the tone of racial or religious bigotry. It was a simple statement:

I should have tried harder.

Marx turned the message over in his mind, but there were too many possible meanings, and without more information to serve as a guiding light into the depraved mind of the killer, he was wasting his time.

The note was written as an *I* statement, not a farewell to loved ones or even an apology, but a vague declaration of the man's shortcomings—something he had failed to do.

It wasn't meant to be confused with a suicide note.

The question was, why leave a note at all? Was it simply a thrill for the killer, an exercise in humility for the victim, or was it a message for the first responders?

The story was hidden in the details, and he just had to piece it together. There was nothing remarkable about the gunshot that ended the victim's life; the important details were the body position, the letter, and the scalpels.

"Holland!"

A young woman shoved past the officer posted by the open doorway and launched into the condo. The officer snatched her out of motion before she made it more than three steps inside.

"Easy," Marx told the officer who had the young woman locked in his grip. As he approached, he caught the shimmer of grief in her eyes. "Let her go."

The officer released her, and she melted to the floor with a cry that resonated with disbelief and pain. She stared at the body, her shoulders trembling with each ragged sob.

Marx crouched between her and the body. No one should ever have to see the mutilated remains of someone they cared about.

The thought sent his mind whirling back in time to Holly lying on a cement floor, bruised and dying. The memory, so vivid in its horror, gripped his heart and squeezed. He pulled his mind from the past and focused his attention on the woman in front of him.

"What's your name?" The Southern lilt of his voice—a leftover from his childhood in Georgia—seemed to soothe her.

On a quivering breath, she answered, "Sarah. I'm . . . I'm Holland's housekeeper. I've worked for him for years."

"So you knew him well."

She nodded and wiped at her damp nose with the sleeve of her shirt. "I called to tell him I would be late tonight, but he didn't answer."

"What time was that?"

"I don't know. Six thirty, maybe. I usually come at eleven to clean, just after he leaves for work, but I have finals tomorrow and I needed to study."

"You're a college student?"

Another nod, this one more subdued as she began to settle. "I'm getting a master's degree in social work."

Marx had dealt with a few social workers before. They were overworked and underpaid, and yet they pushed forward to help children who couldn't help themselves.

"I know you're upset right now," he said. "but this officer is gonna take you outside and get some information from you, okay?"

"Okay."

"All right." He stood and offered her a hand to her feet.

She glanced back at Holland's body one last time before letting the officer escort her out.

"There's something off about this scene," the officer still standing by the body said, his black eyebrows pinched in thought.

Marx looked over at Sam Barrera, the Latino officer who had spoken. Sam was the human equivalent of a brick wall, or so Holly had described him once. He was as broad and solid as a wall, and his face was as immovable and uncrackable as stone.

"You mean aside from the fact that somebody used Dr. Wilder here as a human corkboard?" Marx asked.

Sam's voice was as impassive as his face. "Yes, aside from that."

"Personally, if I feel the need to leave a note, I find Post-it notes to be a lot less messy," a woman said, and they both turned to see a woman in dress slacks and a button-up sapphire blouse striding through the front door of the condo.

She looked like the kind of woman who should be sashaying down a runway in three-inch heels, not wading through a crime scene in blue rubber booties.

"Of course I don't usually stick Post-it notes on dead people," she added after a thoughtful pause. "Just toe tags."

"Mornin', Ella," Marx greeted.

Ella Foster was the assistant medical examiner for the county, and she smiled warmly as she approached. "In my opinion, it's not morning until the sun comes up, Detective."

She brushed her long blond braid back over her shoulder, letting it trail between her shoulder blades, and snapped on a pair of gloves.

"He looks familiar."

"He's a general surgeon at New York City Hospital. Dr. Holland Wilder," Sam explained.

Ella's pale eyebrows knitted together briefly as she peeled open an eyelid to stare into milky brown irises. "I think I met him at a medical conference last year. He offered to buy me dinner."

"You remember anythin' about him?" Marx asked.

"He was extremely flirtatious and pretentious. Very unlikable."

It was no surprise to hear that the man had been pretentious. It was reflected in everything he owned—from the leather furniture to the highest quality electronics.

Marx's mind lingered on that last thought as he looked at the television and stereo system. The killer hadn't been interested in material things.

"Cause of death appears to be a bullet wound in the forehead," Ella said, drawing Marx's attention back.

"I figured that much out for myself," he replied with a small smile.

"I figured you figured that out, Detective. If you hadn't, I would be concerned about your acuity."

Marx's brow furrowed in confusion. "Concerned about my what?"

"Your mental sharpness," she clarified, pulling a meat thermometer from her bag.

The coffee in Marx's stomach rolled over in nauseating waves, and he looked away. He had used a meat thermometer just last night to make sure the dinner roast was thoroughly cooked. Seeing one shoved into a human body like it was nothing more than a Thanksgiving turkey was revolting.

"Who reported the body?"

"One of the couples a few condos down." Sam glanced at his notes. "Sue and Jay. They were out walking their dog when they noticed the door was open. They know that Sarah, the housekeeper, comes by a few nights a week, and they were concerned that something might be wrong."

"Nice neighbors," Marx said. "If I died in my apartment, my neighbor lady would probably pitch a fit that I was rude enough to smell up the second floor with my rottin' corpse, then she'd request to have me evicted."

Ella withdrew the thermometer and wiped it clean. "I would estimate that he's been dead between six and eight hours."

"So he was killed somewhere between four and six yesterday evening," Sam said.

"That explains why he didn't answer when the housekeeper called at six thirty. He was already dead." His eyes swept the living area again. "If the front door was open, it's safe to assume the killer exited through the front."

"Bold."

"Where did he come in?"

"There's an open window in the bedroom, but I'm not sure if it was forced open or left open." Sam nodded in the direction of the bedroom before starting down the hall.

Marx followed him into the large room peppered with mahogany furniture and decorated with neutral colors.

Sam pointed to the window being dusted by a crime scene tech. "There doesn't appear to be any tampering with the lock to suggest it was forced open."

Marx approached the window to peer out. It was on the back side of the condo, facing a grove of bushes that obscured the parking lot, which would make it a relatively covert entry point.

"Even if Dr. Wilder decided he wanted fresh air, there's a chance the killer used it as an entry point. Walkin' out the front door afterward is a lot less suspicious than breakin' in through it," Marx said.

His attention traveled to the en suite bathroom. The small space boasted a walk-in shower, a floating sink, and expensively tiled walls that made *his* apartment bathroom look like an outhouse. "Apparently I need to update my bathroom."

"Do you really spend that much time in there?"

"No, but Holly does."

Holly was the young woman staying in Marx's guest room, and she had a nearly compulsive need to feel clean. Unfortunately, no matter how many times she showered, she couldn't scrub away the memories that made her feel dirty.

"How's she doing?" Sam asked.

Marx considered how much he wanted to share—how much Holly would be comfortable with him sharing. It had been less than two months since her foster brother ripped apart her life, and she was fighting her way through the aftermath.

"She has good days and bad days," he said, deciding that vague was the best approach. He checked the medicine cabinet over the sink. "Somebody had a busy romantic life." He showed Sam the bottles of pills and boxes of accessories.

Sam's eyebrows inched upward. "For a man with such a busy romantic life, he doesn't appear to have been serious about anyone. There's a distinct lack of feminine style in the decor."

"What do you know about feminine style?"

Sam almost smiled. "One of the first things my sister did when she moved in with me was order pillows. Lacey, flowery pillows."

Sam's sister Evey had moved in with him a year ago to escape her controlling husband. She was recovering from the emotional and psychological abuse, but it would be a while before she felt confident enough to move out on her own again.

Marx stepped out of the bathroom and looked around the bedroom. "No pictures of a girlfriend anywhere."

"Plenty of pictures of himself."

There was a different self-portrait of the doctor on every flat surface. "How many pictures does one person need of himself?"

Sam looked around, then said, "Apparently seven."

"That was a rhetorical question, but if we're countin', you missed the one in the bathroom."

"Well, it is the age of narcissism," Sam said.

"Ain't that the truth. Everybody's takin' pictures of themselves and sharin' them all over the place. Like anybody cares what shirt you were wearin' this mornin' while you were walkin' the dog, or that the pancakes you're about to eat look like Elvis. It's just plain obnoxious."

"A lot of people post pictures of themselves because they have low self-esteem and they're seeking encouragement and validation from others."

"How is that lip puckerin' thing girls do in pictures gonna help their self esteem? I can't tell if they're gonna make out with the camera or start quackin'."

Sam smiled. "They do call it a duck face. Jace has never done that, but she does like selfies. And she gets offended if she posts a picture of herself on Facebook and I don't comment or *like* it."

"Why wouldn't you like a picture of your girlfriend? It's not like she's ugly."

"Not *like* as in the opposite of dislike. It's . . . a button."

Marx frowned in confusion. "She's offended if you don't button-like her picture? You realize that doesn't make any sense."

Sam decided just to let it go. Marx barely turned on his computer; he certainly wasn't joining social media sites.

They searched the rest of the condo but found nothing more of interest.

"Anythin' else I should know before I go outside and talk to our young housekeeper?" Marx asked.

"The condo on the left is vacant, and nobody answered when I knocked on the door to the right. It belongs to a Ms. Dory Donovan." Sam revisited his notes before adding, "The couple in the next condo down, Sue and Jay, said she left for a wedding this evening. She's a professional makeup artist. They don't remember any disturbances today, and they don't know the victim personally."

"I'll see if I can catch Ms. Donovan tomorrow," Marx said. "Ella, what time do you think you'll be finished with the autopsy?"

Ella pursed her lips in thought. "Late morning, early afternoon. I'll send you a text."

"Okay." Marx stripped off his rubber gloves and booties before exiting the crime scene.

He spotted the young woman he was looking for, and crossed the lawn to the sidewalk where she sat, her arms wrapped around her ankles.

"Ms. Sarah?"

She blinked up at him with shock-glazed eyes, and he crouched again, much to the protest of his knees.

"You doin' all right?" he asked.

She swallowed and dropped her eyes to study a crack in the sidewalk. "You never expect things like this to happen to people you know."

Marx tapped his hands on his knees as he pondered her, his instincts telling him there was more to this girl's relationship with Dr. Wilder than a mere housekeeper. "How long were you two seein' each other?"

Her eyes darted back to his face, and then she looked around to make sure no one had overheard. "We're not . . . we *weren't* seeing each other."

"Try again."

Her face flushed with embarrassment and anger. "He didn't want anyone to know."

"Because of your age?" He studied the fine, youthful features of her face. "Unless you're extremely advanced in your education, you're too young to be a graduate student. How old are you?"

"T-twenty five."

"I'm gonna find out the truth if that means speakin' to every member of your family, so lyin' is pointless."

Her shoulders slumped and she mumbled, "Eighteen. He didn't want anyone to know we were together because he's thirty-eight, and he said it would look bad for him."

"You said you've been cleanin' his house for years. How old were you when you started datin'?"

She hesitated.

"How old, Sarah?"

She swallowed. "I was a sophomore in high school when I started cleaning for him, and things just . . . progressed. But I knew what I was doing."

Marx released a slow, furious breath through his nose and glared at the condo. Dr. Wilder had been thirty-five when he took advantage of a fifteen-year-old girl, and he had still been stringing her along three years later. If Marx had been this girl's father, he would've pounded the man into the ground.

15

He made a mental note to speak with her father and find out where he had been between four and six p.m. yesterday evening.

But for now, he needed sleep.

2

*M*arx was bone tired by the time he reached his second-floor apartment, and irritation prickled beneath his skin when he found a note taped to his door.

I know you're up to something with that girl in there. I'm watching you, and I'm calling the police next time.

He recognized the handwriting, and he shot a pointed look at the apartment across the hall as he peeled off the note.

The old woman glared at him through the narrow crack of her open door.

"I *am* the police, Mrs. Neberkins," he reminded her.

She huffed and shut her door, but he knew she was hovering by the peephole.

She was convinced he was some kind of nefarious criminal—at the very least a sex trafficker—and she had called the police on him more than once.

He couldn't blame her, given the circumstances. She probably thought the young woman staying in his guest room was being held against her will.

Holly never left the apartment alone, and when she did, she was a twisted bundle of nerves. But more than likely, it was the frequent screaming that made the old woman suspicious.

"Good night, Mrs. Neberkins."

The snap of her dead bolt was her only response, and he shook his head as he stepped silently into his apartment.

The steady rush of water from the shower told him his attempt at stealth had been unnecessary. Something had already woken Holly.

He sighed as he locked the door and dropped his keys on the side table.

He had hoped she might sleep through the night—she needed the rest—but she seldom slept more than a few hours at a time.

Her nights were plagued by nightmares, some of them so terrifying that she woke up screaming and disoriented. Judging by the note from his nosy neighbor, that was what had happened tonight.

Marx slipped out of his shoes and dropped them beside the door. A tail thumped the floor, drawing his attention to the German shepherd lying on the living room rug.

"I see you eyein' my shoes." He pointed a finger at him. "Don't touch 'em."

Riley lifted his head and his tongue rolled out.

"Mmm hmm," Marx grunted. "Look as innocent as you want. I know Holly didn't chew off my shoelace."

Riley's tail thumped the floor in excitement as Marx approached. He might prefer his female mistress, but Marx gave him bacon. Marx paused to scratch behind Riley's ear before carrying a paper bag of shampoo and body wash into the kitchen.

At a drop over five feet and just under a hundred pounds, Holly might not have a lot of surface area, but she used enough body wash to clean a herd of elephants.

He noticed a purple notebook lying open on the counter as he set the bag down, and his eyes grazed the entry before he could think better of it:

He was in my dreams again. He's always there.

He forced himself to look away. Despite the instinctive urge to collect as much information as possible so that he could help her resolve her fears and insecurities, he wouldn't violate her privacy. And her bruised spirit wasn't something he could solve and stamp as *case closed.*

Knowing she would be upset if she realized she'd left her closely guarded thoughts out in the open, he flipped the notebook shut.

The shower turned off while he was unpacking the contents of the bag, and a few minutes later, the bathroom door opened with a rolling cloud of coconut-scented steam.

A petite girl with a cast on her right forearm shuffled into the hall in fuzzy green slippers, rubbing a towel against her damp red hair.

"Hey, sweet pea."

She jumped at the sound of his voice and dropped her towel, her wide, honey-brown eyes sweeping in his direction.

For a second, she stood frozen, but then her fear gave way to relief when she recognized him, and the wary stiffness drained from her body. "Hi."

With the tip of her nose flushed and her eyes still shining with tears, she could've passed for someone much younger than her twenty-eight years.

To him, she looked like the little girl who had been robbed of her childhood, a beautiful soul fighting to survive in a world determined to destroy innocence.

He wanted to wrap her in his arms and protect her from the pain, but it had to be her choice. "Come here, sweetheart."

She folded her arms around her too-narrow waist. "I'm fine."

"I'm glad you're fine, but it's been a long, stressful night, and I could use a hug."

She fidgeted, unsure whether or not she wanted to be touched, then shuffled across the room and into his arms. He folded them around her as she buried her face in his chest with a quiet sniffle.

She had suffered far too much in her short lifetime, and although she survived, she had a long road of healing ahead of her.

Marx closed his eyes and rested his chin on the top of her head. *Lord, give me strength to help her through this.*

She shifted in his arms, pressing her cheek to his chest, and he smiled. She was listening to his heartbeat. Something about the steady rhythm always seemed to calm her nerves.

Quietly she said, "You were gone when I got up. Did something happen?"

"I got called to a crime scene."

He felt her shift again as she tried to look up at him, but he doubted she could see anything more than the underside of his chin. "Another dead body?"

"You know, not every case I work involves a dead body. Sometimes I get an assault or robbery."

"So it was a robbery?"

"No, it was a dead body."

She let out a tiny snort of amusement and then pulled out of his arms. "You're ridiculous."

He lifted an eyebrow at her. "*I'm* ridiculous?" He gestured to the clothes she had put on after her shower. "You're wearin' purple pants, a pink shirt, and green slippers."

"So?"

"Did you get dressed in the dark?"

She rolled her eyes and wandered back into the kitchen. "You know, I remember hearing that you wore mismatched socks one day."

"Because some mischievous little person snuck into my sock drawer and mixed them all up."

"And?"

"And . . . I got dressed in the dark."

She let out another quiet snort as she pulled ingredients from the cupboard to make herself a drink, which he assumed would be a mug of marshmallows with a splash of hot chocolate. She was worse than a heroin addict with her puffed sugar.

He debated whether or not to broach the painful subject of her nightmares as he took a seat on one of the stools at the peninsula. She was doing her best to pretend that March had never happened. As a child, it was how she had learned to cope with heartache and pain, but she was never going to heal that way.

"Mrs. Neberkins left a note on the door."

She paused with a sleeve of graham crackers in her hand, her shoulders stiff. "I didn't mean to wake anyone."

"I know."

For a moment, she just stood there, working through the emotions and thoughts swirling through her. Her voice was barely a whisper when she finally admitted, "I keep thinking . . . about that place. Every time I close my eyes, I'm back there, and I can't get out."

The weight of guilt in his chest grew heavier. If he had stayed with her, *protected* her, like he promised, she would have never been taken.

Holly exhaled and shook some crackers out of the package. She took too long arranging them around the other items on the plate, and he knew she must be fighting back another swell of tears.

A quiet sniff confirmed his hunch, and then she straightened her shoulders like a queen composing herself for her people and brought two mugs of hot chocolate to the peninsula, swiftly followed by a plate of crackers, Hershey's chocolate squares, and fat marshmallows.

Watching her wiggle her way up onto one of the stools one hip at a time made him grateful that he was tall enough to sit down without his feet leaving the floor.

Once she was finally settled, her small feet dangled about a foot in the air. He hid a smile as he considered getting her a step stool. She would probably huff indignantly, but she would use it when no one was around to see it.

She looked over at him. "Have a snack with me?"

It was late, and he was exhausted, but he could see the need in her eyes. If he told her he was too tired, she would let it go, but she was reaching out to him with this small invitation, and he wouldn't pass that up.

"Gladly."

She nudged his hot chocolate toward him. "I only gave you a few marshmallows."

He couldn't even see the hot chocolate beneath the molten layer of marshmallow goo. "We need to redefine your understandin' of a *few* because this . . . is not it."

He scooped some of the marshmallows off the top and plopped them onto her already-heaping mountain.

A soft smile touched her lips, but the pain-filled shadows never left her eyes. Marx waited patiently to see if she felt secure enough to share anything more.

She drew a breath, hesitated, then said, "I'm scared they're gonna let him go."

Her foster brother, Collin, was being held until the trial. He would remain in custody until the trial concluded and a verdict was reached, but Marx understood her anxiety.

"They're not gonna let him go, sweetheart. This isn't like last time."

When Collin was arrested for violating the protection order Holly had brought against him, he was out within a day. And he had come after her.

She rubbed her fingers along the outside of her mug, like she was trying to absorb the heat from the hot chocolate through her fingertips. "I wanna believe you're right. More than anything, I wanna believe that, but I know him, and . . ." She bit her bottom lip. "He gets away with everything. He always has."

She took a sip of her hot chocolate and fell into contemplative silence.

He decided to distract her before she retreated so far into herself that he couldn't drag her back out. He plucked one of the crackers from the plate. "So what are we supposed to do with all this? Make a s'more?"

She relaxed at the change of subject. "A not-quite-s'more. We can't really roast a marshmallow without a fire."

"Who needs a fire?" He grabbed two marshmallows and walked into the kitchen. He turned on a stove burner before spearing one of the marshmallows with a meat fork. "Well, come on, I'm not doin' this by myself."

Eyes alight with curiosity and interest, Holly hopped off her stool and joined him in the kitchen. He handed her the meat fork before setting up his own marshmallow over the neighboring burner.

"You do realize if you keep feedin' me junk food in the middle of the night, I'm gonna get fat," he pointed out. He was forty-eight years old. He didn't exactly have her metabolism.

"We'll get you a stationary bike."

"Stationary bike," he muttered under his breath. "I'm not ancient. I'm still able to run." Just not nearly as fast as he used to.

She smiled. "If you say so."

They slowly roasted their marshmallows until they were melted enough to smash between two crackers. It had been quite some time since Marx had a s'more.

"What a sticky mess," he complained, trying to lick away the marshmallow that had found its way between his fingers.

Holly let out a soft laugh—something adorably like a giggle—and finished licking her own fingers.

Marx glanced at the clock on the wall. He had to be up for work in less than five hours, but he was torn between the need for sleep and his concern for Holly.

Once she was woken by a nightmare, she could never find her way back to sleep. She would be up the rest of the night, and he didn't want her dwelling on *that place.*

"You want me to stay up with you?" he offered.

She shook her head. "I'll be okay. Besides, you said you have a crime scene, which means you're gonna have a busy week. You should go get some sleep."

He tapped his fingers on the counter, still undecided, then finally accepted that she was right. If he was going to solve this *dead body* case, then he was going to need sleep. "Okay. Good night." He kissed the top of her head, but when he pulled back, some of her hair came with him. "What in the . . ."

It was stuck to his lip, and he realized he must have gotten marshmallow on his face too. He blew air through his lips to try to blow the hair off, but it clung.

Holly's eyes widened. "Did you just . . . spit in my hair?"

Marx laughed as he pulled her hair off his face. "No, I didn't just *spit* in your hair. Though I think I got marshmallow in it."

"Ew," Holly groaned with a scrunch of her nose. She touched the top of her head to see if it was sticky.

"Sorry," he chuckled. "But at least you have plenty of shampoo to wash it out." He nodded to the bottles of shampoo he'd just bought.

She smiled and gave him a light shove toward the hallway. "Go to sleep."

"I'm goin'."

He made his way down the hall to his bedroom and passed out on the bed without bothering to change his clothes or check his face for any leftover marshmallow.

3

*A*n unusual sound snapped Marx out of a dead sleep, and his eyes shifted to his bedroom door. He listened, expecting to hear Holly in the hallway, but the footsteps that passed his room sounded nothing like Holly's slipper-footed shuffle.

He pushed back his sheets and pulled his sidearm from the nightstand. He crossed the cool floorboards in his bare feet and pressed an ear to his door, waiting. Silence stretched, and he cracked open the door to peer into the hall.

His heart staggered in his chest when he noticed the front door standing wide open. Someone was in his apartment. Moving silently, he slipped from his bedroom into the hall, keeping his gun pointed toward the floor.

Trusting that he had the layout of his apartment committed to memory, he started forward through the darkness, but his foot caught on something that shouldn't be there, sending him pitching forward to the floor.

He landed hard enough to knock the breath from his lungs and the gun from his hand. He scrabbled to recapture both and then looked back to see what he'd tripped over.

What he saw drained every ounce of warmth from his body. A small body lay on the floor, hair fanned out around her head.

"Holly," he gasped, crawling to her side. He checked for a pulse, and the stillness beneath his fingers wrapped fear so tightly around his insides that he thought he might vomit. "No, no, no."

He dropped his gun beside his knees and mounted both hands on her chest where her bottom ribs connected, and pushed, sinking into the familiar rhythm of CPR.

"Come on, sweetheart. Come on."

As he tried to pump life back into her body, an empty pill bottle rolled out of her loose fingers and up against the barrel of his gun. He stared at it as his mind tried to process what he was seeing. She had taken something.

He knew he should've stayed up with her. He should never have gone to bed and left her alone with her fears. She had been so scared that the police were going to release Collin, and she had told him once before that she would rather die than be at his mercy again.

He tipped her head back and breathed into her lungs before resuming compressions. "Come on, baby girl. Breathe."

A heavy sigh broke Marx's concentration, but it hadn't come from Holly; it had come from behind him. He snapped his gun up, aiming at a silhouette near the open front door, backlit by flashes of lightning.

"What happened to all your promises of protection?" a familiar voice asked, and Marx blinked in confusion. Pale blue eyes that seemed bioluminescent in the darkness laughed at him.

This couldn't be happening. They wouldn't have let him go, not after the things he'd done. "How did you get out?"

Holly's foster brother smiled, his perfect white teeth gleaming. "You should know by now, Detective—I always get what I want."

Marx leveled his gun at Collin's chest, prepared to pull the trigger and end the monster who had destroyed so many lives, but as Collin moved toward him, his features began to melt like hot wax, taking on an entirely new shape.

An old man stood in his place, pain and grief deepening the lines the past sixty-five years had etched into his face. "Are you gonna shoot me again, Rick?"

Marx's grip on his gun grew slippery with sweat as he stared at his best friend. "Matt?"

"Why didn't you find a better way? You could've found one, if you had just taken the time to think."

Marx looked down at Holly's motionless body, the anguish in his chest expanding. "You didn't give me a choice."

"There's always a choice. Isn't that what you told me?"

Marx looked back at his friend when he heard the cocking of a gun, and his finger tightened reflexively on the trigger. "Why are you doin' this?"

Another figure materialized from the murky shadows of the apartment, coming to stand beside Matt. "Because it's the only way." She held out her hand, a ring glistening on her palm. "I want a divorce."

She turned her hand over and let the ring fall. It hit the floor with a thunderous echo, bringing Marx's world collapsing down around him.

"Shannon . . ."

"I don't love you anymore."

Chilling laughter rang through the apartment, and Marx's attention swiveled to Collin, who was leaning against the wall with his arm wrapped around a girl's neck.

Marx pressed a hand to the floor where Holly's body had been just a moment before and realized with a wave of panic that Collin had her. "No!"

A bolt of lightning from outside illuminated the terror on Holly's face as she cried, "You promised."

Marx opened his eyes, the rumble of thunder following him into the waking world. He blinked at his bedroom ceiling as his racing heart slowed.

The torturous scenes of his nightmare had seemed so real, and he was grateful for the storm that had pulled him free.

There weren't many things that frightened him, but being unable to protect the people he loved was at the core of his fears.

Another bolt of lightning lit up his room as he sat up and pushed aside his sweat-dampened sheets. He ran a hand through his graying hair and glanced at the photo of his ex-wife on the nightstand.

There were two sides to Shannon: the district attorney, who was always a picture of professionalism with her perfectly pressed suits and her raven hair wound into a bun at the nape of her neck, and the woman he had fallen in love with, the woman who danced around the house in his T-shirts, singing along to old rock bands, the woman who let her hair flow in the breeze and snuggled deeper when he wrapped her in his arms.

He dragged his mind away from the memories that had become bitter reminders of what he'd lost and went to check on Holly. It might have only been a nightmare, but he needed to be sure she was all right.

He found her sitting in front of the open living room window, watching the storm and basking in the mist that sprayed through the screen. She might live in New York City, but she was still the girl who spent nine years of her childhood watching storms roll across the Kansas sky.

He leaned against the counter and smiled, content to watch her while his coffee brewed.

The weather outside was raging, but at the moment, the storm inside Holly had come to a peaceful standstill.

He wished he could slip out of the apartment without disturbing her, but he knew the sound of the dead bolt would draw her attention. So before he left for work, he kissed the top of her head and told her he would be back for dinner.

He lingered in the hall, listening, and just when he thought she might be moving past her compulsive need to check the locks, he heard her cross the room and fidget with the dead bolt, making sure it was secure. It had only been two months; someday she would feel safe enough to let it go.

It was still storming when he stepped outside, and he glared up at the fat raindrops pelting the ground. He was going to get drenched; there was no avoiding it. But when he reached his car, he realized that this was only the beginning of one long, lousy day.

He'd forgotten to roll up the driver's side window before getting out of the car last night, and his seat had enough water in it to double as a bird bath.

At least the seats were made of leather instead of some cheap fabric, and he wouldn't have to spend the rest of the day sitting on a wet sponge.

He dried off his seat with a blanket he had in the trunk and slid behind the wheel.

He had two stops planned this morning: a visit to Dory Donovan, the dead doctor's neighbor, and a visit to the "housekeeper's" family to see just how angry they were with the man who had taken advantage of their little girl.

As he started to pull out onto the main road, a taxi cut him off, forcing him to slam on his brakes. He smashed his fist against the horn and rolled down the window just enough to holler at the man, but the taxi driver flipped him a crude gesture and kept going.

He quashed the urge to follow him and pull him over out of spite.

Holly had asked him once if he was an angry driver. He was, but it was people like those taxi drivers who made him that way. He scowled at the floorboard of the passenger's side, where his coffee was now splattered, and hit the horn again out of frustration.

He swung by the nearest coffee shop to pick up a large black coffee—which should've taken all of two seconds—but he managed to end up in line behind the one person in New York City who ordered a tall, whole milk, caramel something-or-other before remembering she was "trying this Vegan thing for like a week" . . . and started over.

By the time he pulled up in front of Ms. Donovan's house, his last nerve was twitching.

He turned off his car and sat there for a while, sipping his coffee and longing for the days when a single cup gave him a jolt of energy. Now, it barely put a dent in his exhaustion.

Maybe when he reached the bottom of the cup, he would have the energy to lurch out of his car and up to the witness's front door. Of course, with the day he was having, he'd probably trip over a crack in the sidewalk.

"Somethin' positive," he muttered to himself.

He admired Holly for her ability to find something positive even in the darkest circumstances. She could see the silver lining around every rain cloud. All he saw was how that rain cloud spat water all over his leather seat.

He sighed when nothing positive came to mind, and climbed out of his car into the downpour.

4

*A*s he ascended the steps to Ms. Donovan's front door, it occurred to him that he should buy an umbrella. He was saturated by the time he reached the porch, which did nothing to lift his mood. He raised a hand to knock, but the door whipped open before he could touch it.

A black woman in her thirties stood there with a shower cap over her hair. "I thought you were gonna sit out there all morning." She jerked her head as she stepped aside. "Let's make this quick. I have to be at a wedding in two hours to put some bride's face on, and I can't very well do that without *my* face on."

Marx's eyebrows drew together. "I feel obliged to advise you that you should ask for identification before invitin' a strange man into your home."

She grabbed a cigarette from a box on the nearby shelf and lit it. "You don't look very strange."

Neither did Ted Bundy, and he killed at least thirty people, Marx mused as he stepped inside.

She perched on the arm of her couch and crossed her legs. "Try not to get water all over the floor."

Marx looked down at the puddles forming around his feet as water dripped from his coat. "You realize it's rainin'."

She lifted perfectly plucked brows. "You realize wood absorbs water."

Clenching his teeth against a snappy retort, Marx stripped off his overcoat and, with nowhere else to put it, hung it on the light fixture outside.

"You can shut the door."

Did this woman have no sense of self-preservation? Her neighbor had just been murdered, and she was inviting a man she didn't know into her home and telling him to close the door.

"I'd rather leave it open, if you don't mind," he said.

She shrugged a shoulder. "Suit yourself. I don't know anything about the dead guy. Well, I mean I *knew* Holland, but I don't know anything about his transition into being . . . you know, dead. Was it awful? Was there much blood? Who killed him?"

Marx massaged his forehead. He really didn't have the patience for someone with her personality this morning. "I can't share the details of an ongoin' investigation. And if you don't mind, I have a few questions of my own."

"Well, there's no reason to be snippy about it."

He ran his tongue over his teeth and reminded himself that politeness would elicit more information than his temper. "First of all, I'm Detective Marx with the NYPD, and secondly, I appreciate you takin' time to talk to me this mornin'."

"Sue and Jay told me an officer stopped by hoping to speak with me about Holland's death. I was expecting a handsome Latino officer, but I guess I can spare a few minutes for you."

"I appreciate that." He grabbed his notebook and pen from the inside pocket of his suit jacket. "How long have you known Holland Wilder?"

"Three years maybe?"

"What kind of neighbor was he?"

She took a drag of her cigarette as she considered the question. "Well . . . I particularly enjoyed it when he came out to get his newspaper in the mornings, because he's quite the looker, you know, but really that was the most in-depth interaction we ever had. He wasn't a borrow-a-cup-of-sugar kind of neighbor, and he didn't wave or say hello. I suppose you could say he was distant."

"Distant." Could she be less helpful? "Did you ever notice him havin' any company?"

"Oh, he had a lot of pretty girls over. And that woman who did his cleaning came by a couple nights a week to tidy up. I saw her taking out the garbage every now and then and washing the windows. She usually comes around eleven and leaves sometime during the night. Though between you and me, sometimes her car was still there hours *after* he got home."

"Were you under the impression they were in a relationship?"

"I suppose that depends on how you define relationship. I have a relationship with my mother, but it is *nothing* like what the two of them were doing."

"A physical relationship," Marx clarified, some of his impatience slipping into his tone.

"Mmm, they were physical. I mean I never saw anything other than kissing, but you know how it goes. Where there's kissing, there's usually more."

"Can you tell me if you ever heard the two of them arguin' or noticed any kind of physical altercation between them?"

"I'm not a busybody, and I have a business to run. I don't have time to spy on people. But I did notice they argued on the front porch sometimes. Of course, then they made up. Or maybe I should more accurately say they made *out*. If you know what I mean."

"Did you ever notice any violence between them?"

"No, but most people do tend to keep their dirty little secrets behind closed doors."

He made a quick note before asking, "And what about anybody else? Did you notice anybody unusual around his condo lately?"

"Well, there was a car sitting outside two nights ago for a few hours."

"Can you describe the car? Model, color?"

She bobbed a foot in thought. "Somewhere between Glossy Royal and Darkest Night."

Marx blinked. "I beg your pardon?"

"I do makeup, Detective, not cars. Those aren't my most popular shades of lipstick, very unflattering on most skin tones, but that's the color of the car."

Begrudgingly, Marx wrote down the lipstick names that he would have to look up later. "Darkest Night and Glossy what?"

"Royal. R-o-y—"

"I know how to spell royal, thank you. What time did you see the car?"

"After twelve in the morning. He left around three in the morning. I remember because I couldn't sleep that night, and I decided to do a conditioning treatment for my hair."

"Do you remember who was inside the vehicle?"

"Couldn't tell. Look, are we done here? If I don't get ready, I'm gonna be late, which means I'm gonna have an angry bride, and I've seen this woman angry. It does things to her face that I can't fix with makeup."

Marx offered her his card. "If you think of anythin' else, please give me a call." He tucked his notebook and pen away and showed himself out.

He decided to question Sue and Jay one condo down, but the couple had nothing more to add to the statement they had given Sam.

He dropped into the driver's seat of his car and tapped his fingers on the steering wheel as he thought about the young brunette housekeeper.

There was no delicate way to approach the subject with her family, but he would have to try.

The area where Sarah's parents lived was a much poorer community than the one he had just come from. Police presence was scarce, and the local gang was the authority on the street.

Marx could feel the eyes of the neigborhood residents burrowing into his back as he climbed the steps to the apartment building. Symbols were spray-painted across the locked metal gate, identifying the gang's territory, and there were chips in the building's brick siding from bullet ricochets.

He rang the buzzer next to the surname Akers and waited.

Static filtered through the intercom, and a man snapped, "What do you want?"

"I'd like to speak to Sarah Akers's parents."

The man paused before speaking again, and this time there was more suspicion than anger in his voice. "Who are you?"

"I'm a detective with the NYPD."

"You don't sound like an NYPD detective."

Marx rolled his eyes. As if he'd never heard that before. "I'll gladly show you my credentials if you buzz me up."

The brief silence over the intercom lengthened, and he glanced at his watch as the seconds ticked by into minutes. The moment he tracked down the address for Sarah's family, he'd suspected this trip would be a lost cause. Even if these people trusted that he was a decent cop, inviting a member of law enforcement into their home would no doubt paint a target on their family.

Marx turned toward the street when the heavy thump of music grew closer, the base so loud that it vibrated through his chest. A black car with spiked rims rolled slowly past, and he kept his hand on his gun as he briefly locked eyes with the driver.

"Lord, don't let me get shot," he said beneath his breath.

He watched the car continue on through the neighborhood. When it was out of sight, the lock on the metal gate behind him clicked, letting him into the building.

Sarah's family lived on the third floor, and he found a middle-aged man waiting in the doorway when he reached the top of the steps. He could see Sarah in the shape of the man's eyes and the shade of his hair, but she hadn't inherited the pinched, distrustful set of his mouth. "You're gonna get yourself killed in this neighborhood."

"The thought did cross my mind," Marx admitted, showing the man his badge. "Mr. Akers, I assume."

"Where's our daughter?"

The question—laced with accusation—caught Marx off guard. He parted his lips to ask the man to elaborate, when a woman squeezed into the doorway beside him.

She ran her fingers over the dark shadows beneath her eyes, trying to erase her tears. "Did you find our baby? Did you find Sarah?"

Marx looked between them. "I'm sorry for any confusion, but I don't work with missin' persons. I'm a homicide detective."

Mrs. Akers gasped and covered her mouth.

Marx realized she had taken his statement to mean that her daughter was dead. "Sarah's fine," he said quickly. "I saw her around one this mornin'."

Mrs. Akers choked back a sob and leaned into her husband. The man wrapped an arm around her and glared daggers at Marx. "You should've started with that."

"I wasn't aware that she was missin'."

Mrs. Akers sniffed and pressed a tissue to her left eye. "She packed her bags and left three days ago. We hoped she moved in with a friend, but no one's returning our calls, and her cell phone's been disconnected."

"What do you mean you saw her this morning?" Mr. Akers snapped.

The man's attitude prickled Marx's temper. "I mean she was in my line of vision." When the man's eyebrows dipped in anger, Marx added, "You give me attitude, I'm gonna give it back."

Mrs. Akers placed a hand on her husband's chest, her eyes pleading. "Please, Stephen. I wanna know where she is, and if he can tell us anything . . ."

Stephen silenced her with a look and visibly wrestled to control his anger. "Where did you see Sarah?"

"At the condo of the man she was in a relationship with."

"Wilder!?" he bellowed, his face contorting with rage, and his wife cringed. "She went back there?"

The passing thought that Sarah's father might have murdered the man she was involved with solidified into suspicion once Marx witnessed the breadth of his temper.

He looked at Sarah's mother. She had an air of meekness and subservience about her, but he didn't see any physical indication that she was being forced into that role. "Are you all right, Mrs. Akers?"

"She's fine," her husband spat before she could even open her mouth to respond.

Marx leveled a warning look in his direction. "I didn't ask you."

"I'm okay," she answered, but she glanced up at her husband before she said it, as if seeking permission to speak.

Marx had a feeling Sarah had moved out to escape the controlling grasp of her father. He might not be physically abusive, but it was clear he ruled the household as a dictator.

"How did you know about Sarah's relationship with Dr. Wilder when he encouraged her to keep it quiet?" Marx asked.

"She told Elizabeth."

Marx glanced at Sarah's mother, Elizabeth, and the shame in the slump of her shoulders confirmed that she had shared something Sarah had wanted to remain between them.

"Sarah showed up at my crime scene around one this mornin'."

"It's about time someone killed that pervert."

"Did I say he was dead?"

Stephen's jaw shifted in irritation. "You said you're a homicide detective and that you saw Sarah at Wilder's house, at your crime scene. It's an obvious conclusion."

Marx grunted with interest. He *had* said those things, and the fact that Stephen could so easily connect them and repeat them back to him meant he wasn't the type to be caught in a lie. He was careful, and he paid attention. That knowledge would come in handy if he had to interrogate him later.

He turned his attention back to Elizabeth, aware that it would needle her husband. "Mrs. Akers, can you tell me where you were between four and six p.m. last—"

"She was home while I was out in the city looking for our daughter," Stephen cut in.

Marx cut another sharp look his way. "You have a problem with interruptin' people. But since you're feelin' so chatty, can anybody verify where you were yesterday afternoon?"

The man's eyes narrowed. "You're so bent out of shape about a pervert being murdered. Where were you when he was sleeping with my fifteen-year-old daughter?"

"All due respect, Mr. Akers, but where were *you*? You're her father, which means it's your responsibility to make sure she's safe. But I'm pretty sure she moved out to get away from you."

Stephen clenched his fists and stepped forward, his body language telegraphing violence. Elizabeth caught his arm and tried to pull him back. "Stephen, please . . ."

Stephen shrugged free of his wife's grip and gritted through his teeth, "Get out of our apartment building."

"I'm sure we'll talk again." Marx pocketed his notebook calmly, unintimidated by the man's blustery temper, and nodded to the two of them. "Thank you for your time, Mrs. Akers." Then, less politely, he said, "*Mr.* Akers."

"Don't come back." Stephen thrust the door shut in his face and locked it.

Marx started down the steps. He could understand why Sarah had moved out. He had spent his childhood with a father who had a strikingly similar temper, and he had enlisted in the army the moment he turned eighteen.

His cell rang, and he pulled it from his pocket. It was his lieutenant calling.

He had been making excuses since Lieutenant Kipner mentioned that they needed to talk. "Need to talk" was code for "You screwed up. Now stand there while I list off your every mistake."

He considered letting it roll over to voice mail, but that would only delay the inevitable. He flipped it open. "Yes, sir."

"We need to talk," Lieutenant Kipner said, and Marx gritted his teeth.

You don't say.

"Now's not a good time, sir. A man was killed last night and I'm workin' the case."

"And he'll still be dead an hour from now. I expect you to meet me at the precinct in fifteen."

Lieutenant Kipner disconnected, giving him no opportunity to argue.

5

*M*arx stopped at his desk to check his messages when he arrived at the precinct, and his eyes snagged on the name plaque in the corner. The bronze plate had his name emblazoned on it, but someone had covered it with a strip of masking tape that had a message written across it in black capital letters: *COP KILLER.*

Anger throbbed in his temples. He ripped the tape off, crumpled it in his fist, and tossed it in the trash can.

It was no secret that he was the one who shot and killed their former captain. Some members of the department viewed it as a betrayal that he had ended the life of another cop.

If he could've brought him in alive, he would have, but Matt had no intention of living out the rest of his days behind bars. He forced Marx to pull the trigger when he threatened Holly's life.

Marx tried to push down the memories as he picked up his desk phone and checked his messages. The first message was from a woman.

"Hello, Detective, my name's Erica, and I'm calling on behalf of AmazingNews.org, and I was hoping to talk to you about the woman you rescued. I would love to interview you, get a little insight into how things happened. You truly are a hero. If you could call me—"

He deleted the message. He had no intention of talking with the media. The second message began— another journalist—and he deleted it just as a voice bellowed across the squad room.

"Marx!"

He tracked the voice to a thin, middle-aged man across the room, whose mustache was so big that it swallowed his mouth: Lieutenant Kipner.

Right. They needed to talk.

He hung up and crossed the room to join Lieutenant Kipner in one of the private conference rooms, closing the door behind him. "If this is another conversation about my attitude—"

Kipner held up a hand to cut him off, a gesture Marx used with Holly when she was in one of her contrary moods. He never realized how irritating it was to be on the receiving end.

"There have been a lot of changes since February. Thinning of the ranks, public scrutiny, a new captain."

Matt's death still left an ache in Marx's gut. He had been his closest and oldest friend. He never would've suspected him of the terrible things he'd done.

Thankfully, Lieutenant Kipner had the decency not to say anything more about the situation when he continued. "Everyone's under a lot of pressure. Too many cases, not enough detectives. Too much scrutiny from the public. We're all on very short leashes. Which is why I need all of you focused and on your best behavior."

"There's nothin' wrong with my behavior."

"Less than three months ago, you nearly put a witness through the conference room window because he didn't answer your question fast enough."

"I asked nicely the first time."

The witness had known where Holly was being held, but he had been more concerned about the reward for information than for her life.

Kipner didn't disagree. "The media is gonna be all over Wells's trial."

"They already left messages."

"Your connection with the victim is well-known at this point. When the media comes around asking questions, and they will, I need you to keep your head."

"I always keep my head."

Lieutenant Kipner gave him an incredulous look. "You call busting a journalist's camera and shoving him out into the hallway at the hospital 'keeping your head'?"

"He was tryin' to take pictures of Holly. What would you have done?"

"What I would or wouldn't have done isn't the point. You're a witness in this trial. Everything you've ever done or do between now and your testimony will be under scrutiny. We need this trial to go off without a hitch, which is part of the reason I'm assigning you a partner until the trial is over."

"I don't need a partner."

"It's not negotiable. You and Detective Everly are joined at the hip until we hear a verdict."

Marx scowled. "What's the other part of the 'reason' you're stickin' me with a partner?"

"Somebody needs to keep your temper in check, and I don't trust you to do it." He opened the door to leave, then paused. "And don't give Everly any crap about this. It's my decision, not his."

Marx hadn't had a partner for years—he didn't like working with other people—and he didn't want one now.

His phone buzzed, and he pulled it from his pocket to see a text from Ella: "Finished with my autopsy. Join me if you dare."

Michael Everly cracked open the door and poked his head in. "Morning." When Marx only grunted in reply, Michael smiled. "Not much of a morning person, are you?"

Marx didn't even dignify that absurd question with a response.

Michael cleared his throat. "I was reading up on our victim, Holland Wilder, and I say *our* because I spoke with the lieutenant earlier and—"

"Joined at the hip, I know."

Michael was the most tolerable of the younger detectives. He was honest to a fault and intelligent without being cocky. They had worked Holly's abduction together, but that had been a special circumstance.

He didn't need a shadow questioning his every decision for the next however many months.

He pushed past Michael out of the conference room. "Come on."

"Where are we going?"

"The morgue."

6

*E*lla was seated on a stool, long blond braid draped over her shoulder, scribbling on a clipboard when they stepped into the morgue.

She reached a hand into a bag on her desk and pulled out a Teddy Graham cracker, which she popped into her mouth. She mumbled to herself around the cracker as she wrote.

Marx and Michael exchanged a vaguely amused look as they stood in front of the oblivious woman. She had headphones in, and she was muttering along to a song as she bopped her foot.

"Ella," Marx said.

No response.

He sighed and walked over to her, tugging one of the earbuds from her ear. She gasped and pressed a hand to her chest in surprise.

"You scared me." At Marx's raised eyebrow, she explained, "I'm used to dead people in my morgue, Detective, not live ones who sneak up and pull my headphones out."

She noticed Michael tapping his foot to the rhythm of the music still pouring from her headphones.

"Yes, I know. My dad always said I listen to my music loud enough to wake the dead." She laughed a little to herself. "Wouldn't that make for an exciting day in the morgue."

"If that happens, don't invite me to the party," Marx said.

"Good song," Michael commented.

She switched off her iPod. "Music helps take the edge off the dead silence down here."

Marx grunted in amusement. "Somebody's full of jokes today."

Ella grinned as she stood. "Sense of humor's the only way to survive this job, Detective. How do you survive yours?"

"Coffee. As long as Holly didn't make it. That's liable to put me on your table."

Holly never could manage to brew a proper pot of coffee; either it tasted like battery acid, or there were coffee grounds floating in it.

"Well, there's always room," Ella said as she led them to an autopsy table. "I have a lot of freezer space."

"I'm in no hurry to be a human popsicle, thank you."

They gathered around an occupied autopsy table, and Ella peeled back the sheet to reveal the head and chest of their victim.

"Under sheet number one, we have Holland Wilder, thirty-eight-year-old male—"

Michael raised a hand. "I don't really like the way you said that, 'cause now I'm expecting there to be a sheet number two."

"Don't jump ahead," Ella said, and Michael, thoroughly chastised, lowered his hand and closed his mouth. "Cause of death was a gunshot wound to the head, and the stab wounds in his hands and chest occurred postmortem."

"So it wasn't a form of torture," Marx said.

"Thankfully no. The killer afforded him at least that small kindness."

The gunshot wound was front to back, which meant he had been facing his killer, and he'd had more than enough time to be terrified for his life before it ended. In Marx's opinion, there was nothing kind about that.

"I found traces of gunpowder residue on the victim," Ella continued. "But the amount suggests the shooter was between five and six feet away when the gun was discharged. Also, the trajectory indicates that the victim was on his knees at the time of death."

There was no way to be certain if Dr. Wilder had fallen or if the killer had forced him to his knees at gunpoint. If the killer had forced him to kneel, then it was likely to humiliate him.

"No foreign DNA, but I can tell you that these dark smudges on his hand"—Ella uncovered the victim's hand and turned it for them to see—"are from black ink. CSU should be able to tell you more, but at a glance I would say your victim wrote the note that we found pinned to his chest with a scalpel."

That was the theory Marx was operating under.

"Now, on to sheet number two." Ella strode to the morgue cooler and opened one of the doors, drawing out a metal slab with a set of remains on them. "Meet Terrence James."

Marx scanned the unfamiliar man's features. Death had sharpened the contrast between his ashen skin and the dark bruises beneath the surface.

"Why are we meetin' Terrence James?"

"Because Terrence"—Ella drew the sheet down and pointed to the abrasions on the man's knees—"died on his knees four days ago from a gunshot wound to the head and was stabbed postmortem in the chest."

"You've gotta be kiddin' me." Marx looked over the body a second time.

"I'm dead serious," Ella replied. "I also found paper in the stab wound to his chest. I called Detective Engle last night, hoping to assure myself that the two bodies weren't connected."

Marx tried to keep a straight face at the mention of the detective's name, but his eyebrows twitched. Engle's idea of work was pushing himself up out of his chair to grab a Snickers bar from the vending machine. A crime scene was beyond him.

Ella pulled up a secure email on her laptop and stepped back to let them see the contents. "He sent me this."

Marx cocked an eyebrow. "Engle flexed his fingers long enough to send an email?"

Ella shrugged. "Guess so. Try to ignore the typos. He seems to have fat-fingered some keys."

"He Snickers-fingered some keys," Marx muttered as he bent to look at the email. Attached was a photograph of a handwritten note:

I should have made a better choice.

"Detective Engle had the note and the knife pinning it to the victim's chest bagged by CSU before I even arrived, which is why I didn't immediately link the two," Ella explained.

Unease squirmed in Marx's gut. One body he could dismiss as a random act of violence, but two victims killed and similarly posed was more than a coincidence.

7

The dried blood nearly blended in with the threadbare motel carpet, just one more dark splotch in a collage of stains. Marx stood beside the spot where Terrence James had died four nights ago, absorbing the details of the room as he tried to piece together the man's final moments.

The detective assigned to the homicide had gathered very little information for him to draw from.

"There's not much here," he said as he flipped through the crime scene photos and Detective Engle's "notes."

"I can't tell if there was a struggle or if the guy just lived in filth," Michael said from the doorway.

The smoke-stained wallpaper was peeling at the seams, revealing crude artwork beneath. The sheets, discolored by sweat and other unknown substances, were piled on the floor beside a broken lamp and moldy food containers.

Michael rubbed the back of his hand against his nose. "Engle said this guy was a pimp, right?"

Marx tossed the useless files on the bare mattress. "He's been picked up several times for solicitation. One thing Engle did manage to do was pull together a list of people associated with him. Looks like he managed six or seven young men and women."

"Sounds like a winner," Michael muttered. "You think someone on that list killed him?"

"If so, there has to be a connection between Dr. Wilder and Terrence James that we're not seein'."

A shift in the light pulled his attention past Michael to a figure that had just appeared behind him on the outdoor landing.

Michael followed his gaze, and the girl flitted away before either of them could notice more than the shocking pink-and-blond hair that, paired with her petite frame, made her look like a pixie.

"Something tells me she wasn't happy to see us here," Michael said.

"Which means she probably knows somethin' she doesn't wanna tell us."

"Think she might be one of the women who worked for Terrence?"

"Only one way to find out."

Michael stripped out of his suit jacket and tossed it to Marx before dashing down the steps after her.

Marx locked up the crime scene before going in the opposite direction Michael and the woman had taken, hoping to intercept her.

Sure enough, she turned the corner a few seconds later, high heels dangling from her fingers. When she noticed Marx in her path, she skidded to a stop so fast that she nearly pitched forward. She turned frantically, searching for an escape, but Michael was closing in behind her.

Michael held up a hand. "Relax. We just wanna talk."

"Yeah right! I'm not gonna end up like TJ!" She flung one of her high heels at him, but he sidestepped it, and it hit the parked car along the curb.

Marx grabbed her before she could hurl the second spiked heel and pinned her arms to her sides. "Take it easy. We're cops."

She thrashed and kicked, trying to break free. Michael helped him haul her up against the side of the building. For someone not much bigger than Holly, she fought like a rodeo bull.

"Nobody's gonna hurt you," Marx assured her. "But if you don't settle down, we're gonna have this conversation with you in a jail cell."

She spat curses that would make a nun faint, as if she thought screeching profanity would scare them off, but she stopped resisting.

"Good, now quit screechin' and use your words." Marx released her, and she ripped her arm from Michael's grip.

"Keep your hands off me," she snapped. "I don't give free samples." When Marx plucked the remaining high heel from her hand, she shot him a scorching glare. "Those cost me a week's worth of cash."

He took in her appearance with a quick sweep of his eyes. She stood barefoot on the pavement, her tight skirt and formfitting top leaving little to the imagination. "You work with Terrence James?"

"Nah, I was just out here all night working on my runway walk for *America's Next Top Model*. What do you think?"

"What's your name?"

She folded her arms and let out a protracted *ttt* sound through her teeth. "I ain't gotta tell you nuttin."

"You can tell us now, or we can take you down to the station, print you, and run you through the system to get your name, address, and history."

She looked between the two of them, her irritation giving way to worry. "Look, I can't go to lockup. I gotta get home."

"Name."

She exhaled. "Hope. And yeah, that's the one my mama gave me."

"What happened to your face, Hope?" Marx asked.

She had pasted on layers of makeup to mask the bruises, but they were still visible as dark shadows across her cheekbone and around her left eye.

"Like you care."

Michael folded his arms. "We do care. It doesn't matter what you do to pay the bills, no one deserves that."

She tapped her fingernails on her arms and averted her eyes. "I had to take the other night off. My baby boy was sick. And TJ . . . he got mad. Said he was keeping the earnings from last week to make up for my night off. I can't afford that. I got a baby to support. So I tried to like . . . explain that to him, but it just got him madder."

"What night was that?" Marx asked.

"Saturday."

"What happened that night?"

She gestured to her face, then lifted up the hem of her shirt to show them the span of bruises across her stomach. "This is what happened."

Marx's sympathy for their murder victim was lessening by the second. "Did you fight back?"

She scoffed as she pulled her shirt back down. "You think I wanna end up dead? I got outta there first chance I got."

If she hadn't fought back, then she wasn't the person who had left bruises all over Terrence James's body. "What happened to Terrence?"

Wariness crept over her features. "Oh, nuh-uh. I ain't killed nobody, and you ain't puttin' that on me. That sleezy good-for-nuttin thief was alive when I left. If you don't believe me, talk to the creeper who was hanging around outside when I left."

Marx shared an interested look with Michael. "Do you know who it was?"

"You know, I forgot to stop and ID the guy." She tapped her forehead and added, "Guess it slipped my mind while I was running for my life."

"Did you get a look at him?" Michael asked.

"You mean besides tall, hooded, and creepy? No, I didn't. I could barely walk straight when I left. Like I was looking to check out the guy's face."

Marx tried not to lose his patience. It looked as though she'd had a rough week. "Did he say anythin' to you?"

"Actually, yeah, he did. He grabbed my arm, and I thought for sure he was gonna wail on me too, but then he asked if I was okay, like he was concerned or something." She shrugged. "TJ tried to come after me, and when I saw that guy push him back into the room and shut the door, I got outta there."

Their killer had been concerned about the well-being of a prostitute. Marx filed that interesting piece of information away for later contemplation. "Would you recognize his voice?"

"He sounded like every other New Yorker. 'Cept you. I don't know where you're from."

"Why did you come back today?"

"Cause TJ had my money. I figured it's been four days and ain't nobody should be there. So it was good a time as any to see if he stashed it somewhere in the motel room." She looked between them. "Look, I worked hard for that money. I earned every penny, and I need it."

"You said you have a little boy," Michael recalled. "How old is he?"

"Just turned four. Only good thing in my life." The small smile that lifted the corners of her lips when she spoke about her son faded away as she continued. "I was gonna get him a stuffed T-Rex for his birthday 'cause he loves dinosaurs, but now I don't even have enough money for groceries." She sighed. "I really gotta get home to him before the sitter bails. She works second shift."

Marx glanced at his watch. "We'll give you a lift."

Her eyebrows drew together in suspicion. "I ain't paying you for that lift, so if that's where this is headed, you—"

"It's not," Marx cut in, offended by the suggestion. "You can walk home if you want, or you can get in the backseat and give me an address."

She chewed on her cheek as she considered the offer, then shrugged. "My feet are sore, so a ride home would be nice."

Marx handed back her high heel and nodded toward the curb. "Don't forget your shoe."

She collected both of her shoes and waited by the car.

Marx shook his head and grumbled to Michael, "I didn't think it was possible for a girl to be more stubborn than Holly."

Michael grinned. "I think she's just more distrustful."

"I didn't think that was possible either." When he first met Holly, she didn't even want to share a street curb with him.

"Regretting the offer to drive her home?"

"You never let a lady walk home alone through a dangerous neighborhood, even if she throws shoes at people's heads and swears like a sailor."

Hope hesitated when Marx opened the rear car door for her, then climbed into the backseat.

Michael insisted on stopping to grab something to drink, leaving Marx alone in the car with Hope.

Marx turned his dash cam to face the backseat; he didn't mind giving the woman a ride home, but he didn't want any misconduct rumors floating around because he was alone in his car with a known prostitute.

Michael returned with a few bottles of Pepsi and a plastic shopping bag. He dropped into the passenger seat and handed one of the bottles and the bag to Hope.

"What's this for?" she asked.

"Just a thank-you for your help."

She opened the bag and then stilled for just a second before pulling out the stuffed dinosaur. She blinked a few times before looking at Michael, her lashes damp. "Why?"

"Because every little boy deserves a dinosaur for his fourth birthday."

She swallowed and dropped her eyes. "Thanks."

When they pulled up in front of the address she'd given them, an older woman was waiting on the sidewalk with a little boy, her demeanor impatient.

The little boy lit up when Hope stepped out of the car and squealed, "Mommy!" He ran down the sidewalk and threw his arms around her legs.

"Hi, baby." She bent down and pulled the dinosaur from the plastic shopping bag. "Look what I got for you."

He snatched the stuffed animal from her hands and hopped up and down with excitement. Hope wrapped him in a hug, the dinosaur squished between them, and said with a smile, "Happy birthday, little man."

8

"*S*he doesn't know she deserves better than that, does she?" Michael asked as they walked into the precinct. "Hope, I mean."

"I doubt it," Marx replied.

"Doesn't that bother you?"

It had always bothered him, but it bothered him even more now. He saw Holly in so many of those girls, especially Hope—the expectation of violence, the distrust and fear, and the grim acceptance that being used and abused was just a fact of life.

He wished he could bring an end to that darkness for every man, woman, and child, but all he could do was show Hope a glimmer of kindness by offering her a ride home. Michael's gift had done far more to shatter the illusion that she was only worth what she could do for people.

Michael nudged Marx with an elbow as they walked into the squad room, wrenching him from his thoughts. "There's a pretty lady at your desk."

Marx looked across the room at the tall, lean woman waiting for him.

Even though they had been divorced going on three years, seeing Shannon always made his heart beat a little faster.

She was wearing her court attire, but her dark hair flowed freely around her shoulders, softening the angles of her face.

"I'm gonna grab some lunch," Michael said, but Marx only grunted in reply.

The familiar aroma of Shannon's lavender perfume greeted him as he approached, awakening old memories. "Hey."

She smiled. "Hey yourself."

"Everythin' okay?" She never dropped by for casual visits; in fact, she seemed to go out of her way to avoid him.

"Everything's fine. I just wanted to stop in and check on Holly. I went to your apartment first, but she's not answering her phone or the door."

"She's probably in the shower."

Shannon held up her phone and speed-dialed Holly's number. It rang and then bumped her over to a generic voice mail. "Unless she takes three-hour showers, she's avoiding me."

"I doubt she's avoidin' you." He tried calling Holly with *his* phone and she picked up on the second ring. Eyebrows lifting in surprise, he said, "Hey, sweet pea, what are you up to this afternoon?"

"Watching a movie."

Marx glanced at Shannon. "Did Shannon stop by?"

Silence.

"Holly?"

Her flustered breath filtered down the line. "I don't wanna talk to her."

"Why not?"

"Because she wants to talk about . . . him, and I . . . I can't."

He perched on the edge of his desk and rubbed between his eyebrows. He knew this problem would arise at some point. Shannon needed to prepare Holly for her testimony, but Holly didn't want to revisit the details of her abduction and assault.

"We'll talk about it tonight," he said.

She didn't respond, but he could hear the change in her breathing, the same subtle shift that always preceded a particular question.

He realized that his response to her had come across far sharper than he'd intended. She had every right to be an anxious wreck, and he hadn't meant to use that exasperated tone with her.

Very gently, he added, "I'm not mad at you, sweetheart, okay? Not even a little bit."

She had the phone close enough to her throat that he heard her swallow before she said, "Okay."

He didn't like the lack of certainty in her voice, but he couldn't fix that over the phone. He would give her a hug when he got home. "Enjoy your movie, and don't burn down the apartment when you make dinner."

"No promises."

He closed his phone and dropped it on the desk, rubbing at his forehead with a groan.

"Are you all right?" Shannon asked, gazing at him with concern.

"Yeah, I'm fine. Just . . . frustrated with this mess of a case that dropped into my lap. And it hasn't exactly been a good mornin'."

"Understandable. I have a lunch date with a defense attorney today and I'm dreading it."

"Let's just take the day off."

She smiled as she leaned against the desk beside him. "Go for a drive, maybe grab some apple pie."

It was something they used to do together, and the fondness in her voice as she spoke about the memory surprised him. "You don't even like pie. You just told my mother you enjoyed it to make her like you."

"It worked."

He chuckled. "Yes, it did."

"I also never liked her biscuits."

"Ooh," Marx said with a pained expression. "Don't ever tell her that." His mother loved her biscuits. "She still asks about you."

"I think about her a lot too. She was always so much warmer than my mom. And so sweet." A small smile curled the corners of her mouth as her eyes grew distant with memories. The smile faded into sadness as she said, "I think it broke her heart when she realized we were never going to have children."

It *had* broken his mother's heart, and his. Marx's sister, Cresceda, couldn't have children, and his marriage had fractured and fallen apart. The closest his parents would ever come to grandchildren was Holly.

His mother would fall in love with her the moment she met her, and he would have to pry her loose to bring her back to New York City.

"Have you given any thought lately to . . . giving her some grandkids?" Shannon asked.

Shannon wasn't usually cruel, but that question sent a shock wave of pain through his heart. He had pleaded with her for years to have children, but she had refused.

"And how am I supposed to give her grandkids? Go sleep with a random woman, hope she gets pregnant, and then fight her for custody?"

Shannon rolled her eyes. "Of course not. There are other ways, like falling in love and getting married."

"I tried that," he replied, bitterness edging into his voice.

Realizing that she had upset him, Shannon withdrew behind her impenetrable wall of detachment, ending the conversation. She stood to put space between them and folded her arms. "I'm sorry. That was an insensitive question. I should've known veering off topic was a bad idea."

Marx sighed. "Shannon—"

"We should just focus on Holly."

He didn't want to focus on Holly. He wanted to talk about why their marriage had fallen apart.

"Do you think she'll be willing to talk with me?" Shannon asked.

"About Collin?" At her nod of confirmation, he said, "No, I don't. She says very little about what happened, even to me. And you were right—she's avoidin' you."

Her lips thinned. "Frustrating as that is, I can't blame her. But we can't afford to wait much longer."

"Why the sudden rush? It hasn't even been two months."

"Wells's lawyer is pushing to have the trial sooner rather than later. Probably because they know Holly's in pieces right now, and they're banking on her not being able to take the stand."

"She can't even say Collin's name without gettin' sick to her stomach. There's no way she's gonna be able to be in the same room with him."

"I know, which is why I'm arguing to hold off until after New Year's to give her some time to heal."

Marx shook his head. "That's not enough time."

"It's the best I can do, and it's still contingent on whether or not the judge agrees. She needs to process what she's been through, whether she's ready or not."

"I won't force her to talk about it if she doesn't want to. She's had enough of her choices taken from her."

"You need to think about this objectively, Rick. If she doesn't process what she's been through with a therapist, she's never going to be able to take the stand. And without her testimony, our case could be seriously compromised."

"What do expect me to do? Every time I bring it up, she shuts me down."

Shannon made a note in her phone as she said, "I'll pull together a list of therapists who have worked with victims from some of my previous cases. Maybe one of them will be able to help her." She put her phone back into her purse. "I have court after lunch, so I won't be in touch with that list until later."

"All right."

"Try to broach the subject with her again, please."

She kissed his cheek in a way that was more polite than intimate, and he watched her leave, his heart aching for the life they used to share.

9

He sat in the back row of the courtroom, sketching a picture of the lawyer as she questioned the defendant. He darkened the color of her hair and added texture to the dress suit she wore.

She was beautiful for a woman her age—intelligent eyes, a lean figure, defined cheekbones—and if he were easily persuaded by appearance, like so many men in this world were, he wouldn't be able to see her for what she was.

Dismissive, belittling . . . heartless.

He didn't realize how much pressure he was applying to the pencil in his grip until the lead snapped. He sighed and pulled a small sharpener from his pocket, perfecting the point of his pencil as he listened to the bickering lawyers.

Shannon Marx was a fierce woman who didn't back down easily. She disagreed with the judge almost as often as she disagreed with opposing counsel. It was very entertaining.

He blew the dust off the tip of his pencil and continued filling in the details of his drawing, refining the final sketch of his upcoming target.

10

*M*arx leaned back in his chair as he turned the murders over in his mind. What did a pimp and a surgeon have in common that would inspire someone to kill them? They ran in completely different circles.

Unless . . .

He opened the file he had pulled on their young prostitute. She was pretty and petite, much like the housekeeper Wilder had been involved with.

If Wilder's sexual appetites were as insatiable as his nosy neighbor believed, he could have tried to sate that desire with prostitutes. He certainly had the money to afford regular . . . interactions.

Maybe Wilder had been a client of one of the young women who worked for Terrence. It was a long shot, but maybe Ms. Donovan could identify whether or not Hope had been one of those girls.

He collected the pictures of Holland, Terrence, and Hope, and slipped them into a folder. He looked around the precinct for Michael, but his desk was empty and he wasn't in the break room.

"Jack," he called out, snagging the attention of the older detective whose desk was adjacent to Michael's. "You seen Michael?"

"Said he was gonna grab lunch."

Right. He did mention something about lunch. Marx checked his watch. It was just past one, and he didn't want to sit around all afternoon waiting for his partner to show up.

He decided to do the interviews on his own. He swung by Ms. Donovan's place first and knocked on the door. She opened it and then heaved a sigh.

"You again. Didn't I answer all your questions before I went to the she-devil's wedding? Which I was late to, by the way."

"I'm sorry if I delayed you. And I just have a few follow-up questions, if you don't mind."

"Well, try to be quick this time."

"You mentioned that you saw other women comin' and goin' from Dr. Wilder's place."

"I did." She twirled her hand, impatiently gesturing for him to get to the point.

"Did they seem like they fit into the neighborhood, or were they out of place?"

"I suppose they fit in. And they certainly fit with his type. Pretty and thin."

Marx pulled out the picture of Hope. "Was this one of the girls?"

Ms. Donovan's face soured. "Oh no, this girl looks like a hooker from the wrong side of the tracks. He preferred his ladies classy."

He moved to the picture of Terrence James. "Have you ever seen this man in the area?"

"Can't say that I have. Now if you'll excuse me, I have a hair appointment."

Before he could thank her for her time, she shut the door. He walked back to his car and headed to Hope's apartment, praying for better luck.

He rang the buzzer and waited on the sidewalk. A small face appeared in the lower window, and Hope's little boy studied him with huge eyes, his new dinosaur tucked under one arm.

The inside door opened and Hope appeared, but she made no move to unlock and open the metal gate between them.

"I thought I was done with you. Why you gotta bother me twice in one day?"

She had changed into a pair of baggy jeans and a T-shirt, and the bold shades of makeup had been traded in for neutral colors. It made her look younger.

"I just have some questions."

"Yeah, you blues always got questions. What do you want?" She crossed her arms. "And keep it down. I just put Tyler down for a nap."

Marx glanced at the little face in the window and smiled. Apparently Tyler wasn't in the mood for a nap. "I'll be brief." He held up the photo of Wilder. "Have you ever seen this man?"

"Maybe," Hope said, but the tight line of her jaw told him she was holding back. "I see a lot of people."

"I need to know, Hope. You're not gonna get in trouble."

She looked back into her home, then stepped outside, pulling both doors shut behind her. "I never talk about what I do where my baby can hear."

"That's admirable."

"Whatever. I just do what's best for my boy." She folded her arms and jerked her chin toward the photo of

Wilder. "And yeah, I mighta seen him trolling for girls a time or two. Don't remember when."

"And?"

"And what? I offered 'cause it's my job. He told me I look like trash, and he don't got no interest in trash."

"Did you ever see him pick up a girl?"

"Not from our neighborhood."

"Okay. Thank you." He started to leave, but he had to say what was on his mind, regardless of whether or not she wanted to hear it. "Hope."

She paused, halfway inside.

"I should've said this earlier. This life you live, where every night you go out and men put a price on your body, and every mornin' you come home, so ashamed that you can't talk about it in front of your child . . ." He paused to gather his thoughts. "You deserve more. You're worth so much more."

"Yeah," she said, her voice hoarse with emotion. "Twenty bucks an hour. That's what I'm worth."

Marx shook his head. "What you've been told, how you've been treated, the decisions you've made in the past to survive, you don't have to let them define who you are or how you think of yourself. Let the truth define you."

"And what truth would that be?" She tried to mask her pain and curiosity behind her attitude, but he heard it.

"That you have value beyond measure." Having said what he felt compelled to say, he walked away, leaving her standing in the doorway with silent tears flowing down her cheeks.

11

"*O*h good, you're back," Michael said, intercepting Marx as he made his way across the squad room.

"*I'm* back?" Marx dropped the folder of headshots on his desk and shrugged out of his jacket. "I'm not the one who disappeared for the entire afternoon."

"Sorry about that. I went home to check on my wife. She's not been feeling well."

"She all right?"

"Yeah, she's good. She's, uh, she's pregnant." Michael was aiming for casual, but there was a twinkle of pride and excitement in his eyes. He and his wife, Kat, had adopted a little boy over a year ago, but despite years of trying, they hadn't been able to conceive.

"I thought the doctors said Kat couldn't get pregnant," Marx said, striving to recall the details of that distant conversation. Something about multiple miscarriages.

"Yep, that's what the doctors said, but we got a second opinion."

"From who?"

Michael pointed toward heaven and grinned. "He's got more credentials than every doctor put together, and we've been praying every day. I hope it's a girl. I'll spoil her rotten."

Marx smiled. "Congratulations."

He had only recently reconnected with the God he had shunned for most of his life, and it had been during a fight for Holly's life.

When Marx was a little boy, his mother had described God like air: unseen but ever-present, touching everything around it; unpredictable in how it moved, but reliable because it was always there; a source of life, without which everything would die.

He used to stand on the front porch with his arms spread wide, air whipping around him, and pray that if God was in the wind, He would sweep him away.

But He never did.

Eventually he stopped spreading his wings and waiting for the air to lift him up and carry him away from the life he hated, away from his raging, Scripture-spouting father who swung his fist as often as he swung his belt.

Instead, he sat on the porch steps and looked up at the night sky, wondering why God hated him.

If He was as ever-present as the air, why didn't He *move* to stop the swinging fists? Why did He let his father fall into a bottle every night, knowing that someone else would come out?

Eventually he decided that the Bible his father quoted was nothing but a collection of meaningless words, and the God he alluded to didn't care anymore than anyone else. His mother's stories about a loving God had been nothing but fairy tales to put him and his sister to sleep.

He grew angry with God for all the pain and darkness that filled the world, and he held on to that anger for a long time, until Holly stepped into his life.

She showed him that even in the darkness, there was always a light, a shining beacon of grace and hope, and that light came from God. She was the most innocent soul he knew, and if she loved the same God his father claimed to love, then God was not the issue. People were—people who made imperfect, selfish, emotion-driven decisions, not giving thought to the consequences that would ripple through their lives and the lives of others around them. God was no more to blame for his father's choices than Marx was.

He and God still had a closetful of mess to sort through, and while he knew they would never agree on everything, they did agree that Holly was one of the lights in this world and that she was precious enough to die for.

"Hey, Rickster."

The familiar voice pulled Marx from his thoughts and toward the lanky man with a Mohawk who was approaching on his right. He scowled at Sullivan, the department's contracted technical analyst.

Sullivan, more commonly known as Sully, flashed him a grin. "I know, you don't like Rickster, Ricky, or Ritchie. But Rickster just has so much flare."

Marx folded his arms and leaned against his desk, giving Sully a quick once-over. "You have enough flare for the three of us."

Sully had so many facial piercings that if he walked past a magnet, his head would get stuck. And judging by his daily wardrobe choices, he had never heard of neutral colors.

Sully lifted a foot to display his bright yellow shoes. "This is my newest flare. What do you think?"

Marx's brow furrowed. "I think it looks like a giant stepped on two school buses and decided to wear them as shoes."

Sully grimaced. "I don't like you today. I'm gonna talk to him." He turned toward Michael, who was watching the exchange with an interested expression, and offered him a handful of files. "I found out some interesting details about your two victims. I was gonna just email it, but since Rick here has a nearly allergic aversion to electronics"—he glanced at the layer of dust on Marx's computer monitor with a pained expression—"I went with the antiquated option of printing the information instead of emailing."

Michael opened the top folder and skimmed through the thick collection of papers.

Sully blew the dust off Marx's computer and hit the power button, turning it on. "Did you know that email saves trees and reduces paper cuts by 100 percent? You should try it sometime."

"Mmm hmm." Marx reached over and hit the power button, turning the computer back off.

Sully's mouth dropped open in disbelief. "You cannot treat a computer like that. Do you have any idea what you just did to it by turning it off like that?"

"I stopped the annoyin' hummin' noise." He wasn't sure if it was all computers or just his, but the constant hum it emitted was as distracting as a fly buzzing around his head.

Sully grumbled under his breath and turned back to Michael. "Let's get this over with so I can go back to my office. First we have Terrence James, the dead pimp.

It might surprise you to know that five years ago TJ the pimp was an EMT."

Marx straightened with interest as an automatic connection between a doctor and an EMT formed in his mind. Both men had medical backgrounds.

"He worked for a private company providing emergency services, and he was fired for sexually harassing a coworker," Sully continued. "This guy's idea of romance does not involve flowers and a bottle of wine, I'll tell you that."

"What happened?" Marx asked.

"Becca Hart, the lovely lady who rode in the ambulance with him day after day, reported that he made inappropriate comments on several occasions and that he touched her without her consent. Needless to say, he got canned."

Michael handed Marx the file on Becca Hart. There was a photograph of a dark-skinned woman with vivid green eyes. "Pretty."

"Apparently her partner thought so too," Sully commented.

"So he gets fired from his job as an EMT and decides to become a pimp?" Michael asked, his skepticism not hidden from his voice.

Sully shrugged. "Becca wasn't the only woman who complained about him, so he clearly didn't have any respect for women. Why he decided to become a pimp, I don't know."

Marx frowned as he perused the young woman's file. "This says Becca quit her job shortly after her partner was fired. Considerin' the uncomfortable situation had just been remedied, why quit?"

"She also moved to the slums and got a job as a gas station clerk," Sully pointed out. "Instant pay cut and an unsafe neighborhood."

Michael leaned forward, resting his elbows on his knees, as he eyed Marx. "What are you thinking?"

"I'm thinkin' this entire situation doesn't make sense."

They were going to have to drop by Becca Hart's apartment to see if she could shed some light on what happened five years ago, and whether or not it contributed to Terrence's murder.

"Do you think she had something to do with Terrence's death?" Michael asked.

In Marx's experience, women weren't usually the offenders of violent crimes; they tended to poison their victims or set fires. "I've learned that just about anythin' is possible."

"Well, before you go talk to her, I also found some interesting tidbits about our charming yet arrogant Dr. Wilder," Sully said. "He was involved with several ladies, some of whom were married. Apparently unhappily. And he made frequent calls to a cell number that belongs to a Sarah Akers."

"She's the girl he started dating when she was fifteen, right?" Michael asked.

Marx nodded. "I'm still not sure her father wasn't involved in Dr. Wilder's death."

"Oh, he might've been," Sully pointed out. "Dr. Wilder doesn't have a criminal record, but there is a record concerning an assault. Charges were dropped, but according to the report, Mr. Akers, Sarah's father, showed up at the doctor's house one night and punched him in the face."

That solidified Marx's hunch that Stephen Akers's anger toward Dr. Wilder could escalate to violence.

"If Sarah were my daughter, I would've punched him in the face too," Michael admitted. "What thirty-something-year-old man thinks it's okay to date a fifteen-year-old girl?"

Sully shrugged again. "While some of the women he was involved with were married, none of them were over twenty-one."

Michael leaned back in his chair with an expression of disgust on his face. "What are the chances Sarah wasn't the first or the last fifteen-year-old girl he was involved with?"

"Probably pretty slim, but what are you gonna do, go to every high school in the city and ask around?" Sully asked.

Marx shook his head. "Even if we happened across the right girl, he probably made her promise to keep it quiet just like he did with Sarah."

That answer seemed to agitate Michael, and he shifted in his chair. "You know, maybe it's a good thing he's dead. One less predator in the world."

Michael was a Christian, and like Holly, he valued human life, which made Marx curious about his sudden bout of vengeful anger. Was he worried about bringing a child into a world filled with predators?

Marx could understand that fear. He didn't have any children, but he knew how cruel the world could be to the vulnerable and innocent. He glanced at the picture of Holly on his desk next to the photo of his family.

"So what's next?" Michael asked.

Marx considered the options. They could go talk to Sarah's father, but Marx knew he wouldn't be cooperative. They could try to track down any other girls Dr. Wilder had been involved with—a tedious process that might get them nowhere—or they could track down Becca Hart and see if she could give them any more insight into their first victim.

12

*M*ichael studied the paint-chipped walls of the hallway as they made their way toward apartment 104. Flickering fluorescent lights buzzed overhead—a steady hum in the background of crying babies and shouting voices.

"Why would Becca move here?"

Marx wondered the same thing as he watched a rat skitter along the baseboard of one wall. The floor dipped suddenly. "Watch your step."

The warning came too late, and Michael stumbled, catching himself with a hand against the wall.

"Make sure you wash that hand with bleach."

Michael rubbed it on his pants. "How is this place not condemned?"

"I'm sure it's on a list that's sittin' on somebody's desk somewhere."

"You'd think it would be a priority."

"It will be, when somebody falls through the floor and doesn't get back up."

It had to be one signature away from being condemned and demolished. Nothing had been repaired or brought up to code in years. This building was a death trap.

Michael kept a hand on his gun as he scanned each of the apartment doors for the one they were searching for. "Half of these apartments don't have numbers. How are we supposed to figure out which one's which?"

Marx had been keeping a silent count since the last numbered apartment. "We're lookin' for the fourth door down on the left. Probably."

Michael stepped around a patch of vomit on the floor and pressed the back of a hand to his nose. "How do people live like this?"

"Not everybody has a choice."

They passed by a woman in a stained dress and mismatched shoes who was bouncing a crying baby on her hip. She looked at them with the glazed eyes of someone who hadn't slept in days.

"Isn't there some sort of government aid to get them better housing?" Michael whispered. "A program for lower income families or something?"

"For some, sure. But there are always people who slip through the cracks." He looked back over his shoulder to see that a little boy, no more than five, had joined the woman in the hall.

He sat on a little girl's tricycle, watching them with wide, dark eyes. Marx waved at him, and the little boy's face broke into a smile. He honked the bike horn and rolled back into the apartment.

"You know, I've lived in New York City all my life, and I never knew it got this bad," Michael said.

They reached the fourth door down on the left side of the hallway. "This is the place." Unease washed over Marx when he noticed the apartment door wasn't latched. He rapped light knuckles on the door frame. "Ms. Hart?"

Something crashed inside, followed by the rapid thump of retreating footsteps. Both detectives drew their weapons and pushed into the apartment, branching off from each other to cover more ground.

Marx rounded the corner into the kitchen, his eyes glossing over the contents in search of a human threat. Satisfied that the room was clear, he inched down the hall into the bedroom.

The mattress, layered with sheets and blankets, lay on the floor against the wall, and the contents of the small nightstand were strewn across the room. He tried to step in between the items so he didn't contaminate anything, and looked toward the closet.

A few pairs of shoes rested on the floor beneath clothes dangling from wire hangers. Wherever Becca Hart had gone, she hadn't taken the time to pack first, and given the state of her bedroom, he doubted she had gone willingly.

A flicker of movement in his periphery was his only warning before someone slammed into him from behind.

The impact flung Marx into the wall hard enough to leave him dazed and breathless, and he heard his gun hit the floor. He tried to pull himself together to defend against an attack, but the blurry figure scampered out the bedroom window onto the fire escape.

Still struggling to recapture the breath that had been knocked out of him, Marx managed to grab his gun and stagger to his feet just as Michael sprinted into the room. "Fire escape."

Michael climbed out the open window and dashed down the fire escape in pursuit. Marx followed him out just in time to see him hop down the last few steps and sprint after the man who was pounding the pavement to reach the street.

I am too old for this, Marx thought as he started down. He would be fifty in fourteen months, and chasing down suspects on foot irritated his body as much as his mood.

Michael barreled into the man like a defensive lineman and tackled him to the ground. Marx holstered his weapon as he walked over to join them, and crouched beside the tackled man's head.

He pulled Becca Hart's driver's license photo from his jacket pocket and put it in front of the man's face. "You don't look like Becca Hart, so why were you in her apartment?"

The man whimpered and pressed his forehead to the ground. "I'm sorry, I'm sorry, I'm sorry."

"Where is she?"

"Don't know, don't know, don't know."

Michael shot a concerned look at Marx. The man he was pinning to the ground might be a full-grown adult in body, but not in mind. "I'm gonna get off you now, and I want you to sit against the wall. Don't try to run."

He moved off him and grabbed his arm, helping him sit up against the side of the building. The man looked to be in his late thirties to early forties with dark, close-cropped hair and unusually round eyes.

"What's your name?" Marx asked.

The man ducked his head into the collar of his jacket and began to mutter under his breath, "Don't hurt me, don't hurt me."

"Nobody's gonna hurt you," Marx assured him. "Tell us your name."

"D-Davey."

"Why did you run, Davey?"

"S-scared." He pointed at the gun in Marx's holster. They had frightened him when they burst in with their weapons drawn.

"That apartment doesn't belong to you. What were you doin' there?"

Davey picked nervously at a loose thread on his shirt, reluctant to answer. "N . . . n-nobody home."

"You found the apartment empty and decided to stay?" Michael asked.

Davey nodded and began mumbling apologies again. Marx put a hand on his shoulder to calm him, and asked, "When did you find it empty?"

Davey's forehead crinkled, as if the question confused him. "Mmm, maybe . . . maybe not today. Maybe . . . not-not the day before . . . *before* before." He rubbed at his head, then began smacking his knuckles against it in growing frustration.

Marx caught his wrist to stop him from hurting himself. "Tuesday?" At Davey's blank look, Marx clarified, "Two days ago."

"Two . . . two days. Yeah, two days."

Which meant Becca had been gone for at least two days.

"Did anybody come by?" Marx asked.

Davey hesitated, then pointed to Marx's gun again. "Angry man."

"An angry man with a gun came by?" When Davey confirmed it with a nod, Marx considered how to ask his next question. He wasn't used to interviewing adults with the mental capacity of a child. He looked at Michael.

"What did the angry man look like, Davey?" Michael asked. "Was he . . . purple?"

Davey snorted in amusement.

"Not purple. All right. How about . . . green?" When Davey shook his head, Michael continued. "Brown, peach, strawberry . . ."

"Peach!" Davey blurted with excitement. "Ang-angry peach."

Michael smiled. "Good! Was he skinny like . . . a popsicle stick, round like a cucumber, or fat like a pumpkin?"

Davey laughed again. "Cu-cumber."

"Can you remember if he was tall or short?"

Davey's face creased with concentration. "Tall." He thought some more, then reached for the hood of his sweatshirt and pulled it up over his head. He pulled the strings until the fabric scrunched around his face.

A tall, peach-colored cucumber with a hooded sweatshirt. Marx couldn't exactly put a BOLO out for that.

"Thank you, Davey," Michael said. He stood and offered him a hand up, pulling the man to his feet. "You can go now."

Davey pointed up at Becca Hart's apartment, and Marx shook his head. "You can't go back there."

Davey's shoulders slumped in disappointment.

Michael looked at Marx to see if they were thinking along the same lines, and then patted Davey on the back. "Come on, buddy, we'll drop you at a shelter."

They let Davey out at the nearest homeless shelter where he would have a clean bed and a hot meal, then went back to question the other tenants in Becca Hart's building.

13

*M*ichael let out a grunt of frustration as the last apartment door closed in their faces. No one wanted to speak with them.

Marx approached the tired woman in the hall who was trying to soothe her upset baby. "Ma'am?"

She looked between them with suspicion. "Why are you asking around for Becca?"

"We just wanna make sure she's all right," Marx said. "There was somebody in her apartment who didn't belong there."

She shifted the baby to her opposite hip, the constant weight visibly draining her, and brushed a dark curl back from her sweaty forehead. "Is Becca hurt?"

"We don't know," Marx admitted. "What's your name, if you don't mind me askin'?"

She hesitated. "Maria."

Marx nodded gratefully. "Pleasure to meet you. I'm Detective Marx, and this is Detective Everly. What can you tell us about Becca?"

"She was a good person."

"How so?" Marx asked.

"Sometimes she helps me by watching Robbie." She nodded toward the little boy on the bike. "He can be a handful. Sometimes she watches the baby too while I go to work."

"Where do you work?"

The question put her on guard, and her posture stiffened defensively as she answered, "Wherever I'm needed."

Marx got the sense that she wasn't comfortable sharing what she did for a living because he was a cop. "You're friends with Becca?"

"Like I said, she's a good person."

"When was the last time you saw her?"

"Becca hasn't been here in three days. I haven't been to work because there's no one to watch the kids, and I don't trust these people." Her eyes swept the hall in both directions. "Robbie!"

She rattled something off in Spanish, and the little boy froze on his bike just inches from the dangerous dip in the floor. He looked down at it, then turned around and pedaled in their direction.

Marx waved at the boy again, and Robbie honked his horn with a grin.

"Please stop doing that," Maria said, agitated. "I don't want him to trust strangers. That's how people disappear."

Marx turned his attention back to her. "Is that how Becca disappeared?"

"No, Becca was . . . nervous. I asked her to watch the kids so I could work, and she said no. Becca loves children. She never says no. When I asked her why, she said she thought a man was following her."

"Did she tell you anything about him?" Michael asked. "What he looked like or who he might've been?"

She looked at him, her wariness returning. "No, she didn't. She told me she did something she regretted, and he wanted to punish her for it. I knew something was wrong when she didn't come home, but I don't think he got her."

"What makes you think that?" Marx asked.

"Because a masked man with a gun broke into her apartment looking for her after she was already gone."

Michael frowned. "How do you know he was looking for *her* and that he didn't just wanna steal something?"

She shot him an irritated look. "Because he left with nothing. Robbie!" She broke into Spanish again, her tone sharp as a knife's edge, and the boy looked up at her.

She pushed past Marx and Michael and slapped something from the boy's fingers. A syringe rolled across the floor. She scolded him in Spanish and he started to cry.

She took him by the hand and led him back to the apartment, nudging him inside. "I need to take care of my children. Please, find Becca before he does. Friends are hard to come by."

"We'll do our best," Marx told her, and she offered him the first semblance of a smile before shutting the door.

Michael lowered his voice to a whisper and asked, "How does someone notice that their neighbor's been missing for three days and not report it?"

"Fear. She thinks her family will be safer if she doesn't get involved. She probably already regrets talkin' to us." He stepped back into Becca's apartment and looked around. "Well, let's tear this place apart and see if we can figure out where she went."

Michael grabbed the spare pair of gloves he kept with him when he was on duty and pulled them on. "I got the bedroom."

Marx leaned over to see into the metal bucket in the center of the table. It was half-full of water, and a tiny drip from the ceiling plummeted down with a splash.

There was a second bucket near the couch, and he could see the water stains stretching across the ceiling and down the walls.

Michael had asked why someone would live here, and while some didn't have a choice, he doubted Becca was one of those people. She had quit a well-paying job and chosen to move here.

Maybe as some kind of self-imposed punishment, or maybe because she was hiding from the man who had come looking for her.

Marx opened the kitchen cupboards and scanned the nearly empty shelves. He nudged aside the few boxes of cereal and pasta, looking for anything suspicious.

Nothing but expired or damaged foods that looked like they had come from a food bank or secondhand store.

The kitchen drawers held nothing unusual. He opened the oven and jumped back when the door fell off and nearly landed on his feet. The insides of the oven were blackened and encrusted with burnt food too old to be distinguishable.

He had the passing thought that this was what Holly's oven would look like, and he smiled to himself.

There was something tucked in the back beneath a cookie sheet, and he pulled it out carefully. It was a small metal box layered in dust.

He opened it, and his brow furrowed. It was full of newspaper clippings and printed articles. He thumbed through them, realizing that most of them were obituaries, and they were filed by name.

Becca Hart seemed to have an obsession with death.

He set the box aside for later contemplation and went to check the bathroom. He searched the tub, the toilet, the medicine cabinet, and the shelf beneath the sink, but there was nothing out of the ordinary.

He was just about to move on to the next room when he remembered how Holly squirreled things away in random places. He reopened the medicine cabinet and studied the innocuous-looking items.

Holly hid things in her feminine hygiene box, something he discovered recently when he accidentally knocked them out of the bathroom cupboard and a bag of Doritos fell out.

He turned the box upside down, but only feminine hygiene products tumbled into the sink.

She had two containers of deodorant. He popped the lid off one—normal baby powder–scented deodorant—but the second one had been hollowed out and filled with pills.

He shook a few of the pills into his hand and examined them. There were no numbers to identify what they were. Since doctors didn't prescribe pills in deodorant bottles, though, it wasn't something she had gotten legally.

He finished searching her belongings and carried the deodorant bottle into the kitchen. "Found her stash of feel-good pills. At least I assume that's what they are. You find anythin'?"

Michael held up a gun. "Found this under the mattress. I have a sneaking suspicion she doesn't have a license for this."

Guns and drugs, Marx thought. *Never a good combination.*

Michael set the gun on the table and picked up the deodorant container. He popped the lid and studied the pills. "No idea what these are." He set down the pills and picked up the metal box. He opened it and pulled out the top article, reading the headline aloud. "Father of three dies in motorcycle accident." He moved to the next article. "Sue May obituary. Leaves behind a sister and a husband." He frowned as he continued flipping through them. "Uh . . . everybody in this box is dead."

"Mmm hmm. Kinda concernin' that an EMT was so obsessed with death."

"No doubt," Michael said, setting the box on the table and dusting off his gloves, as if the creepy box of death might somehow infect him.

"I wanna get these pills to the lab. See if we can figure out what they are, and I wanna know if that gun has been fired."

14

The gunshot rang out, and the bullet exploded into the water tank in the lab. Gage, the lab tech, set the weapon aside and removed his earmuffs, gesturing for Marx and Michael to do the same.

"Now I just gotta get it out and run a comparison to see if this is our murder weapon."

He opened the tank and reached in, pulling out the bullet. He observed it with interest as he carried it over to his lab table.

"I can tell you for sure, based on the striations, that the gun used in both homicides was a Glock 22 and that this bullet as well as the ones recovered from your victims are a 180 grain. Superior power right there."

"But is this the same gun?" Marx asked, his patience wearing thin. It was late, and he was tired.

Gage examined the bullets beneath a microscope, comparing the striations to tell if they were fired from the same weapon.

He straightened with interest. "Well, this gun's not a match to your two victims, but"—he rolled his chair over to the computer, typed a few keys, and turned the laptop for them to see—"it was used in a self-defense shooting two years ago."

They didn't recognize the perpetrator who had been shot and killed breaking into someone's home, but they recognized the shooter: Maria Rodriguez.

"Wait . . . isn't that Becca's neighbor?" Michael asked. "The one with the cute kids?"

"Mmm hmm." Marx folded his arms. "I'm guessin' she gave Becca the gun for self defense after she mentioned the man followin' her." It wasn't legal, but he wasn't interested in firearm violations. He needed to catch a killer. "What about the pills?"

Gage turned his attention to the evidence bag full of pills. He dropped one into a flask of water and exposed it to a fluorescent probe. After a few minutes of watching the contents, he announced, "Morphine."

It wasn't what Marx had been expecting, but morphine was a common street drug. "How much?"

Gage pulled one of the whole pills from the evidence bag and left it in the palm of his hand. "Thirty milligrams a pop. Depending on how much of this she was taking a day, she might have been so strung out that she imagined the guy following her."

"She's been missin' for three days," Marx said, doubtful that she'd imagined it. "She's hidin' from somebody."

"These are very easy to overdose on," Gage pointed out. "Most people don't think they're dangerous, but morphine is an opiate. It's addictive, it's powerful, and it trips you up in high doses. There's a good chance she took too much and you're looking for an OD victim."

Marx sighed and looked out at the darkness that had descended over the city. He'd been working for fifteen hours straight, and nothing they had found had brought them any closer to finding the killer or Becca Hart.

There was something important he was supposed to do this evening. As he watched the lights of passing cars flickering past the windows, it hit him. Holly. When he left this morning, he'd told her he would be home to have dinner with her.

He squeezed his eyes shut with a groan. He told Michael and the lab tech good night and headed home.

Marx stepped into a silent, dimly lit apartment and shut the door. His gaze landed on the peninsula, taking in the empty plates surrounded by silverware and glasses of sweet tea. A covered pot rested between the dishes.

He lifted the lid to see macaroni and cheese with hot dogs. *Cold* macaroni and cheese. Even the previously chilled tea had settled to room temperature. He dropped onto a stool with a sigh. She had prepared dinner hours ago.

He was trying to provide her with the stable environment she needed to heal, but his job made that difficult.

He grabbed the serving spoon and scooped a mountain of cold macaroni onto his plate. He stabbed a hot dog and some noodles with his fork and had the bite halfway to his mouth when Holly's bedroom door opened.

She appeared in the doorway, her clothes rumpled from sleep and her hair pulled up in a lopsided bun-ponytail thing. He wasn't really sure there was a name for such a chaotic mess.

Her voice had a cute, groggy slowness to it when she asked, "Eating without me?"

He smiled and set his fork down. "Of course not."

She yawned and made her way over to one of the empty stools. "You had a long day."

"I've had longer." He nodded to the pot. "You want me to warm it up?"

She shook her head, and her hair flopped back and forth with a life of its own. "I like it cold."

"Me too."

They were both too tired for conversation, so they settled into companionable silence as they ate their cold macaroni and cheese with hot dogs.

15

He knew he should try to sleep, but he was drawn to the online articles about his latest endeavors. As he scrolled, he noticed an article about Dr. Wilder's "murder." An inappropriate use of the word, in his opinion. Putting a criminal to death in prison wasn't murder; it was justice. This was no different.

He clicked on the article to see how the media interpreted his mission. His mood darkened with every paragraph. They were painting him as nothing more than an unhinged, sadistic killer. He wasn't unhinged, and he certainly wasn't a sadist. Why did they think he used a gun? It was quick and practically painless, a mercy the guilty didn't deserve.

And of course they had chosen a picture of Dr. Wilder that disguised his true nature behind a charismatic smile. He had left the scene the way he did so they would see his guilt.

He tapped an agitated finger on the mouse pad. Maybe he would just have to send them the correct picture.

He continued perusing the articles, each one more of the same, until he came across an article about the detective working his scenes.

Detective Richard Marx.

The detective had not only led the search for that missing girl in March, but he had found her in a matter of days.

Good for the girl, but this was not the kind of person he wanted trying to track him down. Maybe he could reason with him, make him see that eliminating these people was best for everyone.

But all hope of explaining things to the detective fled when he came across another article. One of the photographers had snapped a picture of Detective Marx as he was ducking under the crime scene tape at the doctor's house. Was that . . . judgment on his face?

He zoomed in on the image, studying the detective's expression. It was judgment. And disapproval.

No, there would be no reasoning with this man.

He skimmed a few more news reports looking for any details about the investigation. His heart fluttered in his chest when a sentence leaped out at him:

Detective Marx refused comment, but according to a source in the department, he is narrowing in on a suspect.

How had he put things together so quickly? How much did he know? Was the media exaggerating? They had to be.

If anyone suspected him, surely he would know, he would sense danger closing in. He had excellent instincts. But then, so did Detective Marx.

He slammed the laptop shut in anger. As a man sworn to uphold the law and apprehend the guilty, Detective Marx should've been on his side, not working against him.

He was going to have to do a little digging to find out how much he knew and whether or not he was going to be a problem that needed to be dealt with.

16

A warning whispered across Marx's mind, and he woke without the fog of tiredness that usually clung to his thoughts in the morning. The anxious flutter in his stomach had to be the remnants of a dream he couldn't remember.

The red numbers on his alarm clock glowed 5:33 a.m. His alarm wasn't set to go off for another hour. Frowning, he pushed back the covers and threw on a T-shirt before stepping out of his bedroom.

Holly was sitting on the couch. "Hey, sweetheart. Can't sleep?"

He ran a hand over his mussed hair as he walked into the living room. She closed her fingers to conceal something in her hand, and looked up at him.

That anxious feeling rippled through him again. Something wasn't right.

He sat down on the edge of the coffee table. One glimpse into her eyes—windows to a haunted soul—explained the feeling in his gut.

"Holly, what's in your hand?"

She didn't answer. He took her hand and pried open her fingers, his heart lodging in his throat when he saw the handful of pills.

It was the Vicodin prescription he had filled for her before bringing her home from the hospital. She had refused to take it despite the physical pain she was in. But

Holly could bear physical pain far better than the fear, shame, and memories that followed the kind of abuse she had suffered.

When she was fifteen, she had tried to escape her foster brother's torment by swallowing a bottle of pills. It was a miracle she had survived. But this amount of pills would kill her.

"Give me the pills, sweetheart."

She lowered her eyes back to the pills, then glanced beside him at the glass of water. "I'm tired."

He could see the weariness weighing down her shoulders, the shadows of painful memories that never left her eyes, and the sheer exhaustion of too many sleepless nights. All beating her down into a pit of hopelessness.

He had thought the nightmares of her dying were just a manifestation of his fears, but some part of his mind had recognized the signs.

"I know you're tired, baby. I know." He tried to clear the tightness from his throat. "But you can't give up. I need you to keep fightin'."

She flexed her fingers, watching the moistening pills shift in her palm. "I can't. I can't make him go away. I can't sleep."

He could tell by the dark circles under her eyes that it had been days since she'd slept. If he could just help her rest, she would feel strong enough to keep fighting.

What was that saying? Something about weariness. "There's a verse my mama used to say. Somethin' about come to me, weary folk."

102

A ghost of a smile touched her lips. "'Come to me, all you who are weary and burdened, and I will give you rest.'"

"You're not alone in this fight, Holly. Maybe you just need to rest and let somebody else fight for you for a little while."

Tears glistened in her eyes. "How?"

He moved to sit beside her on the couch and held out his hand. "Trust that I will keep you safe while you sleep."

The tears spilled over, and she shook her head as she looked back at the pills, her way out. "I can't."

Her words were like a knife straight to his heart. "I know I failed before, but I failed because I wasn't here. I'm here now, and I will shoot anybody who tries to get through that door with the intention of hurtin' you. And Riley will attack whatever's left of them." He gave her a moment to absorb his words, then said, "Please give me the pills."

He could take them from her without much of a fight, but that would be a last resort. He didn't want to take any choices away from her if he could avoid it.

After a long hesitation, she dumped the sticky pile of pills into his waiting hand. He wrapped the pills in a tissue, and stuffed it in his pocket so she couldn't change her mind.

"Come here, sweet pea."

She leaned against him, and he wrapped her in the safety of his arms. He pulled the throw blanket over her and settled in for a long morning and possibly afternoon.

He sent a message to his lieutenant, letting him know that he wouldn't be in until later due to a personal emergency. He wasn't leaving Holly until he saw that familiar shine of determination and stubbornness in her eyes.

"Holly?"

"Hmm?" she responded, drowsiness slipping into her voice.

"Promise me that you won't try to hurt yourself again." He felt the dampness of her tears soaking through his T-shirt, and he brushed the hair back from her forehead so he could see her face. "Promise me."

Holly was one of the most honest people he knew, and if she made a promise, she did everything in her power to keep it. "I promise."

"Will you let me take you to see somebody? Somebody who can help you." When he heard her draw in a breath to object, he said, "I know you don't wanna talk to anybody, because talkin' about it hurts, but do this for me. Please. For my peace of mind."

She sniffled and rubbed at her nose with the sleeve of her T-shirt. "Okay."

He bit back a sigh of relief and turned on a movie before texting Shannon: *She's ready to see somebody.*

She replied swiftly: *I have that list of counselors, and I'll make some calls.*

He started to respond with a thank-you when a call came through, causing his phone to vibrate. He was about to ignore the call, but then he saw that it was his mother.

He accepted the call, but before he could do more than press the phone to his ear, his mother demanded, "What happened? Is she all right?"

"Is who all right?"

She made that exaggerated huff that only Southern women seemed to be able to do, and said, "You know I'm talkin' about Holly."

Marx looked down at the top of Holly's head and then pulled his phone away from his ear, eyeing it with suspicion. He hadn't spoken to his mother in over a week. How did she know something was wrong? "She's fine. Why would you think otherwise?"

"I woke up at four o'clock this mornin' with a hankerin' for biscuits. So I went downstairs to make some."

Of course she did, Marx thought with a smile.

"And while I was mixin' up my biscuits, I noticed Holly's picture on my prayer board. I got this feelin' come over me that somethin' was wrong. I started prayin' and I didn't even know what I was prayin' for."

Marx thought about the whisper of warning that had woken him an hour before his alarm clock. Could it have been because of his mother's prayers? "Everybody's fine, Mama. But I'll call you later."

He said good-bye and hung up, silencing his phone. His mind lingered on that whisper of warning. If he had chosen to ignore it, would he be cradling Holly's lifeless body right now?

Lord, if that was you . . . thank you.

He stroked Holly's hair gently, grateful beyond words that she was still with him. He felt the rest of the tension melt from her body as she drifted to sleep.

His thoughts wandered as he listened to the steady sound of her breathing, finally landing on Becca Hart. When he found the container of pills in her apartment, he assumed she was a recreational user, but now he was reconsidering.

He didn't know much about the woman, but he knew she had quit a successful job and moved to the slums to work as a gas station attendant. One look at her apartment made it clear that she was hiding from something. And he wondered now if those pills were the way she had found to cope with a truth she wanted to forget.

Marx drifted in and out of a light sleep on the couch until a quiet tapping noise roused him.

He opened his eyes and looked down at Holly. She had slid down little by little over the past six hours, and her head was now resting on the fuzzy gray pillow in his lap.

He hated that pillow. It looked like someone had shaved a scruffy mutt and glued the hair into a massive ball. He was tempted to take some hair clippers to it.

He tried to shift positions without jostling Holly. It may have only been six hours, but somewhere along the way, his joints had fused together, and he'd lost all feeling in his legs.

A tap on the door drew his attention. Holly let out a sleepy moan and snuggled closer. When the person outside knocked again, her eyelids fluttered open. Her body went taut with fear, and she stared up at him with huge eyes, like a terrified rabbit caught in a trap.

The cloudiness of sleep cleared from her eyes, replaced by recognition, and she started to relax.

"Mornin'," he said, though technically it was afternoon now.

She pushed herself up slowly, tucking her wild hair behind her ears. "Hi."

He smiled at her awkward shyness, then searched her eyes. The shadows of pain were still there, but the six hours of uninterrupted sleep had rekindled a tiny spark of determination.

"Any nightmares?"

She thought about it for a second, then said, "Not that I remember."

She had murmured and shifted in her sleep, but he was glad that none of the dreams had morphed into nightmares.

Holly rubbed at her eyes. "How long did you sit here?"

"Long enough that I feel rested." *And stiff as an eighty-year-old man.* He stretched until his spine popped in three places, easing the tension in his back.

A fourth knock reverberated through the apartment, and the persistence and patience gave Marx an idea of who was at the door.

He stood and tried to shake the tingles from his right leg as he walked to the door. He cracked it open to see Sam standing in the hall. "Mornin', Sam."

"Hey." Sam glanced past him to see Holly huddled beneath a blanket on the couch. He stared at her for a beat before nodding in greeting, then glanced at Marx, concern seeping into his stony expression. He was seeing what Marx saw every day: Holly was bone thin and exhausted, and the dark crescents under her eyes from too little sleep looked like bruises against her pale skin.

"Let's talk in the hall," Marx suggested, ushering him out the door before he said something that would upset Holly.

"The lieutenant said you reported off for a personal emergency."

Marx recognized the unspoken question hanging at the end of that statement. Though Sam seldom voiced his feelings, he adored Holly, and he was worried about her. "Holly's fine."

"She doesn't look fine. She looks like she hasn't slept in a week. Or eaten."

When Marx first brought her home from the hospital, she wouldn't speak or leave her room unless it was to shower. She spent most of her days curled up in bed, fluctuating between a state of detachment that concerned him and bouts of crying that broke his heart. It might not seem like it to an outside observer, but she was moving forward through the stages of healing.

"She's in the recovery phase," Marx said. Although Holly had refused to see a counselor up until now, he had been in contact with several, trying to figure out how to understand and help her. "I guess what she's goin' through now is normal—inability to sleep, nightmares, changes in appetite, anxiety, flashbacks, depression." Marx paused before adding, "Some days she's gonna feel better, and some days . . . some days are gonna be like today."

"Is there anything I can do to help?"

"I doubt it. I think she's reached the point where she needs to talk to somebody about it. A professional who knows how to help her through the trauma."

"I could—"

"Absolutely not."

"You didn't even let me finish."

"Because I know how you are, and when you try to explain somethin' to Holly, it makes her wanna throw things at your head. And she needs to deal with her pain, not stuff it in a box wrapped in logic."

Sam scowled more than usual. "Fine. On to the point of my visit then. The lieutenant was gonna call you after his morning meetings, but I told him I would come by to let you know that a third victim matching your two other cases turned up this morning."

"Who?"

"Grant Blakely. A cop from the two-three."

"He murdered a cop?" The man may as well have signed his death warrant. Every cop in the city would want to put a bullet in him now.

"Cop survived. He's at Harlem Hospital, but it doesn't look good."

"Why isn't the two-three investigatin' this? He's one of theirs."

"Chief's concerned that the officers from his precinct are gonna take it too personally and it's gonna cloud their judgment. Since the first two cases were yours, he bumped it to you."

Marx bit back a groan at the friction that decision was going to cause between the two departments. He hated politics.

"You want me to let Michael know?" Sam asked.

Marx shook his head. "No, I'll get a hold of him, and I'll meet him there as soon as I can." He said good-bye to Sam and stepped back into the apartment.

He smiled when he saw that Holly had curled up in the corner of the couch with her arms wrapped around the furry pillow, watching a movie.

He grabbed his phone off the coffee table and noticed that he had missed a call from Jordan. Jordan was Holly's best friend from childhood, and while he irritated Marx to no end, he put up with him for Holly's sake.

He called him back as he retreated into the bathroom to shower. "What?" he asked the moment Jordan picked up the call.

"Hello to you too," Jordan replied, a note of amusement in his voice. "I was hoping to spend some time with Holly today."

Jordan's time with Holly had been limited since the assault. It wasn't because he had done something wrong; it was the simple fact that he was male and attracted to her, and Holly felt more comfortable if Marx was present for Jordan's visits.

"I have to work," Marx said, though he didn't like the idea of leaving Holly alone after the morning she'd had.

"I thought maybe we could try going out somewhere."

Marx frowned as he grabbed a towel and washcloth from the cupboard. "I'm not sure that's a good idea."

Holly hadn't been very far from the apartment in the past two months. She felt safer inside behind a locked door, but Marx had been working on that with her.

"It's just a couple blocks away," Jordan explained. "I'm not gonna let anything happen to her."

"She doesn't feel safe with you, Jordan."

Jordan fell quiet. "I know. I need to rebuild that trust with her, but that's never gonna happen if you're always chaperoning."

Marx leaned against the bathroom vanity. "Where are you wantin' to take her?"

"I wanna take her to the agency."

Jordan had recently purchased a property with the intention of creating a detective agency, a profession that would allow him to use his law enforcement experience, and he wanted Holly to work with him. Marx had expressed his concerns—loudly—but ultimately it was Holly's decision.

"I don't think she's ready to be alone with you or that far from where she feels safe. Not yet."

"I wanna try."

Marx looked at the bathroom door when Holly's muffled voice came through it, then opened it to see her standing in the hallway, munching on a cracker the color of her hair. "Are you eavesdroppin'?"

She pasted on an innocent expression and took another nibble of her cracker. He was glad to see that the rest had improved her spirits, but he didn't like the idea of her pushing herself.

Marx lowered the phone to his chest as he asked her, "Are you sure you wanna do that? Go out? Alone with Jordan?"

He saw the uncertainty flicker behind her eyes, but she nodded. "I have to try. I want my life back."

He couldn't argue with that. "Okay. But you call me if you get anxious or if you think you're gonna have a panic attack. I'll come pick you up."

She nodded again and popped the remaining nibble of cracker into her mouth.

He gave her a disapproving look. "And please eat somethin' more than a Cheez-It."

17

*O*fficer Blakely's home was a battlefield—he hadn't gone down without a fight. Furniture was overturned, and pictures and random knickknacks were scattered around the living room.

Marx crouched and picked up one of the picture frames with a gloved hand. Grant Blakely was young. He couldn't have been on the force for more than ten years. The man pictured with him could've been his twin.

"Blakely have a brother?" He looked up at the officer from the 23rd precinct who had been assigned to aid them if necessary.

The officer stood with his arms folded and his teeth clenched, exuding irritation. "Cousin."

Marx grunted and replaced the picture on the floor next to the evidence marker. As he stood, he asked, "Was there a note?"

"There was a lie scribbled on some paper, if that's what you're asking," the officer replied curtly.

Marx spared the officer a brief look, then turned his attention to the crime scene tech beside him. The woman held up a sealed evidence bag with a note inside.

"I should have protected the innocent," Marx read aloud.

"That's bull. Grant's a good cop."

Marx eyed the officer. "I didn't say he wasn't. But since you brought it up, did he ever have any problems on the job?"

The officer pressed his lips together and looked out the window, refusing to speak poorly of a comrade in arms.

Marx resisted the impulse to shake the answers out of him. He'd already been reprimanded by his lieutenant for his temper and attitude; assaulting a fellow officer wouldn't help matters.

He looked toward the door when he heard Michael's voice. His partner ducked under the tape and slipped on the crime scene booties before stepping into the house.

Marx frowned at the bruise brushing up against his hairline and the gash on his forehead being held together with butterfly tape. "What happened to you?"

"I got in a fight with the plumbing last night." He pulled on his gloves. "Fixing sinks is not in my skill set. Dropped the wrench on my head, then I sat up so fast I smacked my forehead on the edge of the cupboard."

Marx winced inwardly. "That had to hurt."

"Left me with one heck of a headache, and probably a permanent reminder to call a plumber next time." He pointed to the gash that would likely scar, and Marx shook his head.

He refocused his attention on the scene. "As a trained officer, Blakely had to suspect the intruder would kill him after he got what he wanted, so why write the note?"

Michael looked at the note in the evidence bag. "Maybe the killer threatened his wife. That's a surefire way to get most husbands to do things they wouldn't normally do."

Even if Mrs. Blakely hadn't been home at the time, the killer could've ensured Grant's cooperation by threatening to wait for her.

"Who do you like for this?" the officer asked.

"Oh, now you wanna talk?" Marx replied with an edge of spite.

The officer shifted his square jaw, clearly biting back his own anger. "Grant is a good cop and a good man, and I won't participate in a conversation that smears his reputation."

Marx wondered if the officer was even aware that his refusal to answer that question told him what he needed to know: that Officer Blakely had done something questionable, something with the potential to ruin his reputation as a "good cop."

"So do you have a suspect or what?" the officer demanded.

"I have some theories, but I prefer to keep them to myself until I make an arrest." He saw Michael frown out of the corner of his eye. He hadn't meant that he wouldn't share his theories with his own partner, but he could clarify that later. "Let's swing by the hospital and talk to Mrs. Blakely."

Blakely's wife sat in the hospital waiting room, cemented to the chair with shock.

"Mrs. Blakely?" Michael said softly, and she lifted her head, gazing at him with a far-off look in her eyes.

There was a sedated glaze over her expression, and Marx suspected the doctors had given her something to help calm her down.

Michael sat down in the chair beside her. "I'm Detective Everly. This is Detective Marx. We're here about your husband."

She lowered her gaze to her lap, fidgeting absently with the wad of tissues in her hands. "He's in surgery."

"I know this isn't the easiest time for you, but . . . can you tell us anything about what happened?"

"I spent the past couple days visiting my sister in Pittsburgh. When I got home . . ." Grief choked her voice and she pressed the tissues to her eyes. "Grant . . . was on the living room floor, and there . . . there was just so . . ." She looked down at her clothes, spattered and smeared with her husband's blood.

After what she had seen, it was amazing she was upright in a chair rather than falling to pieces on the floor.

"I can't believe this is happening."

Michael reached over and took her hand, and she latched onto that small gesture with a desperate need for human comfort.

"I'm sorry that you saw that," Michael said, genuine regret in his voice.

There were some sights that stood the test of time, never losing their horrifying clarity. Seeing a loved one in that brutal condition was a mental snapshot that never faded.

Marx understood that more than most; his mind stitched together horrifying images of Holly's torment and put them on replay in the back of his mind.

"There was a note left at the scene," Michael said. "It said 'I should have protected the innocent.' Do you have any idea what that means?"

She shook her head. "Grant protects the innocent every day. It's his passion. And I don't understand why someone would write that."

"Grant didn't write it?" Marx asked in surprise.

"No." She looked between him and Michael. "It wasn't his handwriting. I don't know who wrote that awful note, but it wasn't my husband."

If Grant hadn't written the note, then the killer had, which meant they had a sample of his handwriting. Marx sent a quick message to the lab to have it analyzed.

"Did you notice anything different about your husband lately? Any anxiety or unexpected tension?" Michael asked.

She shook her head. "He's always tense when he has a rough day at work, but . . . nothing out of the ordinary. Actually, he's been excited. We were planning a reunion with his cousin—they grew up together, like brothers—and he was really looking forward to it. But now . . . he might not . . ." She covered her face and broke down into fresh sobs.

Michael glanced back at Marx, then said to Grant's wife, "Mrs. Blakely, would you mind if I prayed with you?"

She wiped at her tears. "My husband and I aren't believers."

Michael nodded in understanding. "I am, and I believe in the power of prayer."

She swallowed. "Okay."

He bowed his head and whispered a quiet prayer, calling on the Lord to give her comfort and strength, and to give the doctors steady hands. He closed the prayer and released her hand.

"I know you don't believe, but just know that God's always listening when you need an ear, and when you feel alone. It's okay to reach out." Michael handed her a business card. "Please call if you think of anything more or if you just have questions."

"Thank you, Detective."

He smiled and left her alone to wait for the doctor. To Marx he said, "How are we supposed to get ahead of this guy if we can't make sense of his decisions? I mean, a pimp, a doctor, and a cop? What gives?"

"I don't know. If Officer Blakely pulls through, though, I want a guard posted outside of his hospital . . ." He trailed off when he thought he saw a familiar figure walk past the waiting room doorway. "Was that . . ."

The band on Michael's wrist vibrated, drawing Marx's attention back.

"Since when do you wear bracelets?"

"It's a fitness band."

"Callin' it by a different name doesn't change the fact."

Michael rolled his eyes. "It syncs with my phone, and right now it's telling me I have a text from Kat." He pulled out his phone to check his messages, and worry shadowed his face. "Kat's not feeling well."

Marx could see the fear in his partner's expression. After two miscarriages, Michael was probably terrified they were going to lose this baby too. "Go home."

"But the case—"

"I'll handle the case. Go home and check on your wife."

Michael let out a breath of relief, and he muttered a quick thank-you before dashing out of the hospital.

Marx glanced at his watch. He had time to stop by the jewelry shop to pick up the gift he had ordered for Holly a couple weeks ago. He hoped it would give her some comfort. It also gave him an excuse to check on her and make sure she was doing all right.

He pulled into the small parking lot of an old, single-story building that used to be a medical clinic. The letters had been scraped off the front windows, but there was still a faint trace of the previous name: Avery's Medical Center.

This wasn't a neighborhood where he wanted Holly spending her time, but this was where Jordan had brought her. He glanced at the silver vehicle parked in front of the building as he got out of his car.

He grabbed the gift box off the dashboard and tucked it into his jacket pocket before heading into the building.

"Where did all the stuff come from?" Holly asked, looking around at the furniture and computer.

"Well, aside from all the money I've saved up for the past ten years in Stony Brooke, my parents—mainly my mom since my dad and I aren't on speaking terms at the moment—wanted to help out. I also got a start-up business loan," Jordan explained.

"What does Marx think?"

"That it's a bad idea," Marx said, stepping into the musty building with water-stained yellow walls. "I don't relish the thought of you bein' involved with missin' persons cases or people in trouble."

"It's not like I'm gonna send her to go question a pimp or drug dealer by herself, Marx," Jordan replied. "When we do investigative work, the plan is for me to be with her."

"Right, because things always go accordin' to plan when little Ms. Independent's involved," Marx grumbled sarcastically. He pulled the small gift box from his pocket and handed it to Holly. "I had somethin' made for you."

She lit up like a shooting star when she saw the sparkly box. The first time he gave her a gift, it had taken her five minutes to open it. She moved a little quicker with this one.

She moved aside the tissue paper and gasped at the piece of silver jewelry with little charms on it: a cat, a dog, a camera, a rainbow, and a pair of running shoes.

She lifted it from the box with her left hand, then cocked her head curiously. "I'm not sure this will fit my wrist." She looked from her left wrist to the giant bracelet, and then to her right wrist, which was still in a cast. She made a thoughtful noise as she considered whether or not it would fit with her cast.

Marx smiled. "It's for your ankle. Let me help you with it."

She handed it to him, and he crouched to fasten it around her left ankle. She stiffened when he lifted her pant leg, but she didn't pull away.

"There." He tugged her pant leg back down and stood. "There's a charm on here that has a small GPS tracker in it, but it's not activated. Whether or not you activate it is entirely your decision, but if you decide to and somethin' happens, we'll be able to find you."

He saw her swallow and look down toward the anklet. If, as she feared, Collin escaped or was released from the county jail before the trial, and he managed to grab her again, they would be able to find her. It was as much for his piece of mind as hers.

"It would only be for emergencies?" she asked.

He nodded. "I promise. None of us would ever use it to infringe on your privacy."

She was quiet for a moment before she said, "Thank you."

"You're welcome, sweetheart."

"So, about the job . . ." Jordan said, bringing the conversation back around.

Holly looked from him to Marx with uncertainty. Marx wanted her to take more time to focus on healing, but maybe this would help her regain some sense of normalcy.

"Whatever you decide, I'll do my best to support it," he said.

"Do I get paid?" she asked, and Jordan laughed.

"Of course."

"Are you gonna want me to make you coffee?"

"Um, assuming the rumors I hear are true"—he glanced over her head at Marx— "why don't you leave the coffee making to me?"

"Wise decision," Marx commented.

Holly chewed on her lip as she considered the job offer, then announced, "I can't work in a place with pee-yellow walls."

Marx bit back a laugh. Yellow was Holly's least favorite color, with brown coming in at a close second. Whenever she had a bag of M&M's, she picked out the brown and yellow ones and gave them to him.

Jordan held up a finger as he walked away and then came back with a tub of slate-blue paint, a paint tray and three rollers. "I wasn't planning on keeping them yellow." He offered a paint roller to each of them.

Marx checked the time. He didn't have a whole lot to spare, but he could help for a few minutes. He stripped out of his jacket and began rolling up his shirt sleeves. "Well, let's get started."

Holly dipped her roller into the paint and climbed up onto a chair. "I'll get the top!"

Jordan and Marx exchanged an amused look. The shortest person in the room was going to paint the highest point of the wall? They both watched her as she stood on tiptoe and stretched. She grunted as she tried to make herself tall enough to get that last inch, but she couldn't.

She sank back to her heels and glared up at the wall, seemingly offended by its lack of cooperation. She tried one more time, then abruptly announced, "I'll get the bottom."

She climbed down off the chair and went to work on the wall above the baseboards.

Marx smiled and shook his head. They were halfway through one wall when the front door opened and an Asian woman in a wheelchair rolled into the office.

"I brought goodies!" she declared, waving a tray of drinks in the air.

Holly popped up and went over to give her friend a side hug. "Hi, Jace."

Jace grinned and plucked a cup from the tray. "Hot chocolate with extra, extra marshmallows and caramel for my bestie."

"Ooh." Holly took it and popped the lid off, drawing in the sweet aroma. "Mmm."

"I know. I had one too, but mine had two shots of espresso and a drizzle of hot fudge. A dose of heaven for less than six bucks. Beat that."

"I don't think you need caffeine," Marx said to Jace. She was hyper enough without it.

"Plain, bitter, and boring for Mr. Southern." She held up a cup for him, and he took the offering.

"Black coffee is neither plain nor borin'."

"Oh, I wasn't talking about the coffee." She winked at him to make sure he knew she was joking. "And cream and sugar for the second-place best friend."

Jordan snatched the dangling cup with a crooked grin. "What makes you think you're first place?"

"Obviously because she likes me more. I mean, I am pretty fantastic."

"Maybe it's not a matter of more or less and she just likes you differently than she likes me."

"I hope so, 'cause . . . you're a boy." She set down the empty drink carrier, interlaced her fingers, and cracked her knuckles. "Now, let's get down to business. Where's *my* paint roller?"

Marx handed his off to her. "You can use mine. I gotta get back to work." He wrapped an arm around Holly, giving her a gentle hug. When she looked up at him, he asked, "You gonna be all right?"

He saw the uncertainty in her eyes, but she forced a smile. She was doing better than she was this morning, but she was putting on a cheerful face for her friends. He wished she didn't feel the need to do that.

"I bet I can paint faster than you," Jace said behind them, and they both looked back to see the inevitable paint battle. Jace was competitive to a fault.

"Yeah? I bet I can paint higher than you," Jordan replied teasingly.

"That's cheap. I'm only four feet tall."

Holly gripped a fistful of Marx's shirt, and he was about to ask if she was all right when he noticed her staring through the glass door.

The familiar figure he thought he had seen outside the hospital waiting room grabbed the door handle, his thick arms flexing and a vein throbbing in his forehead.

Stephen Akers, Sarah's father.

He looked like he was itching for a fight. Marx swept Holly behind him in case the guy came in swinging. "Jordan."

The lighthearted conversation behind him died, and he felt Jordan approach on his left just as Stephen wrenched open the door and stepped inside.

"We're not open for business, and this is private property," Jordan informed him.

Stephen's eyes flickered briefly over the other people in the room before landing on Marx. "My daughter still hasn't come home."

"I'm sure there's a good reason, which we can discuss *outside*." Marx nodded toward the parking lot.

Stephen's gaze swept over the people in the room again, lingering briefly on Jace and Holly, then moving to Jordan. Whether he realized he was outnumbered, or he just didn't want to frighten the girls, he decided not to argue. He shoved the door open harder than necessary and walked out to wait on the sidewalk.

Jordan turned to Marx. "Who is that guy?"

"A suspect in my case."

"Is he dangerous?" Holly asked.

Marx offered her a reassuring smile. "I'll be fine."

Stephen pounded on the glass impatiently, demanding Marx's attention, and Marx shot him a glare of warning.

He set aside his coffee to free up his hands, and told Jordan to stay with the girls before going out to talk with Stephen.

"I don't appreciate you showin' up here and scarin' the girls."

"I don't care if you don't appreciate it," Stephen snapped back. "Sarah hasn't come home, and you know where she is."

Marx did have her contact information, but Sarah was avoiding her family for a reason, and unless she asked him for help, he wasn't getting in the middle of it. "So you followed me."

For the first time, Marx saw a glimmer of something other than anger in the man's eyes—regret. "I told her that if she didn't stop seeing that pervert, she could find a different place to live. I didn't actually expect her to leave. And when she did, I thought she would come back."

Had Stephen realized his mistake in giving his daughter an ultimatum, and then tried to fix it by getting rid of the problem? "You thought if Dr. Wilder was out of the picture, she might come home."

Stephen shifted his jaw in irritation. "Sarah's not ready to be on her own. She's . . . naïve and easily manipulated. She won't survive out there."

"When you were out lookin' for your daughter the other night, did you happen to stop by Dr. Wilder's condo?"

"No."

He was lying. He hid it well from his face, but the muscle that flexed in his neck betrayed the truth. "I think you *were* there. Wouldn't be the first time. And your car was spotted outside Wilder's house two nights before he died."

It was a leap, but it paid off when Stephen's attention shifted to the vehicle parked along the street, a car that resembled the color Ms. Donovan had identified as Glossy Royal—a blue approaching black.

"You can't prove anything," Stephen said.

"That's where you're wrong. You knew where the victim lived. You assaulted him on his own doorstep last year. You sat outside his house. You went there lookin' for your daughter, and you had motive to get rid of him."

Fury ignited in Stephen's eyes, and he clenched his fingers into fists as Marx spoke.

"How hard do you think it's gonna be to link you to his murder?"

Stephen was bigger and younger, but when he came at Marx, he came at him with anger instead of skill.

Marx parried to avoid the man's meaty fist, and Stephen stumbled. "Come down to the station and we'll talk about what happened."

He caught a glimpse of Holly standing by the door, watching with wide eyes. Jordan was talking to her, probably trying to convince her to move without having to move her himself.

Holly didn't budge from in front of the door until a skinny pair of arms locked around her waist from behind and pulled her backward. She landed in Jace's lap, and Jordan grabbed the handles of Jace's wheelchair and wheeled both of them away from the door.

Distracted by what was happening with the girls, Marx almost missed the second fist flying at his head. He dodged it just in time and then leveled Stephen with a right hook to the face.

And his lieutenant thought *he* had a temper. At least he didn't explode and try to attack people like this putz.

Stephen hit the ground hard, cupping his nose as he curled in on himself like an overgrown potato bug.

Marx tried to flex the pain from his knuckles as he glared down at him. "I grew up with a father just like you—a bully who thought everythin' could be solved with a raised voice or swingin' fist. You can shout and throw punches all you want. You don't scare me."

He pulled his handcuffs from his belt and forced Stephen onto his stomach.

He had a feeling Lieutenant Kipner was going to reprimand him for punching his suspect in the face. He probably could've subdued him without breaking his nose, but he didn't regret it.

He hauled Stephen to his feet. "In case you haven't figured it out yet, you're under arrest."

18

*S*tephen sat in the interrogation room chair, arms locked over his chest, and glared at the one-way mirror. Marx stared back from the other side, watching the man's agitation build.

"Was it necessary to hit him?" Lieutenant Kipner asked, frowning at Stephen's swollen face.

"He swung first."

Lieutenant Kipner's mustache twitched, which Marx could only assume meant he was smiling. "Try not to break anything else. We don't need a lawsuit. And if you can't find definitive proof that he's our killer, cut him loose."

"Sir—"

"Father looking for his daughter unjustly locked up for the murder of a man who preyed on his fifteen-year-old child. That is not something we can afford to see in the papers right now."

After the events this past year, the NYPD couldn't afford any more negative attention, and throwing Stephen Akers into a cell on suspicion alone would cause just that. "I understand."

"Good." Lieutenant Kipner paused with one foot out the door and asked, "Where's Detective Everly?"

"He went home to check on his wife."

Lieutenant Kipner grunted in acknowledgment before leaving. Marx grabbed the file folders off the chair and walked into the interrogation room.

Stephen shot him a look of smoldering hatred. "What took you so long?"

Marx sat down at the table, donning a mask of indifference. He only allowed suspects to see the emotions he wanted them to see. "Did I inconvenience you?"

Stephen shifted in his chair. "I don't know what you think you're gonna prove by dragging me in here, but—"

"Did I forget to mention that I'm a homicide detective? My goal is to prove that you committed a homicide. So let's get started. Why were you in Dr. Wilder's house?"

"I've never been in his house."

"Hmm." He pulled a photo of a fingerprint from the top folder. "Then explain this."

"It's a fingerprint."

"*Your* fingerprint. Found inside Dr. Wilder's condo, where you have apparently never been."

Stephen swallowed.

Marx laid out several more pictures, displaying powdered fingerprints on a window sill. "You climbed in through the bedroom window, which we found open at the scene."

He opened the next file, which was a rap sheet.

"You were arrested in 1995 for breakin' and enterin'. Isn't that interestin'."

"That was a misunderstanding."

"I suppose Dr. Wilder's dead body was a misunderstandin' too."

Stephen made a sucking sound with his cheek and stared at the picture of his fingerprint. "I went to Wilder's house that night. Looking for my daughter. I got there around eleven, which was around the time she usually shows up."

"And?"

"I waited, just like I did the two nights before that."

Marx tapped a finger on the picture of the window sill. "You didn't just wait."

"The window was already open, so I climbed in to see if Sarah was staying with him. None of her things were in the master bedroom. I figured maybe she was staying in a spare room. I went to check."

"And what did you find?"

Stephen sighed and slid down an inch in his chair. "Wilder was already dead. I rushed through the house, looking for Sarah, but I couldn't find her. So I left."

"You just . . . left."

"Yeah, I just left. I climbed in through a window and found a pervert dead. Did you think I was gonna call the cops and wait? I'm not an idiot."

And yet he had left his fingerprints all over the condo. Who breaks into a house without wearing gloves?

"What exit did you use?" Marx asked.

"The front door."

His story matched with the prints found at the scene, but the timing was questionable. "I find it hard to believe that two people broke into that house in one night.

And your statement that you were out lookin' for your daughter at the time of his murder is not an alibi."

Stephen tapped his fingers on his biceps. "I was at a bar on Twenty-Ninth."

"What bar?"

"Riggies. More of a tavern."

"Were you drinkin'?"

He shifted in his chair again, agitated. "I wasn't supposed to be. I was five years sober, but then Sarah ran off and I couldn't find her."

Marx set pictures of the other two victims in front of him. "Tell me about these two."

Stephen's brow creased as his gaze flickered between the photos. "How am I supposed to know who these people are? I never met them."

Marx studied his face, trying to gauge whether or not he was being truthful. "You didn't run into either of them while lookin' for your daughter?"

"No."

Terrence had been dead before Sarah ran off, but Marx kept that detail to himself. He pointed to Terrence. "We haven't figured out how yet, but he was somehow connected to Dr. Wilder."

Stephen's head snapped up. "If those two knew each other, is it possible Sarah was with this guy?"

"Doubtful." Marx gathered up the photos and papers and stood. He knocked on the door and someone let him out.

"Where are you going?" Stephen demanded. "You have to tell me where my daughter is."

"No, I don't," Marx said before closing the door.

Stephen slammed into it from the other side. "I wanna see my daughter!"

The officer who let Marx out lifted his eyebrows. "Guy's got a temper."

"If he keeps it up, handcuff him to the table. I gotta go make a call." As he walked to his desk, Marx dialed the number the patrol officer had collected from Sarah.

"Hello?" a quiet female voice answered.

"Sarah?"

"Yes."

He dropped the folders in his desk drawer and grabbed his gun. "It's Detective Marx. I just wanted to call and let you know your father's been arrested, if you wanna see him."

He waited for her to ask why her father had been arrested or if he was okay, but she didn't.

"Oh," she said. "Thank you for calling, but . . . I don't wanna see him."

"Well, maybe you can go see your mother while he's in here. Let her know you're okay."

"I think I will. Thank you."

Marx hung up and grabbed the phone book from his other desk drawer. He searched for a bar called Riggies, finding it halfway down the page. It wasn't too far from the precinct.

The door drifted slowly shut behind Marx after he stepped into the bar. He hated the smell of liquor, but he approached the counter and took a seat on one of the stools.

The bartender, a man somewhere over twenty but under forty, placed a napkin in front of him. "What'll it be?"

"I'll take a glass a water."

The bartender's lips quirked up at the corners, and he poured him a glass of ice water. Setting it in front of Marx, he asked, "How long you been sober?"

"Forty-eight and a half years."

The bartender offered him an interested look. "Okay. I'll bite. What brings you to a bar?"

Marx set the picture of Stephen Akers on the counter, and the bartender turned it to get a better look.

"Yeah, he's a regular." He turned the picture back toward Marx. "He owe you money or something?"

"He owes me an alibi."

"Ah, a cop. I should've figured." The man folded his arms and leaned on the counter. "What did he do? Kill somebody?" He meant it as a joke, but Marx's expression wiped the humor off his face. "Oh, he *did* kill somebody. That's . . . unsettling."

"Was he here last night?"

"Yeah, he was here. Sat right there." He pointed to the far stool closest to the back door. "He doesn't usually drink, but he likes to come in here to watch sports and chat with the other guys."

"But he drank last night?"

"Yep. Sad to see him fall off the wagon. Been sober for years. Guy could rage like a drunk, though. Had to kick him out a few times 'cause he started taking swings at the other patrons." Alarm skittered across the bartender's face, and he straightened. "Wait, he didn't kill one of my patrons, did he?"

"No. What time was he here?"

The bartender exhaled through his nose and stared at the ceiling as he thought about it. "Got here a little after three in the afternoon, stayed till around eight."

Marx looked at the stool Stephen had occupied the night before, and then past it to the door that led into the alley. "Was he here the entire time?"

"Honestly, I can't say for sure. We got really crowded after five. He could've slipped out the back and come back later, but if he did, I never noticed."

"Was anybody else workin'?"

"Trina usually works the tables, but she's got pneumonia or something. So it was just me."

"Surveillance cameras?"

The bartender glanced up at the camera above the bar. "That belonged to the previous owner, and I never figured out how to work it."

"All right. What's your name?"

The man pointed at the name frosted across the front window. "Riggie."

"Thank you, Riggie." Marx stood and gulped down the glass of water, left a tip on the counter, and headed back to the precinct to release Stephen Akers.

19

*M*arx set a plate of waffles in front of Holly and sat down beside her with his mug of coffee. "How does it feel havin' your cast off?"

She grimaced in discomfort as she flexed her right wrist. "Stiff, but I'm glad it's off. It's really hard to write in my journal with my left hand."

He had taken her to the doctor first thing this morning for a checkup, and they decided it was time for the cast to go. He was sure the doctor's strict orders for her to be careful had gone in one ear and out the other.

She offered her right hand, and Marx took it carefully, bowing his head so she could pray over breakfast.

"Dear Jesus," she began, and Marx's lips twitched.

She always spoke to God like she was writing Him a letter. He half-expected her to end the prayer with "Sincerely, Holly" instead of the traditional amen.

"Thank you for this food and for this beautiful sunny day. And thank you for Marx, and please help him learn to trust you more. Amen."

Marx was trying to put aside his old ways and adopt new ones now that he was a Christian. It was hard, and he found himself backsliding into his old habits more often than not, but when Holly was around, she reminded him.

She released his hand and cut into her breakfast. Marx devoured his homemade chocolate chip waffle in five bites, but Holly nibbled hers down in size like a mouse, eating one little square at a time.

Eating that slowly had to require patience, which he didn't have. He sipped his coffee as she ate, hoping she would polish off the entire waffle, but she surrendered halfway through with an if-I-eat-another-bite-I'm-gonna-explode sigh, and set down her fork.

He immediately began plotting how to squeeze more calories into smaller portions. She only ate when she wasn't anxious—which wasn't often—and she had such a small appetite. He used to nag her about eating well-rounded meals, but now he just wanted her to eat. More.

"Thanks for breakfast," she said.

"If you're not gonna eat that, hand it over. No sense in savin' it for later; it'll be a soggy mess."

She slid her plate over to him with a smile, and he finished the rest of her waffle. She snatched the plate the moment he set the fork down and carried the dishes to the kitchen.

He tried not to wince as she stuck them straight into the dishwasher—sticky syrup and all—and left them tilting at odd angles in the wrong places. He was going to have to fix that later.

He finished his coffee and walked to the sink to clean the cup, but Holly plucked it from his fingers and put it in the dishwasher. He paused, considered commenting, then decided he didn't want to risk ruining her mood this morning. She was trying to be helpful.

"I gotta head to work," he said. "Are you gonna be okay by yourself today?"

She let out a flustered breath that said she wished he would stop asking, but he had good reason to ask, especially after yesterday morning. She closed the dishwasher and looked up at him. "I'm sorry . . . about"— she folded her arms over her stomach—"the pills. I was just . . ."

"Sleep deprived, weary, and tired of fightin' what feels like an endless battle. I know. But just remember that it won't always be this hard, and you're never fightin' that battle alone."

Her eyes dropped to her slippers and she nodded.

He ran an affectionate hand over her shower-dampened hair, and then let his arm drop back to his side. "I'll be back later."

20

A quick call confirmed that Detective Marx was at his desk, no doubt searching for him among the details of each death, which gave him just the opening he needed.

He meandered through Marx's bedroom, perusing the orderly contents that spoke of a personality at least bordering on obsessive-compulsive disorder.

He studied the framed photos on the dresser, one clearly depicting his family. Strong gene pool; they all looked strikingly similar. The second photo was of a woman with coal-black hair and slate-colored eyes.

"Well hello, Shannon."

She looked just as fierce and determined in the photograph as she had in court the other day. It was interesting, finding her picture in Marx's bedroom. They were divorced, after all.

What man was foolish enough to let the love of his life go? Maybe he hadn't loved her enough.

He opened the drawers quietly, examining the contents but disturbing very little. There was a gun beneath a stack of T-shirts, and he pulled it out. It was a very nice piece: lightweight, sleek, and fully loaded. He considered taking it, but he didn't want anyone to know he'd been here.

He replaced the gun in the drawer and slid it shut before moving to the nightstand. There was a spiral notebook in the drawer. He opened it and flipped through the pages. It appeared to be filled with notes on Marx's current cases: Holland Wilder, the surgeon who should've tried harder, and Terrence James, the former EMT turned pimp who should've made a better choice.

Precisely what he was looking for.

The handwriting was barely legible, and he squinted as he read through the contents, looking for any mention of himself. There was nothing about Officer Blakely yet.

He froze midsentence when he heard a quiet click from outside of the room. His fingers tightened on his gun, and he set the notebook back in the drawer before sliding it shut.

He pressed back against the wall and cracked the door to peer out. He silently cursed himself for not checking the other room before searching this one. But there wasn't supposed to be anyone here.

He crept down the hall toward the door that now stood ajar and slunk into the room with his gun raised. He stilled, his eyes flickering over the room in confusion.

The purple blankets on the bed were rumpled, and a beaded purple pillow lay on the floor next to a small pair of fuzzy green slippers. A woman was staying here. There wasn't supposed to be a woman. Detective Marx was divorced, and he didn't have any daughters.

Did he?

A worn notebook lay on the end of the bed, and he picked it up. He opened the cover to the first page—a journal entry dated almost a month ago. It was definitely a woman's handwriting, delicate and neat, and he read the first few lines.

Some days I barely feel anything. Like a breathing carcass surrounded by life, but no longer alive. My heart is still beating, but my spirit has shriveled up like a dried leaf and crumbled to dust in my chest.

He didn't even know this woman, and her heartbroken thoughts resonated through him, touching the dark, lonely place in his chest that had once been abundant with warmth and love.

He wanted to keep flipping through the pages to see if she had captured any more of his soul with her pen, but that wasn't why he had come. He set down the notebook and pressed the back of his wrist to the sheets. Warm. She'd just been here.

Frantic thoughts tumbled through his mind: Does she know I'm here, is she armed, who is she, did she call the police? Get out now, before—

A lock clicked behind him. She was across the hall in the bathroom, and she was coming out. He didn't have time to make it to the front door and escape, so he melted into the closet and pulled the sliding door shut until there was only a sliver for him to peer through.

Quiet feet padded into the room, and he saw the woman appear. It wasn't any of the women from the photographs in the bedroom. From the back, she looked more like a little girl—barely over five feet with long, red hair that fell in graceful waves down her back.

She wore a pair of black leggings and a sapphire blue tunic top that draped around her thighs. On a shapely woman, it might have been flattering, but on this girl, it hung like a pillow case.

He wondered absently if she was ill. Not that he should care. He wasn't interested in physically sick people or their problems; he was more focused on the ethically and morally sick.

She sat down on the end of the bed, and he was surprised to discover he recognized her: Holly, the victim whose face had been plastered across newspapers for months, the girl who had been abducted and held captive in March.

He cursed himself for not realizing she would be here. After everything she had been through, and everything Detective Marx had done for her, it should've occurred to him.

If he hadn't been close enough to see the silent tears spilling down her cheeks or hear the tiny hitches in her breathing, he wouldn't have known she was crying. She drew her feet up onto the bed and curled in on herself, her silent pain turning into sobs.

He felt like a voyeur witnessing this intensely private moment of pain, and he averted his eyes.

He couldn't stand to watch an innocent suffer, but he couldn't exactly hold her and soothe her pain like he did with the woman he loved.

Listening to her grief gave him the urge to add her attacker's photo to his wall. He had room. And his death might give her peace.

She didn't let herself grieve for long before she wiped at her cheeks and whispered, "It won't always be this hard, and I'm not alone. I'm not . . . alone."

He frowned in confusion. She wasn't alone? He hadn't noticed anyone else in the apartment. Unless she realized he was here, but . . .

"God," she said, blinking up at the ceiling, and he relaxed. She wasn't talking about him, she was talking about God. "I'm trying. I'm trying to be okay for everyone, but I don't feel okay." She released a shuddering breath. "I feel . . . like I'm falling apart."

He knew that feeling too well.

"Please, Jesus, give me peace," she pleaded. She closed her eyes and whispered a prayer too soft for him to hear.

He watched, fascinated, as her breathing slowed and the tension gradually melted from her body. What was happening? Was God actually there, listening and answering prayers?

A German shepherd trotted into the room and then went dangerously still, his nose scenting the air. He could probably smell an intruder. The dog looked toward the closet, and his lips curled back in a snarl.

Anxious sweat slid down the back of his neck, and his fingers twitched on his gun. What would he do if the girl opened the closet door? He could shoot the dog, but what about the girl?

He didn't want to kill her. He could knock her out—one blow would probably take her down—but his conscience rebelled at the thought.

Innocent, she's innocent. Punish the guilty, avenge the innocent, *the quiet voice in his mind whispered.*

But he had more guilty people to take care of, and he couldn't let this idiotic mistake stop him. He couldn't let this girl stop him.

"What's the matter, Riley?" Holly asked, fear shimmering in her eyes as she looked at the closet door.

He never realized how hard it was to stand perfectly still until that moment. He could feel the hangers digging into his back between his shoulder blades, but if he so much as twitched, he would give himself away.

He needed her to leave, to take the dog for a walk. Something. He couldn't hide in this closet all evening.

She slid off the bed, and he tensed. He had never hit a woman in his life. What if he hit her too hard? He'd been in fights before, but it wouldn't be like hitting another man his size; she was . . . dainty.

His heart thumped hard as she approached the closet. No, no, no, *he thought desperately.* Walk away. Just walk away. I don't wanna do this . . .

21

*M*arx taped the pictures of his victims to the whiteboard by his desk and placed the snapshots of their notes beneath them.

He hesitated with Becca Hart's photo. They hadn't found a body or a note when they searched her place, but his gut told him she was a part of this.

Davey had seen a man break into her apartment two days after Terrence was murdered. Maybe the killer had intended for her to be the second victim, but something had gone wrong.

He moved the pictures down and added her photo next to Terrence James. Beneath her picture he wrote *M.I.A.*

He filled in their career information next: medical background, medical background, medical professional . . . cop.

He tapped the marker against his palm as he searched for the common thread. He was concerned that the connection between these victims only existed in the killer's mind, in which case they wouldn't find him by analyzing the victims.

"Four targets in a week," he muttered to himself. "Why in such a hurry?" His kill rate—or rather, his intended kill rate—was extreme, even when comparing him to some of the most prolific serial killers.

He had to know everything about his victims ahead of time in order to be this efficient. He knew their schedules, their habits, and he knew how to bypass their home security systems.

He added *stalked his victims* to the board.

Becca was the break in the chain, which made him question his gut instinct that she was involved. He dropped the marker on his desk and rubbed the back of his neck as he stared at the details.

I could use a hand here, Lord. Or two. A young woman's life might be on the line.

If the killer had stalked his victims, why kill them now? Why so quickly? Why so close together? It was almost as though he waited until the last minute, and this was his cram session before the final the next morning.

"He has a deadline," Marx realized. The killer was working toward a deadline that was fast approaching.

Marx jotted the word down and circled it with a question mark. He hadn't the slightest clue why the killer had a deadline or when it might be. Or worse: how many more people would die before he reached it.

Getting nowhere with the case, Marx decided to head home a little early. He shifted the bag of Chinese food to his left arm and pulled out his apartment key. He was too tired to cook tonight, and if he came home empty-handed, Holly would insist on making him dinner.

She meant well, but she had butchered that box of macaroni and cheese, and the last time she made him biscuits and gravy, the biscuits tasted like buttered sawdust, generously drenched in gray, chunky snot.

Chinese food was a good compromise. Holly wouldn't eat vegetables, even slathered in sauce, but she could devour sesame chicken and fried rice.

"You should be ashamed of yourself."

He looked back over his shoulder at Mrs. Neberkins, who stood in her doorway with a pinched expression.

"Using that girl the way you are," she continued. "I heard her crying in there while that man was with her."

Concerned, Marx asked, "What man?"

"Don't play the fool. You know very well what man—that hooded hooligan. He was in there with Holly for an hour, and then he snuck out like no one would notice." With a note of disapproval, she added, "Probably married."

Marx looked at his apartment door and then back at Mrs. Neberkins, but before he could ask her to describe the man, she spat "despicable" and slammed her door.

Mrs. Neberkins had an interesting imagination; sometimes she accused him of using the pizza delivery man to smuggle drugs, but more often than not, she accused him of worse things.

He brushed off her ridiculous imaginings and slid the key into the lock. It turned without resistance, and fear congealed in his stomach.

Holly never left the door unlocked. He had watched her check it multiple times a day, just to be sure it was locked.

Mrs. Neberkins's words rang through the back of his mind: *That man was in there with Holly for an hour . . . I heard her crying.*

He dropped the bag of Chinese food and drew his weapon. The door clicked open with a turn of the knob, and he slipped inside, closing it behind him.

"Holly?"

He waited, praying for a response, but the only sound was the gentle whir of the refrigerator. He scanned the living room and kitchen, finding nothing out of place.

Heart beating in his throat, he glided forward. The spare room door was open, and he took in the rumpled bedding and pillows on the floor. He couldn't tell if there had been a struggle or if Holly had just slept fitfully.

He pushed open her closet and looked inside. There was nothing but her clothes and shoes and . . . pink dust on the floor.

He crouched and ran a finger through it, rubbing the substance between his fingertips. It felt like greasy chalk.

He had bought Holly a box of pastels and charcoal as a welcome-home present when he brought her back from the hospital, and she kept them in the bottom of her closet.

The container was smashed, and the pale pink pastel had been crushed into the floorboards. Looking closer, he could see the pink shadow of a boot heel stepping out of the closet.

Someone had been in Holly's closet.

He stood and stepped into the hall. The bathroom door was closed, but his bedroom door was wide open.

He tiptoed into his room and visually scanned the shadows. A quick search yielded nothing suspicious.

Moving back to the bathroom, he turned the knob. The dead bolt had been flipped from the inside.

"Holly, are you in there?" He tapped his knuckles on the door. "Sweetheart, answer me."

The only response was the scrabble of claws on the tile, and Riley let out a snort as he sniffed at the crack beneath the door.

Was Holly in the bathroom with him, or had someone locked him in there to get him out of the way?

He pounded louder on the door. "Holly?"

No response. He walked to the kitchen and grabbed the spare ring of keys—one for the bathroom and one for the bedrooms.

If Holly was okay, he would apologize profusely for invading her privacy, but if she wasn't . . . he couldn't wait around, hoping she would come out.

Please God . . . let her be okay.

He unlocked the bathroom door and pushed it open. Riley launched forward and wedged himself in the opening.

Marx peered inside, his eyes tracing over the counter and floor, finally landing on the bathtub.

All he could see was red hair wound into a messy bun on top of Holly's head, and a pale arm hanging limply over the edge of the tub.

Fear lodged in his throat, and he pushed Riley back so he could step inside.

Water splashed and Holly shifted, resting her chin on her arm, her eyes closed. She was covered up to her neck in lilac bubbles, and she was wearing a pair of wireless headphones.

He glanced at the laptop on the counter. It was playing through a list of music Sam had downloaded for her to help her relax. At least now he knew why she hadn't heard him.

He could've melted into a puddle of relief on the floor when he realized she was okay.

With a gentle pat of Riley's head, he withdrew, locking the door and replacing the keys on top of the refrigerator. He slipped his gun into its holster and walked back into her bedroom, flipping on the light.

The heel print was barely visible, and it probably wouldn't show up in a picture, but he pulled out his phone and snapped one anyway.

He called to report the break-in as he walked to his bedroom. He opened his dresser to make sure his gun was still there, and frowned at his clothes. He was meticulous about how his T-shirts were folded and organized—a leftover habit from his years in the military—but now they were wrinkled and out of alignment.

His gun was where he had left it, which was a small comfort. He checked over the rest of the room. Nothing was missing, not even the cash he kept in a box on the closet shelf, but someone had been in his nightstand.

He was certain he had left off reviewing his notes about Dr. Wilder's murder, but now it was turned to his notes on Terrence James, and the corner of one page was bent, as if someone had hastily shoved it back into the drawer.

The tub draining told him Holly was done with her bath. A few minutes later, she popped into the hall, humming along to the music in her headphones.

His lips twitched in amusement. Either she was humming along with someone who was horribly off-key, or she was a terrible singer.

She noticed his bedroom light and stiffened for a beat before her surprise gave way to embarrassment.

She pulled her headphones out, her cheeks pink. "When did you get home?"

"Apparently while you were havin' a concert in the bathtub." The flush on her cheeks deepened, and he smiled at how adorably innocent she was. "You have a good day?"

She shuffled into his room and sat down on the end of his bed, drawing her slippered feet up onto the blanket. He loved that she trusted him enough to sit on his bed with him, that she wasn't afraid he might hurt her.

"It was okay," she answered. "How was yours?"

Pointless, he thought. He'd made no headway with the investigation, and Michael had called to let him know he was staying home with his wife, so he wouldn't have anything to contribute when he returned. The day had felt like a waste of time.

"It wasn't too bad," he said.

He glanced at his watch. CSU and a couple patrol officers would be here soon, and he didn't want Holly to be here. She had no idea a man had been hiding in her bedroom closet, and he wanted to keep it that way.

"I could go for some ice cream to top it off. How about you?" he asked.

She looked down at her pajamas. "I'll have to change."

"Be quick. I want my mint chocolate chip."

She grinned and scampered off to her room. Riley plopped his head on Marx's thigh, and Marx scratched him behind the ear.

He wondered if the only reason the intruder hadn't hurt Holly was because Riley would've attacked him to protect her.

22

He *slammed his hands on the roof of his car in anger. What had he been thinking? Detective Marx hadn't had a clue about him before today, but now . . .*

The old woman across the hall had seen him slip out of the apartment; she had looked right at him.

Stupid, stupid, stupid.

Maybe the woman was as blind as she was old and hadn't been able to see his face. And the girl had never even realized he was there.

He was grateful that she had decided to run the bathwater before coming back for her clothes. It gave him time to slip into Marx's room. Once she settled into the bathroom with the dog, he made his escape.

But it had been too close. He *couldn't afford to make mistakes. He* couldn't *fail.*

23

*M*arx sat in the booth at the all-night ice cream shop, poking at his glass goblet of mint chocolate chip as he stared at the speckled tabletop.

Holly had gone to the restroom, leaving him alone with his thoughts.

He hadn't told her about the intruder—he didn't want to give her a reason to think she wasn't safe—but the more he thought about it, the more it troubled him.

If a man had forced his way into the apartment so easily, then she *wasn't* safe there. She had been alone and vulnerable, and the man could've done anything he wanted.

How many times had he promised her that she was safe, that he would protect her? And how many times had he failed?

God, you gotta help me here, he thought, floundering for a way to protect Holly from the dangers of his job and the threats of this world. She was far too fragile to protect herself right now.

He was going to have to add another dead bolt or two to his apartment door, but even then, someone with a skilled hand could bypass a lock.

He could have an alarm system installed. His only concern with that option was that it might make Holly feel like she was being imprisoned or monitored.

He would just have to find a way to explain the decision to her without letting her know that someone had broken in while she was home alone.

His phone chirped with an incoming text message, drawing him from his thoughts. He opened his phone to see a message from Sam.

CSU found scratches on the dead bolt consistent with the lock being picked. Aside from that and the shoe print, there's no other evidence of an intruder. They'll run fingerprints and get back with me.

Marx hadn't expected them to find much, but he hoped the intruder had left a fingerprint or identifiable fiber. He responded with a question: *Did Mrs. Neberkins give a description of the intruder?*

He would've asked her for the detailed description himself, but she would have only slammed the door in his face. Ever since he moved in across the hall and she asked him to help find her Pomeranian—Perry-Quinn or some equally ridiculous name—there had been a persistent tension between them.

He helped to find her dog; it had curled up under her bed and died, probably from the stress of living with *her*. He had gotten rid of the remains for her, but she was convinced he had stolen her dog and sold it.

There was no persuading her otherwise.

Sam replied, *she says it was a man, average height, average build, with a hooded sweatshirt that said, 'Freedom is never free.' The letters were army colored or camouflage. She wasn't sure. But considering the phrase, I'm banking on army. She also said we should arrest you for sex trafficking. She's concerned that Holly never leaves the apartment alone, and that she frequently hears her crying or screaming. And she thinks the man today was there for sex. I tried to explain the situation to her, but she really doesn't like you.*

Marx let out a frustrated sigh and typed back a thank-you before closing his phone. That woman was a paranoid old bat.

Holly stepped out of the bathroom and wrapped her thin sweater tightly around herself as she shuffled toward the table. As she passed by the two men seated at the counter, their eyes followed her with interest.

When the larger of the two men, an overweight man with wiry hair and a pen tucked behind his ear, got off his stool, Marx noticed a laminated badge hanging on a lanyard around his neck. He squinted, making out the word journalist.

Annoyance flitted through him.

The moment the man started after Holly, Marx stuck his spoon in his ice cream and slid out of the booth. At Holly's puzzled look, he said, "I'm gonna grab a drink."

"Okay." She dug into her rocky road sundae, scooping up such a large spoonful that it took her three bites and a lick to clean off the spoon.

Marx intercepted the journalist, and the man tried to step around him with a muttered "Excuse me."

Marx blocked him. "You're not talkin' to her."

The man's beady eyes narrowed to slits. "Freedom of the press. I have the right to talk to her if I want."

"And I have the right to hold you behind bars for twenty-four hours without pressin' charges."

The man glanced at Marx's badge. "You can't arrest me for asking questions."

"That depends on the questions."

The journalist shrugged his bulky shoulders. "She's the girl who got abducted, the one the NYPD practically had the whole city searching for. I wanna know the details."

Marx flexed his fingers in anger. All this man cared about was a story. It didn't matter to him that his questions would be excruciating for Holly or that they would probably send her into a panic.

"You ask her those questions, it's gonna upset her and cause a disturbance, which will be your fault. Then I'll arrest you for disturbin' the peace."

"You're bluffing."

"I don't bluff."

The journalist's eyes shifted to Holly, and his tongue flicked out to moisten his lower lip. Marx didn't like the way he was looking at her, like she was a paycheck rather than a person.

"You can't stop the media from talking to her forever. We'll get the story."

"I'm sure you will," Marx said. "But let her enjoy this night in peace."

The man grunted and slapped a quarter tip down on the counter. "Come on, Joel. Let's go find a story worth our time."

A little bell over the door announced their exit, and Marx watched the journalist and his friend cross the street, leaving him and Holly as the sole patrons in the shop.

He tapped his hand on the counter to get the waitress's attention. "Two waters, please."

He took the glasses back to the table and sat down. His sundae looked a few nibbles smaller than he remembered, and he lifted an eyebrow at Holly.

She let out a giggling snort and covered her mouth.

"Mmm hmm." He took his spoon and stole a huge spoonful of hers to return the favor.

"Hey!" She grabbed for the spoon, but he popped it into his mouth before she could reach it.

He made a face. Marshmallows. S'mores and marshmallow hot chocolate he could tolerate, but marshmallows did not belong in ice cream any more than they belonged in chocolate milk. He swished some water and swallowed. "You realize you're a marshmallow addict."

She only smiled and took another bite. "So what ever happened with your dead body?"

"It may have escaped your notice, but I'm not dead yet."

She rolled her eyes and clarified, "I mean your case that wasn't a robbery."

"Well . . . he's still dead." At her disgruntled frown, he smiled. She liked to poke her nose into his cases; it was a side effect of her insatiable curiosity. "A couple more bodies that may be related have turned up."

She nodded. "I heard Sam say that. But how do you know they're related?"

He interlaced his fingers and looked at her. "I don't think a deranged killer is the best thing for you to be focusin' on right now."

She lifted her chin defiantly. "I might be short, but I'm not a kid. I get to decide what I wanna focus on."

"Is that so?"

Her certainty faltered at his question. "Yeah, that's . . . so."

"Good argument."

She sighed at his sarcasm and slumped down in her seat, folding her arms over her stomach. "I'm not fragile."

That was debatable. But if she was feeling stronger right now, the last thing he wanted to do was belittle that strength. She was clawing her way back from the bottom day by day, and if feeling useful helped, he could share a few details with her.

Capitulating, he said, "We know they're related because of the killer's signature." When her eyebrows pinched in confusion and she started to ask a question, he clarified, "And no, I don't mean he signed his name."

The way she puckered her lips inward between her teeth told him that he'd correctly anticipated her question.

"A signature is somethin' a criminal does at a crime that makes him unique, somethin' he needs to do for the crime to satisfy him," he explained, belatedly realizing he was explaining it to someone who had lived it.

He saw the pieces fall into place behind her eyes, and she automatically rubbed her throat where the layers of black and purple handprints had been.

She pushed through the discomfort, determined to take her life back, and asked, "What's his signature?"

"Leavin' notes on the bodies."

"Like . . . love letters?"

"Cryptic notes." He didn't want to read them aloud in case the waitress was an eavesdropper, but he pulled the pictures of the notes up on his phone and slid it across the table to her.

She studied them with a curious furrow between her eyebrows. "Hmm."

"Hmm what?"

She shrugged. "No one's perfect. There's a point in everyone's life when they think they should've tried harder or made better choices, when they should've stood up to a bully to protect someone smaller, but didn't."

He glanced toward the waitress, but she had disappeared through the swinging doors into the kitchen. "Go on."

"He's no different, so . . . what did these people do that made him, um . . ."

"Fixate," he offered when she struggled for the word.

"Yeah. With a city full of people making these *should've* mistakes every day, why did he fixate on these people?"

"I don't have an answer for that."

Her eyes dropped back to the images on the phone. "Maybe he's angry with them because these people's mistakes affected his life personally."

Marx had been thinking along the same lines. He might not know the connection between the victims yet, but they weren't chosen at random. His gut told him that much. "I agree. I think he specifically targeted these people, and he watched them to learn their schedules."

She cocked her head in thought. "What about the notes?"

"He forced the victims to write them."

"Because he was making them apologize or because he wanted the world to know they failed?"

"Maybe both."

She took a bite of her ice cream absently, dribbling it across the table. "So . . . he's forcing them to admit their guilt and then deciding their fate, like a judge."

"That might suggest he has a conscience." Which was an unusual thing to find in someone who had killed multiple people.

"Or he just thinks he's better than everyone." She shrugged and slid the phone back.

Marx pondered the possibility that the killer might have a conscience. If he did, he had a moral compass. He could justify killing the guilty, but what about an innocent?

He looked at Holly as she dove back into her ice cream.

He had no doubt the man who had broken into his apartment was the killer he was looking for. Who else would be interested in his case notes? But what puzzled him was why the man had chosen to hide.

Even if he hadn't wanted to shoot Holly, for fear someone would overhear the gunshot, he could've subdued her, and then he would've been able to move freely through the apartment rather than hiding in closets.

Maybe he *did* have a conscience that forbade him from hurting someone he perceived to be innocent. Or maybe he just didn't want anyone to know he'd been there.

160

They finished their ice cream and left the little shop. Holly shivered in the chilly night air, and he wished he had a jacket to give her. He wrapped an arm around her to share his warmth, and she looked up at him.

"Thank you."

"For what?"

She wrapped her arms around his waist in a hug and exhaled a quiet breath. "For helping me feel normal for a night."

Holly rarely hugged anyone, even him, and he folded his arms around her, appreciating the rare gift of her affection.

24

He saw them at the quaint ice cream shop, eating their hot fudge sundaes. Detective Marx hid his unrest behind a smile every time Holly glanced his way, but he noticed the man's guarded and watchful demeanor when she wasn't looking.

Detective Marx knew someone had been in his apartment, and it had triggered a bout of paranoia.

There would be no way he could sneak back in to study the case notes now. He would probably keep them under lock and key. He should've just taken them.

He considered walking in to the ice cream shop to see if Detective Marx had figured out who he was, but it wasn't worth the risk. He had too much left to do.

If only he could hear the conversation between him and Holly without being seen. It might be informative.

No, he wouldn't talk to her about the case. She's a civilian.

He had followed them here on impulse, a decision he regretted. If Detective Marx had figured out who he was, he would've sent someone after him. He must not be as close to narrowing in on a suspect as the media believed. Maybe he was safe for now, but he would have to be more cautious.

He pulled up the picture of his next target, contemplating how to proceed. Her schedule was unpredictable, which made his job more challenging.

The doorbell of the ice cream shop dinged as the two men from the counter exited.

"*You believe that guy?*" *the large man asked with obvious irritation.*

"*Cops,*" *his friend grunted.* "*Think they can control everyone and everything with that badge.*"

"*Not me.*"

The smaller man's eyebrows lifted. "*What are you gonna do?*"

"*We are gonna wait for them to leave, and I'm gonna get my story. Everyone is practically drooling for the details, and I'm gonna be the guy who gets them.*"

"*How are you gonna do that?*"

The large man smiled wickedly. "*We're gonna follow them, and when Mr. Detective steps out of the picture, I'm gonna get what I want.*"

"*You sure that's a good idea? What if you scare her?*"

"*I don't care if she hides under the bed and cries afterward. She can go whine to her shrink. I'm gonna have the goods, and that's what matters. You just make sure you get pictures. Good ones. Tears sell, you hear me?*"

He watched the two men cross the street and duck into the shadows, then looked back at Holly, conflicted.

He had seen her pain when she curled into a ball on the bed and cried, so broken that she was barely holding herself together, and these men wanted to rip her apart for a front-page story.

It stirred the coals of anger inside him, rekindling the fire. He hated people who hurt innocents.

He was about to cross the street to deal with the problem, but the door dinged again. He shrank back out of sight as Detective Marx and Holly stepped outside.

His heart pounded beneath his ribs like a jackhammer. Detective Marx wrapped an arm around Holly as she shivered, and they started off down the sidewalk.

The two men followed, stalking their prey, and he fell in step behind them.

He followed at a discreet distance, but he could hear the two men concocting a scheme. The smaller man was going to draw Detective Marx's attention by taking pictures while the larger man cornered Holly to get the information he needed.

Holly's bubbly laugh carried on the quiet street as she and Detective Marx turned the corner. The two men picked up their pace, and he did the same.

He couldn't just walk away knowing that they were going to terrorize her.

He lunged and collided with the smaller man, knocking him into the side of the building. The man's face cracked off the glass and he crumpled to the ground, unconscious.

Before the larger man could react, he tackled him to the ground, pinning him facedown on the sidewalk. "Hands on your head. Interlace your fingers."

When the journalist complied, he gripped his interlocked fingers in one hand to prevent him from pulling them apart, and pressed the edge of his blade against the man's throat, cutting off the squeak of terror rapidly building toward a scream.

"Quiet," he said, and the man whimpered. "I don't like you, and I don't like your intentions."

"I'm j-just a journalist."

He leaned down and whispered in the man's ear, "You're a predator. Maybe you're not a criminal, but you're no better, and maybe the law can't do anything about you, but I can."

"No, p-plea—"

He pressed the blade in deeper, drawing a thin line of blood. "You torment the grieving and the suffering for the love of money and fame. Do you know what that makes you?" He paused before answering his own question. "Evil."

He rifled through the man's pockets with his free hand and pulled out his wallet.

"Do you know what I do to evil people?" He opened the wallet to see the man's driver's license. "Miles."

"No."

"I get rid of them."

Miles let out another whimper. "Please, I promise I'll do whatever you say."

"Holly is a sweet kid, and she's suffered enough. If I let you live tonight, you're never gonna so much as look at her again. And you're gonna keep this conversation between us."

"O-okay."

"Good, because if you don't keep that promise, I know where you live."

"I'll keep my word. I p-p-promise."

"You should really learn to respect other people's privacy, Miles. And unless you want those to be the final words left on your corpse, you'll be more cautious with your decisions from now on."

Miles started to sob.

"I'm gonna get off you now, and you're gonna walk away without looking back. If you try to look back, I'll jam this knife into each one of your disobedient eyeballs. Understand?"

Miles nodded, then clambered to his feet the moment he was free. He took off like his life depended on it.

It did.

Now, for the lawyer . . .

25

*M*arx sat down at the peninsula with a tired sigh and rested his head in his hands. He needed sleep, but despite his body's exhaustion, he knew his mind wouldn't be able to rest.

A barely audible tap on the front door drew his head up. He glanced at the clock on the kitchen wall—nearly midnight—and then at Holly's bedroom door. She had gone to bed half an hour ago, and he didn't want the knocking to wake her if she had managed to fall asleep.

He crossed the room and peered through the peephole. Surprised, he stepped back and opened the door.

Shannon stood in the hall, her arms folded across her chest. This was the first time in years that he had seen her without her court attire.

She wore a pair of formfitting jeans that immediately attracted his attention, a thin sweater, and moccasin-style shoes. She used to dress like that when she was lounging around the house, engrossed in a book.

Worry sharpened the lines in her face, but before Marx could ask if everything was all right, she flung her arms around his neck with a breath of relief that sent tingles of warmth across his skin.

Without her high heels, she had to stand on her toes to hug him this way. It reminded him of just how delicate she was despite her fierce personality.

This was his second unexpected hug tonight, and he savored both of them for entirely different reasons.

"I just heard from Sam. He said someone broke into your apartment." She pulled back to look at him, and he let her go reluctantly. "Are you all right?"

"I'm fine. I was at work when it happened."

"And Holly?"

"She was home, but he didn't hurt her. In fact, he seemed to go out of his way to *avoid* hurtin' her. I think he just wanted information."

Shannon's thin eyebrows knitted together in confusion. "What kind of information? Does this have something to do with the case you're working?"

"Probably." He invited her in and closed the door. It was strange—this pleasant interaction.

Over the years, he had gotten used to the cool demeanor she adopted in his presence, and he had stopped calling her because she deliberately avoided him.

Now she was standing on his doorstep minutes from midnight, worried about his well-being. He wasn't sure when he gave up hope of ever having her back, but recently that hope had sparked to life again.

A couple months ago, she had canceled her court appearance and shown up at the hospital while Holly was in surgery. She had held him when he broke down outside the operating room, and she had listened as he tried, between sobs, to describe the horrors he'd seen.

Something had shifted between them that night, but there was no telling where it would go.

"You want some coffee?" he asked.

She sat down on the edge of the couch. "I shouldn't."

Neither should he, but he poured himself a mug anyway and joined her in the living room. "Court tomorrow?"

"I'm trying to put away a man who robbed his own family to pay off his debts."

Marx grimaced. "That's awful."

She smiled tiredly. "There's a lot of awful in this world. All we can do is try to make it better one decision at a time."

He didn't disagree.

"What makes you think the break-in had something to do with your current case?" she asked.

"Because whoever broke in went through my case notes. I think he wanted to make sure I wasn't gettin' close to him." He unfolded the newspaper on his coffee table and showed her an article.

"'Detective Marx refused comment, but according to a source in the department, he is narrowing in on a suspect.'" She looked up. "You think he read this article and it had him scared."

"Mmm hmm. But we're not even close to findin' a suspect."

"Well, I'll let you rest so you can think clearly enough to catch him. I only wanted to make sure you and Holly were all right." She stood, then remembered something. "Oh, I made some calls and found a therapist who might be able to help Holly. She works with a lot of women who have been through similar circumstances."

Marx took the card she offered. He didn't recognize the name, but that wasn't a surprise. "What's she like?"

Shannon gave it some thought before saying, "Patient." She hesitated, and then kissed him on the cheek, her lips lingering just a moment longer than usual. "Please be careful with this case you're working."

"I will." He opened the door for her, and she smiled.

"Ever the gentleman."

"Just because I live in the city doesn't mean I've forgotten my roots." He tipped his head and added with emphasis, "Ma'am."

She barely withheld a smile. "That had better be the last time you ever call me ma'am."

"I make no promises."

She laughed. "Good night."

He lingered in the doorway, enjoying the view of her gorgeous figure as she walked away and descended the steps. No matter how often he reminded himself that *she* had left *him*, he still loved her.

26

*S*weat dampened his palms as he waited for the lawyer to come home. Her schedule was frustratingly unpredictable. He checked his watch and then rechecked the list of times written in his notebook.

She'd been home an hour earlier yesterday and an hour and a half early the night before that. He'd rushed to get here after the fiasco outside the ice cream shop, afraid he was going to be too late to catch her. And she wasn't even home yet.

He paced her living room in a state of growing agitation.

He could be home right now, gazing at the love of his life, but no, he was waiting on a woman who didn't have the decency to show up on time.

Movement out of the corner of his eye startled him, and he brought the gun up as he turned toward it. A woman stood at the edge of the hallway, her blond hair spilling down around her shoulders.

He blinked and lowered his weapon, his heart palpitating in his chest as he stared at his wife. "What are you doing here? You shouldn't be here."

"I go where you go." She crossed the room toward him, her feet soundless on the wooden floor.

"You don't need to see this."

She rubbed a hand over her pregnant stomach and looked around the dark house. "What's there to see? You're standing in an unlit room."

Headlights splashed across the front of the house, piercing the front window, and his breath caught. The lawyer was home. "Hide. I'll come get you when it's done."

Sadness glinted in her eyes, but she turned and walked back down the hallway, disappearing into the darkness. He watched from the window as the lawyer pulled into a space along the curb and shut off the car.

She climbed out of her high-priced car, no doubt bought at the expense of the innocent, and her high heels click-clacked up the sidewalk to her front door.

She stepped inside, deactivated the alarm system, and kicked off her ridiculous shoes.

He knew she would strip out of her clothes and head for the shower, as she did every night when she got home. Maybe she was hoping to wash away the filth, but she couldn't wash away the toxic scum that leaked from her soul.

He didn't want to wait for her to get comfortable. He stepped out of the corner and aimed the gun at her. "It's about time you got home."

27

$\mathcal{M}$arx slammed his car door and squinted at the flashing lights that blurred into endless streaks of color.

It was bad enough being called to a homicide at three in the morning, but with so little sleep he was at risk of committing a homicide himself.

People, drawn from their homes in the middle of the night by sirens screaming through their "safe," affluent neighborhood, crowded around the outside of the crime scene tape.

He waded through them and checked in with the officer securing the scene.

Sam waited for him on the front steps. "You look like death."

"How appropriate. Because I feel like death." No sleep would've been better than the few hours he managed to get. "What do we know so far?"

Sam led him into the house. "According to witnesses, the victim arrived home a little after midnight. She's a local attorney, and . . ." Sam paused to look at him. "You know her."

Marx felt anxiety churn in his stomach as they approached the scene.

The woman lay on the kitchen floor, arms spread wide, her vacant eyes staring at the ceiling. He took in her details—dark hair with a touch of gray; a long, lean figure, and a small birthmark on her forearm that looked like a bouquet of balloons.

He scrubbed a hand over his face, his fingers coming to rest over his tightly pressed lips.

"If you need a minute—"

Marx waved away the offer as he sank to a crouch beside the victim. "Her name is Lola Eubanks. I haven't seen her in . . . five years, maybe. She and Shannon used to be friends, until their careers drove them apart."

"Well, prosecutors and defense attorneys don't usually get along very well."

Marx wasn't sure how Shannon would take the news. The two of them might no longer be friends, but there was a time when they were inseparable.

His eyes moved down the length of Lola's body, snagging on the note pinned to her stomach with a pen.

I should have told the truth.

Anger burned away the remainder of his tiredness. Lola had made some poor life choices that led her down a path of greed and self-importance, but she didn't deserve to die.

There had still been a chance she might recognize that she was defending the wrong people and turn her life around.

Now it was too late.

He knew he wasn't supposed to touch the body, but he dragged light fingers over her face, closing the eyes that had once been filled with a bright-eyed passion for justice, just like Shannon's.

"Well, it looks like our murderer just graduated to the status of a serial killer," Marx said.

"Did Officer Blakely pull through?" Sam asked.

"He's in intensive care, but they're not sure, with the brain damage, if he'll ever wake up."

Marx's phone chirped, and he pulled it from his pocket. He had sent a text to Michael to meet him here, but the response wasn't what he'd been expecting.

Problem with the baby. Will come when I can.

Marx prayed they wouldn't lose their baby. To become pregnant after years of trying only to lose the baby would be cruel. He told Michael to stay with Kat and then snapped his phone shut.

He stood to survey the home. Being a defense attorney for the affluent, Lola had no financial struggles. She had funneled a lot of her income into her home: renovations, an expensive art collection, and a media center that would make any man salivate.

He stepped into the living room and picked up the framed photo resting on the mahogany bookshelf. The photographer had captured the joy of two young women hugging and holding up their diplomas. Shannon looked so young and full of hope, and Lola looked as though she might bubble over with giddy laughter.

The two women might have gone their separate ways, but Lola clearly treasured the memory of their friendship.

"How'd the killer get in?" Marx asked, returning the picture frame to its spot. "Another window?"

"The lock on the back door shows signs of tampering," Sam answered.

"This guy does know how to pick a lock."

It didn't help that people could learn how to skillfully break the law by watching online videos. Dummy guides for the criminally inept: how to pick a lock, how to build a bomb from household products, where best to hide a body.

Once he'd even seen a how-to video with step-by-step instructions on how to kill an irritating neighbor and get away with it. The internet really did make his job harder.

"She has an alarm system, but it was disarmed when we got here." Sam pointed to the number pad by the front door.

"So either somebody else with the code disarmed it, or she never turned it on."

"She lived alone, and according to her neighbors, she never had visitors, unless you count the guy who delivers her groceries each week," Sam said. "Somehow I doubt she entrusted *him* with the code."

Marx pondered why a single woman, who was intimately familiar with the depravity of mankind, would neglect to activate her security system.

He walked over to examine the alarm panel, but there were no obvious signs of tampering. He was missing something.

"Call the security company this belongs to and find out when the system was last armed," he said, without looking away from the panel. He would bet his paycheck that Lola had set the alarm and someone had managed to bypass it.

That didn't give him much hope about installing one in his apartment for Holly's safety.

He looked around the room, and his eyes landed on the sheer curtains covering the picture window.

"I wonder . . ."

He opened the front door to step out but stopped at the threshold. Media vans were scattered all over the street, and journalists were buzzing through the onlookers like bees, pestering them with questions.

Apparently the death of a high-priced defense attorney was more interesting than the death of a surgeon or the attempted murder of a cop.

Standing in the spotlight of the open door, Marx drew the attention of every journalist within a one-block radius, and a chorus of voices called out, "Detective!"

He tuned them out as he descended the steps and crossed the front lawn. He had no patience for journalists. They were bloodthirsty maniacs with insatiable curiosity. He would rather deal with a serial killer.

He positioned himself near the large picture window just off the living room, and with the lights on, Sam and the alarm panel were visible through the sheer curtains.

If Lola had stood even slightly to the left or right of the number pad when she entered the code, the killer would've been able to see the numbers.

But standing in the middle of the yard, staring through a woman's window, would've drawn suspicion, especially in this neighborhood.

Marx walked along the edge of the bushes in front of the window, scanning the ground for any sign of a disturbance. He crouched by two shoe impressions behind one of the bushes.

Whoever had hidden there had a shoe size somewhere between an 11 and 12. That didn't eliminate the possibility of the killer being female, but it made it less likely.

He pulled out his cell phone and called up the image of the heel print the intruder had left in Holly's room. The tread on both shoe prints matched.

Fear tightened his grip on his phone.

Whoever had been lurking outside of Lola's house was the same man who had been hiding in Holly's closet. He'd suspected his intruder was the killer, but now that he had proof, he couldn't dismiss his fears with the possibility that it might have been someone else, someone nonviolent.

He dialed Jordan's number and waited anxiously for him to pick up.

"Yeah," Jordan answered groggily.

"I need you to go to my apartment and stay there until I get home."

The tiredness evaporated from his voice, and he sounded alert. "What's going on? Is Holly okay?"

Marx glanced at the onlookers and then lowered his voice. "Somebody broke into my apartment last night."

He jerked the phone away from his ear when Jordan shouted, "What!?"

He waited to make sure Jordan was done shouting, then explained, "Holly's fine. She's not even aware that it happened, and I'd like to keep it that way."

"Was it the guy who showed up in my parking lot and took a swing at you the other day?"

"I don't know. But I'm concerned it might have somethin' to do with my case."

"You know, you're really dangerous for her health."

"I'm not the one who screwed up and got her abducted," he snapped back, wincing in regret the moment the words left his lips. What had happened that night could've happened with any one of them.

"Yeah," Jordan said, his voice thick with pain. "I know."

Marx blew out a breath and rubbed at the tension in his forehead. "I'm sorry. That was uncalled for." He took a moment to gather his thoughts, then said, "I don't have a spare key for you to get in, and I'd rather you not wake her up."

"I won't. I'll just have a seat in your hallway and point my gun at anyone who walks by."

Jordan, still upset with Marx's offhand comment, disconnected without so much as a good-bye. Marx put his phone away and rose.

He tried to remember the crime scene tech's name; it was on the tip of his tongue, but his brain was running on emergency power. "You!" He snapped his fingers to grab the man's attention. "With the camera."

"Seth," the man said as he walked over. "But 'you with the camera' works just fine." The young man noticed the shoe impressions in the grass and lifted his camera for a shot. "Oh, would you look at those. Very nice."

"Detective!" a woman shouted, practically lunging at the crime scene tape to get his attention. "Can you tell us how Lola Eubanks died? Was she murdered by—"

"Sources say she was shot. Can you confirm that?"

"Do you have any leads as to who the killer might be?" a male reporter interjected, pushing his way to the front.

"Is her death connected to the death of Dr. Wilder and the cop who was shot?"

Marx scanned the faces in the crowd. It wouldn't be the first time a killer lingered to watch the reactions to his handiwork. "Photograph the spectators too, Seth."

Somewhere in the back of the crowd, a man called out, "Aren't you the detective who was kidnapped by Edward Billings this past fall?"

Marx glared in the man's general direction, but it was too late to do anything; his inquiry changed the tide of interest, and the questions followed to cover a potentially more sensational story.

"Is it true that the young woman you were kidnapped with in Kansas was recently abducted a second time?" a woman asked.

"There's a rumor that Holly's abductor is her foster brother, Collin Wells, and that this isn't the first time he assaulted her. Can you confirm that?" The man thrust his microphone at Marx as he walked back toward the front door.

Irritated, Marx slapped it aside. "Get that out of my face."

"Is Holly all right? Can we speak with her?" another voice chimed in.

"Will she testify in court?"

Marx stepped inside and shut the door on the barrage of questions. He closed his eyes and rested his head back against the door.

"Should I even ask?" Sam said.

Marx tried to let the tension roll out of him with his next exhale, but it was too tightly woven into his muscles. "I hate reporters."

He had a feeling someone had filmed his short-tempered slap of the microphone and he would be getting a call from the lieutenant in the morning.

"Just imagine how they'll react if they catch Holly in public."

Marx grimaced. If the media ever managed to corner Holly with those questions, Holly would spend the rest of her life hiding between the toilet and the bathtub with a butcher knife.

"The panel is visible through the curtains," he said. "Looks like the killer hid in the bushes out front and watched her enter the code."

"Makes sense. The alarm company said she armed it at 12:15 this morning. It was disarmed a few minutes after one a.m. According to witnesses, there was a 'popping sound' around one. Pretty obvious what that was." They both looked at the small bullet hole in the victim's forehead. "Which means the killer disarmed it and let himself out after he was finished."

Marx grunted in thought. "He probably came back while she was at work, let himself in through the back door, deactivated and then reactivated the alarm, and waited for her inside."

"Her schedule would be unpredictable, so waiting would've been his best option. One of the neighbors said he saw the headlights from her car around midnight last night."

And an hour later she was dead.

28

*S*ince half the neighborhood was already awake, Marx decided to question the neighbors. He made his way onto the porch of the condo next door to his crime scene and raised a hand to knock.

He paused at the sound of feet clomping up the steps behind him and turned to see a woman standing on the second step from the top.

She stood in three-inch heels, hot pink pants, and lipstick the same startling shade. There was even a shimmer of gold glitter on her eyelids and a thin strip of too-tan midriff showing.

Although she was dressed like a teenager, her caked-on makeup sank into the creases around her eyes, betraying the fact that she was approaching fifty.

Marx cleared his throat. "This your house?"

Her heavily lined eyes regarded him with a twinkle of admiration. "Sure is. I'm Kandy. Zipowski." She stepped onto the porch and held out her hand. "And you are?"

He shook her offered hand and forced a polite smile. "Detective Marx. Do you have a minute to talk?"

"Oh, absolutely." She brushed against him as she moved to open her front door, and he took two steps back.

This woman was a lawsuit waiting to happen, and he was not going into her home alone.

"Excuse me," he said by way of warning before placing two fingers in his mouth and letting out a shrill whistle.

He motioned over the lone female officer. She didn't look thrilled to be summoned, but she abandoned the police tape and started his way.

Stomping up the steps like a thundercloud, she said, "Detective."

"Officer . . ."—he glanced at the name tag on her uniform—"Simmons. I apologize for the whistle, but I didn't know your name."

The slender blond hardened her jaw and crossed her arms. "That's fine. Every woman enjoys being summoned like a dog."

He flinched inwardly. He hadn't even considered that the gesture might come across that way. "I meant no disrespect."

"Well, now that I'm here, how can I *serve* you?" she asked tartly.

He sighed. He'd managed to offend her before even speaking, and he wasn't smoothing that over any time soon. "I would appreciate it if you would join me for my conversation with Ms. Zipowski."

Simmons looked at the woman standing just inside the house in her bubble-gum–pink ensemble, her equally pink lips puckered in a disgruntled pout, and gave Marx a slow, knowing smile. "Sure."

They stepped inside, and the woman closed the door. "I'm Kandy," she told Simmons.

Simmons's lips thinned in a reflexive smile. "Of course you are."

Kandy gestured toward her living room just off the entryway. "Make yourselves comfortable."

Marx bypassed the nearest love seat in favor of a flower-printed chair. Kandy hid her disappointment poorly as she sat on the love seat alone.

"I'm so glad you're here, Detective. Knowing what happened to Lola . . . well, it's terrifying. I'm a single woman living alone too, and to think it could've been me." She pressed a hand to her chest. "I feel much safer knowing there's a strong, handsome detective here looking out for us single ladies."

A tiny, amused cough escaped Simmons, and Kandy shot her a vicious look.

Marx pulled out his notepad and pen. "Well, the police department is here to protect and serve. What is it you think happened to Ms. Eubanks?"

"Well, she was murdered, obviously."

"What makes you think that?"

Kandy frowned. "Because of the police. If it were just an accident, you wouldn't be here, right?"

"We're here in response to an unexpected death. It's the duty of the medical examiner to determine if that death was the result of an accident, suicide, or foul play," he explained, although it was clearly a homicide.

She blinked, clearly confused. "But I heard the gunshot, and what about the man running out of Lola's house?"

Marx leaned forward with interest. "What time did you see a man runnin' from her house?"

"Around one a.m. I had just gotten a text from my . . . my ex-husband. Sometimes he texts me when he's drunk, but we're not together anymore. There's . . . nothing between us."

He'd gathered that from the "ex" part, but he only smiled. He didn't want to put her on the defensive by being rude.

"And that's when I heard the pop," she continued. "I thought maybe I was just being . . . well, I don't wanna say paranoid. But then I walked to the window, and I saw a figure running out of the back of Lola's house."

"Can you describe this figure?"

"Oh, I know who it was. One of those delinquents she works with. He was there last Wednesday night too, slamming his fist on the door like some kind of gorilla."

"Do you know his name?" Marx asked.

She laughed softly. "I don't associate with those kinds of people, Detective. Frightening. Honestly, I feared for my own safety last night. I mean, what if he had wandered over to my house?"

"Did you call the police Wednesday night?"

"Of course. They chased him off."

Marx made a note to check the police report for that night. It might not be any more helpful than Ms. Zipowski's vague description, but it was worth a try.

"Are you married, Detective?" She gestured to the wedding ring he still wore.

Shannon might have taken hers off and tossed it in a drawer the day she left, but he had made a promise to love and cherish her for all the days of his life. He wouldn't part with the symbol of that vow.

"I'd rather stay focused, if you don't mind," he replied.

"Of course, I understand. Could I get you a drink? Some brandy maybe?"

Simmons leaned in and whispered, "Careful, she might roofie you."

Marx shot her a censoring look; he was in no mood for jokes. "I appreciate the offer, but I'm fine. The man you saw runnin' from Lola's house tonight—are you sure it was the same man you saw Wednesday night?"

"Oh, absolutely."

"Can you describe him?"

She tapped an overly long pink fingernail against her lips. "Five ten, maybe six feet. Bald, tattooed."

Marx wrote down the description. At least it was more detailed than Mrs. Neberkins's "average" description.

"You have remarkable eyes, Detective."

"Oh, for the love of . . ." Simmons muttered as she walked to the other end of the room.

Marx tried not to let his already-thinning patience evaporate. "I've heard that, thank you. Did you happen to notice which direction the man fled? Did he get into a vehicle?"

"No, he just ran off." She gasped. "Do you think he could be the man who killed her? What if he knows I called the police? What if he knows I saw him running from the house?" She stood and pressed a hand to her chest. "Could I be in danger? I'm so vulnerable here. All alone. What if he breaks in and tries to . . . to attack me?"

Marx couldn't decide if she was truly frightened or if she was just being theatrical.

"Oh, Detective." She stepped toward him. "If that happens, can I call you for help? How will I reach you?"

He stood and tucked his notebook into the inner pocket of his suit jacket. "If you feel unsafe or threatened, it would benefit you to call 9-1-1. They can get here faster than I can." And he really didn't want to give this woman his card with his cell number on it. "And if you think of anythin' else, please call the local precinct."

She tried not to look too disappointed at the gentle rejection. "Of course. And if you're in the neighborhood, you're welcome to stop by." She offered her hand again, and he shook it after a moment of hesitation.

What is wrong with these women? he thought as he pried his fingers from her lingering grip. One woman was in such a hurry that she invited a complete stranger into her home without seeing his badge, and this woman was . . . desperate.

Maybe he was just so used to the women in his life that other women seemed bizarre. Shannon was usually so coolly collected, and Holly was the polar opposite of forward.

"Have a good night, Ms. Zipowski, and thank you for your help," he said, before letting himself out. He stepped out onto the porch and let out a relieved breath.

Simmons stood on the porch with him and made a little choked noise before bursting into laughter. Her laughter was deep and loud and interspersed with heavy snorts.

"What's so funny?" Marx asked.

"Are all your interviews that interesting?"

"Thankfully, no."

She pressed a hand to her chest and said in a mocking soprano, "Oh, Detective, how will I ever reach you? I'm so vulnerable here. All alone." She broke into snorting laughter again as she walked down the steps and back to her post.

Sam passed by her on his way over, joining Marx on the sidewalk. "I see you met my new partner."

"Simmons? She's your new partner?" Sam's last partner had died back in February, and it was only a matter of time before he was assigned a new one, but Simmons was unexpected. "She's . . . quite a character."

Sam looked over at her. "One minute she's bent out of shape about . . . woman things, and the next it's like talking to one of the guys. When I say something offensive, I can never tell if she's gonna cry or punch me."

Marx laughed. Adjusting to a new partner was difficult enough, but the fact that she was a woman complicated matters even more. Sam was fiercely protective of the women in his life, but if he tried to safeguard Simmons the way he did Jace or his sister, she would probably level him.

"Speaking of offensive," Sam said, folding his arms and raising an eyebrow. "I heard you whistled at her."

"I did not whistle *at* her. I whistled to get her attention."

"I'm not sure I understand the distinction."

"It was a misunderstandin', and I apologized."

"I would've gotten punched for that misunderstanding."

Marx chuckled again. "Lucky for me, she's not my partner." He checked his watch. "The rest can wait till mornin'." He slapped Sam on the back. "Have a good night."

As he was about to slide into his car and head home for the night, a shrill whistle drew his attention back to the crime scene. Simmons gave him a smug grin and a wave.

He sighed and got into his car.

When he got home, he found Jordan seated against the apartment door, his long legs stretching the width of the hallway.

Jordan tipped his head back to look up at him. "You done for the night?"

"I am."

Jordan hopped to his feet with the lithe agility of a man under thirty, and holstered his gun.

"About what I said earlier," Marx began, guilt tangling around his words.

"Save your apology. You weren't wrong."

"You know Holly doesn't blame you for that."

"I know. She's told me. But she doesn't have to blame me. I'm reminded of the consequences of my decision that day every time I see that haunted look in her eyes."

Marx tossed his keys in his hand as he said grimly, "So am I."

"I'm gonna head home. If you need me tomorrow, give me a call."

Marx stepped into his apartment after Jordan left, tossed his keys on the side table, disarmed, and dropped onto the couch. He stretched out and practically melted into the cushions.

29

He pulled at his eyes with his fingertips as he paced from one end of the room to the other, anxiety gnawing at his insides. No matter how many times he told himself he had done what needed to be done, something bothered him about this one.

Maybe it was because his latest target had been a woman. His eyes darted to her Polaroid on the board next to Dr. Wilder's as his dad's teachings whispered in his mind: Never hurt a woman.

She had knelt on her kitchen floor, begging for mercy as tears streamed down her face, and he'd hesitated. But when she begged for her life for the sake of her children, he remembered what she was: a poisonous arachnid, spinning her webs of lies with every breath, webs so airtight that they smothered the truth.

She had no children.

And after everything she had done, she deserved her fate even more than the doctor. Her guilt was there for all to see, written by her own hand:

I should have told the truth.

She wouldn't be telling any more lies now. The thought should have brought him a sense of satisfaction, but all he could see was the blank space on the wall where Becca Hart's picture was supposed to be.

He had been planning to punish her first, but Terrence James had crossed a line. He hadn't intended to kill him that night, but standing outside the motel room, listening to him beat a woman for wanting to stay home with her sick toddler, it pushed him over the edge.

The woman, a teenager who sold her body by the hour, was far from innocent, but she had a child to care for.

He knew he had gotten carried away with Terrence, but five years of rage building within him had to be released. He tried to clean up before he slipped out, and he was confident he had left nothing behind.

But when he went back for Becca Hart the next night and the night after that, she never came home. He had no idea where she was. She must have seen him on one of the days he followed her, or he had touched something in her apartment that gave him away.

Frustrated, he dropped into his desk chair and glared at the blank space on his wall. He couldn't waste time looking for Becca Hart right now—not with his deadline approaching. All he could do was move onto his next target, and then circle back for Becca later.

He opened his laptop to review his information on his next target, and an email banner flashed across his screen with a recent news headline: "NYPD Officer Survives Home Invasion."

He might not be able to find that slippery EMT, but there were a few loose ends he could take care of.

30

*H*olly shuffled out of her room at a little past four in the morning, and Riley followed along at her heels, his nails clacking quietly on the floorboards. He was her ever-present shadow.

She was restless again, and she had wanted to write in her journal, but she couldn't remember where she put it. She was pretty sure she had set it down somewhere on . . . the left side of the apartment. Or maybe the bathroom.

She wandered from room to room looking for it, then paused by the couch when she realized it was occupied.

Marx was stretched out on the cushions, shoes still on. He must have walked through the door and collapsed. Even asleep, his features looked tight with stress, and she felt a pang of guilt.

Was that her fault?

He had so much going on with work and the trial, and yet he went out of his way to take care of her, which wasn't an easy task. She decided it was her turn to take care of him.

She eyed his shoes. She couldn't fathom how she might get them off without waking him. She carefully undid the laces and, biting her lip, slid them off his feet one at a time.

He didn't stir.

Marx had one house rule: no shoes on his leather couch. The one time she'd accidentally broken that rule, he'd stolen her shoes and hidden them. She grinned as she looked down at the shoes in her hands.

Yep, those were going to disappear.

She set them aside for now and grabbed the blanket off the back of the couch. She draped it over him, then realized his shins and feet were uncovered. She tugged the blanket down, which then left his chest uncovered. She almost snorted in laughter. *Tall people.* The blanket fit *her* perfectly. She pulled it back up to cover his chest and then stepped back with her hands on her hips to survey her handiwork.

He looked cozy . . . except for his big feet sticking out.

As she watched him sleep, her heart warmed. There were very few people she truly cared about, and even fewer she cared about this much.

She parted her lips to speak, hesitated, and then whispered softly, "I love you." She couldn't remember the last time she'd told someone that, and it felt good to shape the words on her lips even if he couldn't hear her.

Marx awoke with a groan and pressed a hand to his aching head. He had a headache fast approaching a migraine. Was that his body's way of saying he needed to sleep more often?

He checked his watch. The numbers were blurry, and it took him a moment to read the time: 8:30. He had managed to snag about five hours of sleep. With a pot of coffee, he could function on that.

His phone chirped.

He started to sit up and realized he was covered in a blanket. Had he put that on? He barely remembered anything from last night. He pushed it aside and dropped his feet to the floor.

He fished his phone from his pocket and flipped it open to see the text from Ella: *show and tell in the morgue at 10:30. You bring the coffee.*

She was done with the autopsy already? Maybe she had found something useful to help them catch this guy before another innocent person died.

He had one unread message from Michael; he had been so dead to the world that he hadn't even heard his phone go off at six o'clock this morning.

Had to take Kat to the hospital. Be in later.

Marx noticed the sticky note on the coffee table when he set his phone down. He peeled it loose and read it:

Good morning! I made breakfast. It's in the oven.
~ Love, Holly ~

He smiled at her signed name at the bottom of the note, as if it could've been anyone else who left it. Then his brain registered the last two dangerous phrases: *I made breakfast. It's in the oven.*

Holly was an explosion waiting to happen in a kitchen. She had a tendency to burn things and nearly start fires. She was too easily distracted.

He looked over his shoulder into the kitchen. It looked . . . intact, and he didn't smell smoke. What had she made, a bologna sandwich?

He stood, stretched, and walked into the kitchen to check the oven. It was set on the lowest temperature, and when he popped the door open, he found a Hungry-Man frozen breakfast warming on the rack.

To his dismay, he even found brewed coffee in the pot. He checked to make sure she'd remembered the filter this time—she had—and then examined the amount of coffee grounds. It looked normal. Maybe she was learning.

He grabbed the nearest mug—the one she'd gotten him that declared, "I am a hot Southern mess"—and filled it to the brim. He almost laughed when a marshmallow he hadn't noticed in the bottom of the white mug popped to the surface of his coffee.

"Always somethin' floatin' in my drink."

Marshmallows, coffee grounds . . . next he'd find a Cheeto floating in his sweet tea. He downed his miniature marshmallow and some Tylenol with a gulp. The coffee tasted old, but it was palatable.

But if it was old, Holly had been up in the middle of the night. He glanced at her door, knowing what that meant.

He approached her room and raised a hand to knock but then thought better of it. If she had managed to fall back asleep after her nightmares, he didn't want to wake her. He tried the door handle and was surprised to find it unlocked.

She never slept with the door unlocked. He tapped lightly. "Holly?" When no reply came, he cracked the door and peered inside to make sure she was all right.

She was curled up on the floor with Riley, her right hand still resting between two pages of an open album. She must have fallen asleep unexpectedly.

She was surrounded by printed photos she'd taken with her camera, scissors, glue sticks, and her colored pastels.

He tilted his head to study the scrapbook she had been assembling since February. She had very few pictures of her family, and none of her foster placements had lasted longer than a year. This small group of people she had now—Jace, Sam, Jordan, and himself—were the closest people she had to family, and it was pictures of them scattered around her like a moat.

One of the pages he could see was filled with pictures of Jace, Jordan, and Sam, but the second page only had one picture: a photo of him beneath a pink-and-purple pastel title that read Family.

He rested his head against the door frame and smiled. He loved this girl more than words could express.

He wished he could've met her when she was just a kid, drifting through the foster system. He would've adopted her in a heartbeat.

Of course, Shannon wouldn't have approved. She had never wanted children, biological or adopted. Over the years, it began to drive a wedge between them.

He took another gulp of his coffee and snapped his fingers softly, drawing the dog's attention.

Riley's head lifted, and then he climbed to his feet gently, as if he were intentionally trying not to disturb Holly. Marx attached his leash and took him out to go to the bathroom. When they returned, he let him back into Holly's room and went to get ready for work.

He couldn't seem to find his shoes, though. He'd worn them yesterday. He'd come home, dropped his keys on the side table, removed his gun and holster, and . . . that was the last thing he remembered. He should've taken off his shoes after dropping his keys. That was his routine. But if he'd forgotten to take them off, then why . . .

He looked down at his socks. Then he noticed the blanket he also didn't remember covering himself with, and realized why he couldn't find his shoes.

Holly.

She was up to her mischief again. It had been a while since she'd played one of her innocent little pranks on him: putting marshmallows in his drinks, mismatching his socks, tilting the pictures on the walls. He checked them just to make sure they were straight.

He never thought his shoes missing would make him smile, but it did. It meant she was healing. As hard as Collin had tried to break her, he'd failed.

He retrieved a pair of sneakers from his bedroom and put them on. They didn't exactly match his dress pants, but he didn't have time to look for his loafers.

He ate the breakfast she'd warmed for him, drank another mug of coffee, and scribbled a note for her:

Thanks for breakfast and coffee. The marshmallow was a nice touch. I'll be out late. Call me if you need me.

P.S. I will find my shoes.

31

*M*arx found Ella hovering over the remains of his latest victim, tapping her toes as she sang along to the music pulsing through her headphones. He knocked on the edge of the autopsy table, and her head snapped up, eyes wide with surprise.

"Detective." Concern creased her forehead as she draped her headphones over the back of her neck. "Oh, you have periorbital dark circles."

Marx blinked. "I have what?"

She slid her index fingers under her eyes. "Under-eye shadows. It can be caused by allergies, but the most common cause is a lack of sleep. You're not sleeping."

"I hadn't noticed," he replied dryly. He offered her a Styrofoam cup of coffee as his eyes fell to Lola's face.

When he saw her last night, there had still been traces of color in her face and warmth in her skin, but any illusion of lingering life was gone now.

He had seen more dead bodies than he could count, but he would never get used to seeing someone he knew lying on one of these tables.

"What did you find?"

Ella set her coffee aside after a sip that burnt her tongue left her slurping in air through her mouth to cool the flames. "Wow. That's hotter than I expected."

"You didn't ask for iced coffee."

Her face contorted in disgust. "I think I'd rather drink saltwater than iced coffee. Of course, then I would vomit or my stomach would rupture, both of which are extremely unpleasant."

"Mmm hmm. Can we . . . ?" He gestured to Lola's body.

"Oh, of course. Let's start with what I didn't find. No signs of drugs, alcohol, or poisons in her system, which is consistent with what I found when I ran Dr. Wilder's tox screen. Mr. James, however, was higher than a 757, but I expect that was self-administered."

"Wouldn't surprise me."

"No foreign DNA beneath her nails, and despite the torn panty hose, there was no evidence of sexual assault."

Marx felt a small sense of relief. Lola hadn't been tortured before she died. He wasn't sure he could handle another sexual predator right now.

After Collin, he couldn't be sure he wouldn't shoot the next scumbag who raped a girl or an innocent child.

"She has abrasions on her knees consistent with both victims. But here's where things get weird." She pressed two fingers to Lola's chin and opened her mouth. "Go ahead, take a look."

Warily, Marx leaned over and peered into the victim's mouth. He swallowed against the bile burbling up his throat as he said, "There appears to be somethin' missin'."

"That would be her tongue." Ella pushed Lola's slack jaw back into place. "It was removed postmortem with a sharp implement."

Marx frowned in thought. The killer had left a message on Lola's body—*I should have told the truth*—and then removed her tongue. The symbolism wasn't lost on him. A person without a tongue couldn't lie, at least not with their words.

Somehow she had offended the killer by speaking.

If Dr. Wilder had offended the killer by not *trying harder* with his hands, it might explain why the killer had pierced his hands with scalpels.

He'd nearly beaten Terrence to death before putting a bullet in him, possibly because he had been abusing one of the girls who worked for him. Could that have had something to do with the *better choice* he should've made?

Marx gazed at Lola as he tried to find his way into the mind of her killer. "What happened that made him hate you so much?"

"Are you talking to me or the dead body?" Ella asked, her blond eyebrows arching with interest. "I talk to dead bodies all the time. It's nothing to be ashamed about, and sometimes it's even therapeutic. Unlike living people, they don't interrupt or offer unsolicited advice."

Marx snorted in amusement. "You are the strangest person, Ella."

"It's not just me. Why do you think people visit cemeteries? I mean, aside from visiting a dead relative. It's a way to be around people without all the noise and drama of people. It's peaceful."

"I suppose. You have anythin' else for me?"

"I sent the pen to the lab for analysis, but it's probably going to match this." She lifted Lola's hand and turned it to show him the dark ink smudges on the side.

"It's probably her pen. Shannon has a similar one that she only uses when she's in court." His own words struck him.

Defense attorneys were often accused of being deceptive or manipulative in court, and the killer had stabbed her with her own court pen. Whatever she had done to upset him, it had happened in a courtroom.

32

$\mathcal{M}$arx knocked on Sully's door and pushed it inward when no one answered. His gaze traveled the walls cluttered with sci-fi movie posters and character figurines, and then over the desk, which was a pending avalanche of books and files.

Sully's chair was empty.

Stepping into the windowless cavern to wait, Marx noticed a frozen image on the computer screen, and his stomach turned over.

A small girl, red hair tangled around her face, curled into a fetal position on the floor to protect herself from the booted foot frozen midkick.

"Holly," fell beneath his breath.

This was one of three DVDs, each one depicting more brutality than the last, and he had sat in this room with Sully less than three months ago, trying to find something in the video that would lead them to Holly.

Sully, a man who prided himself on wit and humor, had been sick before the first video was halfway over. He may never have met Holly, but he knew her through the digital details of her life.

Marx caught movement in his periphery and looked up. Sully stood in the doorway, his skin tinged green.

"Hey, I wasn't expecting you," he said, before tipping a bottle of Pepto-Bismol to his mouth and taking a swig.

"I don't think that's gonna do much for emotional nausea."

"Yeah, well, I got ten more hours of this . . ."—he dropped into his chair and waved a hand at the screen—"mental torture, and I don't have the energy to hurl again. So Pepto is better than nothing."

"Why?" Marx asked.

"The DA—your ex-wife actually—wants me to go over the footage again to see if I can do more to clear up the deliberate distortion of the attacker's face and voice. She's concerned the judge won't admit them as evidence the way they are now."

That was the first Marx had heard of the videos being potentially inadmissible. He would have to discuss that with Shannon. "Take a break. I need your help with somethin'."

"Gladly." Sully closed the DVD program and straightened in his chair. "What do you need?"

"I need a list of Lola's clients for the past ten years."

Sully lifted one pierced eyebrow. "Seriously? Ten years?"

"Mmm hmm."

"Okay." Sully's fingers danced across the computer keyboard as he collected the names of Lola Eubanks's former clients from public records.

He shifted in his chair and flicked an uncomfortable look at Marx, who was hovering beside him. "I get that you really want this information, but if someone's gonna be close enough for me to feel their body heat, I'd rather it be a hot chick."

Marx cracked a smile. Everyone knew the only way Sully ever came close to a "hot chick" was by sharing a Skype connection. He seemed to prefer it that way. Marx stepped back to give him some space.

"So, uh, how's Holly?" Sully asked, his eyes glued to the computer screen.

"She's doin' all right."

"What are the chances she would do a video chat with me?"

Marx puzzled over the question. "Meanin' what? Will she . . . online date you?"

"Well, I know she has man-anxiety, which, who wouldn't after that? But we won't even be in the same room, and I can be very charming."

Marx couldn't decide if he was genuinely interested or if he was just trying to lighten the mood. "I didn't think Holly was your type. Don't you prefer tall blondes?"

"There are always exceptions."

Marx leaned over his shoulder and whispered, "Before you go and make an exception, you should know that when Holly decides to start datin', I will investigate the man she's interested in down to the very first F on his report card."

Sully pointed a thumb at himself and winked. "Straight-A student."

Marx laughed. "Just focus, please."

"It's gonna take me a while to get every name for the past ten years. I'll cross-check the names of Lola's clients with associates of the other victims to see if there's a common denominator. You're welcome to hang out if you want, but . . . please don't."

Marx had no desire to linger in this dungeon any longer than necessary. "See if she had problems with any of her clients. A neighbor reported some domestic disturbances at Lola's house, but she didn't have a name."

"Will do."

"Were you able to find any connection between Stephen Akers and any of the victims besides Dr. Wilder?"

"Not yet."

"What about Becca Hart?" Marx asked. "Any sign of activity on her credit or debit cards?"

"None so far. Either she's using cash or . . ."

Or she was dead.

The alarm on Marx's phone went off, reminding him that he needed to take Holly to her counseling appointment. "I'm gonna be out of the office for a few hours. Call me if you find anythin' useful."

33

$\mathcal{M}$arx sat in his car, waiting for Holly's counseling session to conclude. He didn't want to crowd her by hovering in the waiting area, but he didn't want to just drop her off and leave either.

His gaze drifted to the clock on the radio. She had been with her therapist for almost thirty minutes. He figured she would make a dash for the exit within fifteen.

He considered going in to check on her but decided to give her the hour. Then he would go in and start searching bathrooms, which were her typical hiding places when she was upset or scared.

Someone knocked on the passenger window, and he looked over to see Shannon. She opened the door and slid into the passenger seat.

"You said we needed to talk."

Marx considered how to break the news. "You remember that attorney you used to be close with, the one who left the prosecutor's office to become a defense attorney?"

Shannon grunted, the sound a mixture of disappointment and disapproval. "Lola. We're actually at odds in the courtroom right now. She's the one defending the man who robbed his own family to pay off his debts."

"Have you two spoken on a personal level at all over the past ten years?"

"Not really. We had lunch before this case went to trial, trying to work out an agreement." Shannon's eyebrows drew together. "Why the sudden interest in Lola?"

He paused a beat before explaining, "She was murdered in her home last night."

Shannon inhaled sharply and looked out the window, trying to process the news. "I don't understand. Who would want to kill her?"

"I imagine every person she prevented from gettin' justice, which brings me to my next question. Can you think of anybody she might have had problems with?"

"I'm really not the person to ask. What about her law firm? Surely someone there would know *something*."

"We're workin' on that."

She rubbed at her neck as she tried to think of anything helpful. "I'm sorry. No one comes to mind."

"That's all right. I knew it was a long shot."

"Do you have any suspects?"

"A man was seen fleein' from her home. We're tryin' to track down his name."

She swallowed hard and nodded. "Good. I should get back to work. With Lola . . . gone, there's going to be a mistrial. I can't let that predator walk."

As she grabbed the door handle, Marx asked, "Are you gonna be okay?"

"I lost my friend a long time ago," she said, but the glimmer of sadness in her eyes told him she would still grieve for the loss of an old friend. "Call me if you find anything out about who did this to her."

"I will."

She stepped out and closed the door. Marx watched her walk down the sidewalk toward a nearby coffee shop. The squeak of a door drew his attention back to the counseling center.

Holly emerged, her eyes flickering nervously over the passersby as she shuffled to the car. She had on a pair of skinny khaki overalls, ruby-red flats, and an oversized cabby hat that practically swallowed her head. He knew she was going for inconspicuous and unattractive because it made her feel safer, but she was too cute not to draw some attention.

He considered getting out and walking her the rest of the way, but he knew she wouldn't want him to. She opened the passenger door and melted into the seat with a heavy sigh of relief. She slammed the door, snapped down the lock, and slouched down to prop her feet on his dashboard.

Marx arched an eyebrow at her, a silent reminder to keep her tiny feet off his dashboard, and she dropped her feet to the floor as she squirmed upright in her seat.

"Sorry," she mumbled.

"Everythin' go okay in there?"

She folded her arms over her stomach and shrugged. "Fine."

Which meant it had been a disaster. He could imagine her curled up in a big chair, staring intently at a piece of lint on the upholstery, as the therapist tried to pry information from her.

They had already been through that song and dance at the hospital a couple months ago. She had refused to say a single word to the crisis counselor who came to assess her.

"Did you talk to her?" he asked.

While he tried not to invade her privacy, the point of counseling was to talk through her experiences so she could heal, not stare at the hideous upholstery.

"She wants me to talk about my feelings," she said grumpily. "I told her I feel like this is an irritating waste of time, but she didn't seem to like that answer."

"Holly—"

"She should've been more specific."

He sighed. When Holly was scared or upset, she became defensive and snippy. It was how she tried to protect herself. Surely, a therapist would recognize that too.

After a quiet moment, she said, "We talked about . . . him." She shifted in her seat to gaze out the window, and he caught the flicker of vulnerability in her reflection. "About what he . . . did."

He could hear the shame in her voice as she pulled her feet onto the seat and hugged herself.

"You have nothin' to be ashamed about, sweetheart." He started to tuck a stray hair behind her ear, but she cringed, not wanting to be touched.

He hesitated, then returned both hands to the wheel. He pulled the car out of the parking space into late-morning traffic.

Holly stared out the window at the passing trees, but he could see the distant look in her eyes. Her mind wasn't on the scenery. The tension in her body suggested her mind had crawled into a much darker place.

Probably into her memories.

He wished there was something he could do to protect her from those, but all he could do was remind her she was safe now. "What are the chances I can get you to eat somethin' this afternoon?" he asked.

"I'm not hungry."

His fingers tapped a steady rhythm on the steering wheel as he tried to think of a way to get her to eat. The doctor was already concerned about her low body weight.

"Well, if you're not gonna eat, neither am I," he decided, and he hoped the tactic would work, because he really wasn't into fasting. His Southern-bred family did not skip meals. They rarely skipped second helpings.

Holly lifted her head and frowned at him. "Don't do that. You have to eat or you'll pass out when you're chasing a suspect."

"Well, let's hope I'm chasin' him across a patch of soft, fluffy grass when that happens." Holly cared far more about the well-being of others than she did about herself, and he was banking on that compassion.

"You're being ridiculous."

"You're bein' stubborn."

"Marx."

"Peanut."

She huffed and scowled at the nickname, which made it hard for him not to smile. She tried to be fierce, but she was about as intimidating as a toddler throwing a tantrum.

"Cute. Are you gonna stomp your feet on my dashboard next?" he asked.

She scrunched her nose at him before dropping her chin back on her arms and gazing out the window.

"We have a whole ninety minutes to not eat lunch," he pointed out casually. "I suppose we could just drive around aimlessly. And then I'll go back to work until seven p.m. without anythin' to eat."

"Fine," she sighed. "Let's go eat."

Thank the Lord, he was hungry. If only it would be that easy to convince her to eat every time.

They stopped at a small diner and found a table on the patio. Holly stared at the menu with disinterest, so he ordered for both of them. She didn't touch the burger he chose for her, but she picked at her fries and finished most of her milk shake.

At least she'd eaten a few hundred calories. He had one more stop planned to brighten her mood before he dropped her off at home.

He drove down a side street and pulled up in front of a cozy little bookstore. Holly's chin lifted from the door, and he saw some of the sadness slide away from her. She loved bookstores.

She shot him a hopeful look. "Really?"

"No, I thought I'd tease you before we walk down to the liquor store."

A ghost of a smile touched her lips. "You don't drink." Then the smile faded as wariness took its place. "Do you? I've never seen it."

"No, I don't drink," he assured her with a gentle smile. Alcohol had turned his father into a completely different man, and that was a man Marx was determined never to become.

212

He stepped out of the car and walked around to open the door for her, but she already had it open. He would've offered her a hand out of the car, but she always refused, so he waited on the curb.

She glanced around as she shut the door and tugged her huge hat further down over her head. He opened the shop door for her, and she stepped inside onto the checkered tile floor. He thought he saw her inhale the scent of books as her eyes danced over the packed shelves with the excitement of a kid in a candy shop.

A man stepped out from behind the counter to offer assistance, but Holly wandered straight past him and into the heart of the store.

Marx glanced at the frowning man and said, "Don't mind her. She likes books more than people."

Holly let out a quiet "Ooh" before he heard the telltale scrape of a book sliding off the shelf. He smiled and said, "Excuse me," to the employee, and headed for the aisle Holly had disappeared into.

He found her nose-deep in a women's mystery novel. He was almost positive it was the purple-and-pink color of the cover that had first grabbed her attention.

"You like that one?" he asked.

She nodded as she turned the page. She flipped the book over to look at the price sticker on the back, frowned, and then slid it back onto the shelf. He plucked the book back off the shelf after she wandered away down the aisle.

He motioned the employee over and whispered, "Hold this at the counter for me." He handed it to him before following after Holly.

He found her standing with her hands on her hips, her eyes fixed on a book that was tucked onto a shelf about a foot and a half above her reach. She chewed on her lower lip as she narrowed her eyes at it. He knew that look. She was contemplating doing something she knew she shouldn't.

"Don't even think about climbin' that bookshelf, young lady," he chided.

She shot him a mischievous grin. "Too late. Already thought about it."

"Of course you did."

He noticed she was deliberately ignoring the "Please ask an employee for help" sign posted right in front of her. She was the most hardheaded individual when it came to asking for help.

He wondered what she had done when she encountered this problem before meeting him and Jordan. Did she just climb up every shelf? Being her height would get on his nerves in about ten seconds flat.

"Which one?" he asked.

She stretched onto her toes and pointed. "That one. With the shiny cover."

"Girls and shiny things," he teased as he got the book down for her. He dropped it into her waiting hands, and she cracked it open to skim through it.

She didn't like that one, so he put it back. He saw her lose herself in a few more books—mostly soft mysteries with quirky crimes and even quirkier characters—but she put most of them back after checking the prices.

He waited for her to walk away and then added them to the stack of books being kept at the register. She would probably argue with him, but he was buying the books for her regardless.

She spent so much time cooped up in his apartment, trying to heal and move past painful memories, and she could use a few enjoyable distractions. She found two books in the bargain section with prices that didn't scare her and clutched them to her chest happily.

"You probably have to get back to work," she said, and he glanced at his watch.

"It is about that time. You ready?"

She nodded and trotted toward the register. Some of her tension returned when she reached the checkout counter, and he suspected it was because the cashier was a man.

"Find everything okay?" the young man asked.

She nodded, set the books on the counter, and stepped back—out of grabbing distance, Marx realized.

The cashier rang up her books, and she paid. There was an awkward moment when he tried to hand her the change back, but she refused to hold out her hand. Finally, he just slid it across the counter to her with a puzzled smile, and she scooped it up.

Marx watched her anxiety with an ache in his chest. She said very little about what happened during those four days she was held captive, but he knew. Collin had recorded twelve hours of footage, and he had seen the depth of the torment.

He paid for the other books, and as expected, Holly tried to argue with him. "Stop bein' difficult," he said.

"But—"

"They're a gift, and you know I don't want anythin' in return. Besides, my family lives in Georgia. Who else do I get to buy gifts for?"

She closed her mouth and folded her arms, unsure how to respond to that. It had taken Marx less than two months to figure out how to combat her arguing: make it about him instead of her. She surrendered much easier if the outcome benefited him in some way.

He gathered up their bags and they headed back to the apartment. Holly curled up on the couch under a blanket with a sweet tea and one of the books she had told him *not* to buy, and Riley sprawled protectively at her feet.

"Call me if you need me." He pressed a gentle kiss into her hair and left her to read.

34

*M*arx paused partway up the precinct steps when he heard someone slap a hand down on a hard surface and shout, "No, I need to see Detective Marx."

Marx backtracked down the steps to see a large man with light-socket hair standing in front of the reception desk. Even without the journalism badge around his neck, he recognized him from the ice cream shop.

"Sorry, he's away from his desk right now," the receptionist informed him. "I can page a different detective."

"No!" The man slapped the counter again. "I need to see him. Right now. My life is in danger."

Wonderful, Marx thought. The last thing he wanted to deal with right now was a journalist with a theatrical flair.

He considered leaving it for another detective to handle, but the man's next words stopped him cold.

"You call him and tell him that this involves the girl he's protecting. Holly Cross. He'll make time if it means protecting her."

Marx walked down the steps and across the lobby, interrupting the frazzled receptionist midreply. "That's all right, Jenny. I have a few minutes to talk with him."

The man exhaled in relief. "Thank you."

"I didn't catch your name last night."

The man looked around nervously and licked his lips. "Miles. Can we talk somewhere private?"

Marx led him to the conference room just off the lobby and shut the door. He crossed his arms and shot the man a look that conveyed his annoyance. "Sit."

Miles obediently dropped into a chair. "I really need your help, and you're the only person who can help me."

"I got that," Marx said dryly. "I'll give you five minutes, so start talkin'."

Miles leaned forward, his hands shaking as he explained, "My friend and I were jumped last night after leaving the ice cream shop. This guy just came out of nowhere and attacked us."

"Attacked you how?"

Miles tilted his head and pointed to the thin scab across his neck. "He put a knife to my throat, and my friend has a concussion."

"There are plenty of detectives who can help you. Why are you tellin' *me* this?"

Miles's attention shifted nervously to the conference room window that opened into the lobby, his eyes bouncing between the uniformed officers. "I don't trust them. Any of them but you."

"Oh, for the love of all things holy," Marx muttered under his breath. *Why do I always get the crazy people?*

"You have to listen to me."

Sighing, he asked, "Why don't you trust them?"

Miles's voice lowered to a whisper. "Because the guy who attacked us . . . is a cop."

Marx's blood turned to ice. "You wanna run that by me again?"

"The way he jumped us . . . he knew what he was doing. He took out Joel without breaking a sweat, and then he tackled me and told me to put my hands behind my head. He said I might not be a criminal, but I was just as bad, and he frisked me, pulled out my driver's license. This psycho cop knows where I live, and he threatened to kill me."

If Miles truly believed a cop was behind the attack, then he had a lot of guts walking into a police station and asking one for help.

Marx locked the door and closed the blinds. "Why did he attack you?"

Miles moaned and rubbed his face. "We were following you. Joel was gonna distract you while I talked to Holly."

A muscle ticked in Marx's jaw. "I told you to leave her alone."

"So did he. He told me not to even look at her and that if I bothered her again, he would kill me. He knows her. He called her by name."

"Because he overheard you talkin' about her."

"We didn't say her name. He just knew."

"What else did he say?"

"That I should mind my own business if I didn't want that to be the last message on my corpse."

Marx began to sweat as he realized what had happened. The killer had been following them. He had probably trailed them from the apartment.

But why the interest in protecting Holly? She was important to Marx, but to the rest of the world, she was just another girl. "Did he say anythin' else about Holly?"

Miles stared at the tabletop, and Marx slammed both hands in front of him, making him jump.

"Think, Miles!"

"I don't know! He said she's a sweet kid, but that's it. I told you everything else."

A sweet kid. If the killer viewed Holly as a kid, then he was at least over thirty. There were several men on the force who thought of her as a kid, but he didn't believe any of them capable of murder.

It was just some deranged vigilante who thought he was making the world a better place by . . . his thoughts drifted back to the conversation about Dr. Wilder in the squad room, and Michael's uncharacteristic statement: *You know, maybe it's a good thing he's dead. One less predator in the world.*

No, that was just a coincidence. He had said similar things himself. Sometimes certain cases burrowed under a cop's skin worse than others, and this was that case for Michael.

"You're not gonna do anything, are you?" Miles asked. "Because it's a cop, you're just gonna let him go."

"You don't know that it was a cop, and neither do I. There's no proof."

Miles pushed out of his chair. "This was a bad idea. I thought maybe you could be trusted, but you know, now that I think about it, this is all because of you. That guy was probably a friend of yours. Did you text him after we left?" Miles backed toward the door. "Did you send him after us 'cause you knew we were gonna follow you?"

Marx held up a hand. "Miles—"

"You did, didn't you?"

"I had nothin' to do with what happened to you and your friend."

Miles fumbled with the door handle, shaking so badly that he could barely grip it. "Of course, you didn't, because nothing happened. I don't remember anything. Neither does Joel. It was all just a big misunderstanding. And I . . . I won't bother that girl again. I swear on my life, okay? I swear."

Miles flung the door open and launched out of the room, running as fast as he could through the lobby toward the exit.

"Miles!" Marx shouted, but Miles shoved through the doors and disappeared down the steps. Marx thought about pursuing him, but his phone rang before he could decide. "Marx," he answered.

He heard Michael speaking in the background, his words muffled by panicked voices and the intermittent buzz of a fire alarm.

"Michael."

Michael shouted for someone to stay back, and the whoosh of water flooded Marx's ear.

"Michael!" he shouted, growing more concerned with each passing moment. "What's goin' on?"

Heavy breathing crackled down the line, and Michael said, "Officer Blakely's dead."

35

*T*he hospital was surrounded by fire trucks and squad cars, and there were people gathered on the street, staring at the building with fear.

Marx pushed through them and sprinted into the hospital. He took the stairs to the intensive care unit, where Officer Blakely had been.

He showed his badge to the woman at the reception desk, and she buzzed him in.

The stench of burnt plastic hung as thickly in the air as the smoke, and Marx tried not to breathe too deeply.

Water pooled on the floor from the sprinklers, and nurses scrambled to attach oxygen masks to coughing patients without slipping on the tile.

"There we go," Michael said, and Marx tracked his voice to the other end of the ward.

Michael settled a sobbing, choking woman into a chair and affixed an oxygen mask to her face. "Deep breaths."

As Marx made his way toward them, he realized with a knot in his throat that the woman was Officer Blakely's wife. He couldn't imagine the devastation she was feeling.

Michael straightened when he approached. "Hey."

"What happened?"

Michael put a little distance between them and Blakely's widow, and lowered his voice. "I was downstairs with Kat when I heard fire alarms. Someone started a fire in the storage closet."

He gestured toward the storage room, and Marx walked over to take a look. Flames had licked up the walls and over the door, and all that remained at the ignition point was metal shelving and ash. "You think it was a distraction?"

"It had to be. It was complete chaos when I got up here. People were panicking. The officer we posted outside Blakely's hospital room was down, Blakely's wife was screaming . . ."

Marx glanced at the pool of the blood on the floor outside Blakely's hospital room. "Benson?"

Benson was the young officer who was supposed to be stationed outside the room during the day.

"He's in surgery. The killer stabbed him from the side with a seriously sharp implement. It went right into his lung. Nobody even saw it happen."

"Probably a bump-n-stab durin' all the chaos." It wouldn't be the first time a killer bumped into his victim and slipped the knife in at the same time. "What about the fire? Did anybody see who started it?"

"I asked around, but no one noticed anybody out of place."

"Excuse me, ma'am," Marx said, catching a nurse's attention as she passed. He pointed at the storage closet. "Is this door kept locked?"

"Always."

"Thank you." He looked back at Michael. "What happened with Blakely?"

"His wife was in the bathroom when the fire alarms went off. She came running out and straight to her husband's room, but . . . he was already dead. He'd been stabbed in the heart."

Marx glanced at Blakely's wife with a pang of sympathy. The past twenty-four hours had no doubt been the worst day of her life. "Does she have any other family?"

"One of the nurses called them."

Marx turned to survey the damage. "So this guy comes to a public place—a hospital full of innocent people—and endangers their lives to get to one man."

"One of the firemen said the fire looked like it was a scare tactic. It was too contained to cause much damage."

The brisk clack of heels on the tile pulled their attention to the double doors leading into the ward. A woman strode toward them, her expression as severe as the black suit she wore.

Michael leaned toward him and asked out of one corner of his mouth, "Lawyer?"

"I bet you breakfast tomorrow mornin' that she's the hospital administrator."

"Pancakes?"

"Waffles."

They waited in silence as she covered the last few feet between them. She offered her hand to each of them, shaking firmly. "Valerie Cray. I'm the hospital administrator."

"Dang it," Michael muttered, his voice so low that only Marx could understand him.

Valerie Cray shifted her piercing eyes to him and said curtly, "Excuse me?"

Michael cleared his throat. "Nothing."

Marx noticed his slight grimace as he cradled his arm to his chest. "Did you get burned?"

"I was trying to help put out the fire."

"Nurse." Marx waved over a lady in Star Wars scrubs. "Can you check out his arm, please?"

"Let me see." She held out her hand, and Michael reluctantly uncurled his arm and rested his wrist in her palm. A patch of his forearm was raw and blistered. "Come with me and we'll get this treated."

"It's really not that—"

She fixed him with a motherly look that could freeze any toddler midtantrum. "Since you're not a medical professional and I am, you're going to do what I tell you to do."

Michael glanced at Marx, then followed the nurse like a scolded child. Marx rubbed the back of his neck and returned his attention to the hospital administrator.

She was obviously displeased that she had been forced to leave her office and tend to this mess, but she pasted on a false smile and asked, "How can I help you find out who did this?"

"None of your staff recalls anybody out of place who might have set the fire," Marx said. "We would like the personnel files for every one of your employees who works in the ICU."

The smile melted from her lips. "Are you suggesting that a hospital employee set the fire and murdered a man?"

"The fire originated in a storage closet, a closet that your staff assures me is locked at all times."

Her cold eyes slid toward the scorched door. "Perhaps someone forgot to lock it. Oversights do happen."

"Perhaps." But he had no intention of letting the matter drop that easily. Two of his victims had a history in the medical profession, and one of his victims had just been murdered in a hospital. "We still need the personnel files."

"I don't think they'll be of use."

"That's not for you to decide." Marx pointed to the cameras on the ceiling. "And we'll need the footage for this afternoon."

Her teeth clenched, giving her jaw a masculine edge. "We have some affluent patients, and they wouldn't appreciate their vulnerability being on display."

"We're not gonna upload it to YouTube," Marx replied impatiently. "We're gonna use it to find a killer."

She folded her arms. "I'm sorry, Detective, but I'm not going to give you that footage. Or the employee files."

Irritation prickled beneath Marx's skin. "So when you asked if you could help, you meant help in any way that didn't involve makin' the hospital look bad."

"If there's anything more I can do, feel free to call the hospital and they'll transfer you to my office."

Marx glared after her as she turned and strode back toward the double doors. He was going to have to get a warrant, but one way or another, he was getting that footage.

"You a cop?" a small voice asked from his left.

He looked down at the old woman who couldn't be more than four foot ten, her white hair styled in thin, short curls on top of her head. "I am."

Her eyes slid left and right cautiously, and then she whispered, "I saw the man who caused all this."

"Can you tell me about him?"

She motioned him down, and he bent so that he was closer to her level. "He said he's a cop too. But I saw him with that fire, and the other cop on the floor." She lowered her voice even more. "And he was in the room with the dead man."

Marx straightened, and she lifted her pale eyebrows at him, nodding.

"And he's right over there." She pointed to a room across the hall.

Michael sat just inside the room, the nurse tending to the burn on his arm. Doubt and confusion threaded through Marx. "There must be a misunderstandin'."

She lifted her chin. "I know what I saw. That man is a killer. And just you wait until he kills someone else. You'll believe me then."

A nurse swept in with an apologetic glance at Marx and took the old woman by the arm. "Come on, Mrs. George, let's get you back to bed."

Marx watched as the old woman was escorted down the hall through the reception doors and into a hall that wasn't clouded with smoke.

He frowned and followed, slipping out the doors and walking to the reception desk. The young woman who had buzzed him in still sat at her post.

"Can I help you?" she chirped with strained cheerfulness.

"Everybody who comes through here comes through you, correct?"

She shifted nervously in her chair. "Yes."

"Can you tell me who all came through here today?"

"Um . . . I can try. I'm new and, um, sometimes people come through without signing in, and I'm not sure what to do about that." She grabbed the clipboard and set it on the counter for him. "These are the ones who signed. But I know at least a couple followed other people through the doors."

He scanned the list of names, but nothing stuck out. "Make me a copy of this, please."

"Sure." She bounced up and took the sheet to the copier behind her, running off a copy for him.

He doubted the killer had signed in with his own name, if he had signed in at all. He may have just waited until another group of visitors was going through and trailed in behind them.

"Did anybody strike you as suspicious?" he asked, taking the paper from her.

"No, not really. Just a lot of sad people."

"Thank you. You mind lettin' me back in?"

"Of course." She smiled and pressed the buzzer. The doors parted, letting him back into the intensive care unit.

Michael met him halfway, a bandage wrapped loosely around his forearm. "Think it'll leave a scar?"

"Probably."

"You find anything?"

The old woman's words replayed in the back of Marx's mind: *He said he's a cop too. Just you wait until he kills someone else. You'll believe me then.* He cleared his throat. "No, nothin'."

36

"*W*hat am I supposed to do?" Marx asked, pressing the knife down a little too hard on the cutting board as he diced onions for dinner tacos.

Sam sat at the peninsula with a Coke, a grim set to his features. "You know what you have to do, as uncomfortable as it is."

"He didn't do this. I know Michael."

"You're *acquainted* with Michael. I know you're partial to him because he helped you find Holly, but how well do you really know him?"

The knife stopped halfway through the onion as he thought about it. "I know he's a good man."

Sam leaned forward, meeting his eyes. "How do you know that? Because he has a good solve rate for his cases? Because he's friendly? Because he's a Christian?"

Marx slammed the knife down in frustration. "I don't know!"

Sam pressed his lips together and sat back, giving Marx time to rein in his temper. "No one really knows what's in another man's head or heart. We lost ten percent of the department because 'good men' wanted to supplement their income by dealing drugs."

Marx leaned on the counter, torn between his obligations and his desire to protect a man he thought was a genuinely decent person. "If I investigate Michael for these murders, it could ruin his career."

"Well, let's talk about the facts before you decide anything." Sam got up and grabbed a second knife and cutting board, then reached around Marx for the tomatoes.

"What are you doin'?"

"Saving the tomatoes from your wrath." He shot a pointed look at the maimed onion scattered across the counter.

Marx sighed and resumed dicing. "What facts are we talkin' about?"

"Let's start at the beginning. Michael was assigned as your partner after the second victim. When the two of you went to visit the motel room where Terrence James was murdered, the prostitute ran from Michael, saying he was gonna kill her too."

"She ran from both of us, and she didn't see the killer's face the night Terrence died."

"People have instincts."

Marx shook his head as he scraped the onions into a bowl and grabbed a pepper. "I don't buy it."

"Okay. After that incident, you went to Becca Hart's apartment to look for her. Another witness ran from Michael, and you said he was so scared he could barely talk."

"The guy has the mind of a child, Sam, and after a man broke into the apartment with a gun, he was scared."

"A scary man with a gun." Sam flicked a look his way. "Like a cop?"

"No, like a killer with a gun."

"After that, a cop is shot. Where was Michael when that happened?"

"Probably at home asleep. Like I was. Does that make me a killer?"

Sam moved aside a small pile of tomatoes with the knife and started on a fresh one. "You're taking this too personally. Try to be objective."

"I am objective," Marx snapped.

"When someone broke into your apartment, where was Michael?"

Marx opened his mouth to answer, but nothing came out. Michael hadn't been at the precinct with him because his wife had been sick.

"Did the killer break into your apartment while Michael was at the precinct with you?" Sam asked.

"No, he wasn't there. But why would he need to go through my notes? We're workin' the case together?"

"If you suspected him at the time, would you have told him?"

"Of course not." As he answered, he remembered the way Michael had shifted with unease when he answered the officer's question about a suspect at Blakely's house: *I have some theories, but I prefer to keep them to myself until I make an arrest.*

"That's why," Sam said. "He wanted to see if you were keeping anything from him. If you suspected him, walking into the precinct would've been a game ender for him."

Marx finished with the pepper and dumped the cutting board into the sink. "I'm done talkin' about this."

Sam sighed and set down his knife. "He knew Officer Blakely survived because you went to speak with his wife at the hospital. He knew an officer would be guarding the room. Don't you think it's a little convenient that he was in the same hospital with a 'sick wife' the same night the killer came back for Officer Blakely? You have a witness that put him at the scene as the killer. He even has a burn from starting the fire."

"He was tryin' to put it out."

"After the fact, so he could explain the burn and his presence."

Marx wiped off his hands and threw the towel on the counter. "This is ridiculous. Michael is not a murderer. What reason could he possibly have to kill these people?"

"I don't know. The notes on the bodies suggest the killer thinks they're guilty of something and he's punishing them for it. How many times have we been infuriated to see a criminal skate on charges and wish we could take matters into our own hands?"

"You're sayin' Michael did."

"I'm asking if you think it's possible," Sam clarified.

Before Marx could respond, the front door opened and Holly stepped in. Jordan, keeping the respectful five feet of space between them that Holly preferred, followed her in a moment later.

Marx watched the weight of anxiety and tension slide from Holly's shoulders now that she was safely home. "Hey, sweet pea."

She set her knapsack on the couch and shrugged out of her jacket. "Hey." She drew in a long breath through her nose. "Do I smell tacos?"

Marx smiled. "Yes you do."

She shuffled across the apartment and plopped onto a stool. "I love tacos. Hi, Sam."

"Holly."

While most people would read the lack of expression and flatness of his voice as indifference, Marx knew Sam regarded Holly as a second little sister.

"My shift starts soon, so I'm gonna go get a little sleep," Sam said. To Marx, he added, "Think about what we discussed."

Marx grimaced. "I will." Whether he wanted to or not, unfortunately. It was going to linger in the back of his mind for the rest of the night. He turned his attention to Holly as he shredded the lettuce. "Go wash up for dinner. You've got paint on your nose."

She threw a scowl at Jordan. "You said I got it all off."

He grinned. "Did I?"

She hopped off her stool and went into the bathroom to wash her face and hands.

Jordan took her seat. "I wonder if it drives her crazy that her feet never touch the floor."

"It does. How did today go?" Marx asked, lowering his voice.

"I hung out in the hallway until early this afternoon, then I knocked on the door and pretended like I hadn't been sitting out there all morning. We went for a walk in the park, but that didn't go very well."

Concerned, Marx asked, "What happened?"

"A group of girls recognized her and came up to talk to her. I gotta be honest, I've never had the impulse to hit a girl, but the one who told Holly, 'It's not really rape if the guy's as hot as Collin,' is lucky to still have her teeth."

Marx groaned at the stupidity of some people. "How did Holly react?"

"I don't think I've ever seen her that angry. She actually lunged at the girl, but an off-duty cop caught her and hauled her back. Nance Miffton?"

"I know her. Holly met her at the winter memorial."

"Yeah, she's also the cop who took our statement when someone tried to run me over in March. She told the girls off, but Holly was already spiraling toward a panic attack. All I could do was sit there while Nance tried to help her through it." Jordan ran a hand through his hair. "It's hard—not being able to do anything."

"I know."

"I took her to the agency after that to do some more painting. It was a good distraction."

Holly trotted out of the bathroom and climbed onto the furthest stool from Jordan. "I'm starving."

Marx prepared a taco for her, minus all the vegetables, and set it in front of her. When he brought out the bowl of cheese dip and tortilla chips, she locked on to them like a hawk. She loved cheese dip.

Once everyone had a plate of tacos in front of them, Marx asked, "Holly, would you do the honors?"

She clasped her hands together, and they all bowed their heads. "Dear Jesus, thank you for all my wonderful friends, for whoever created marshmallows . . ." Jordan tried not to laugh. "And thank you for these tasty tacos. Amen."

37

*H*olly stood on a stool as she searched Marx's kitchen cupboards for dust or crumbs. There had to be something she could clean, but there were no dust bunnies under the bed, no junk drawer to organize, not even water spots on the glasses that she could wipe off. She'd checked. All of them.

The only room that ever seemed to need dusting and organizing was hers. How was his apartment so immaculate? If she believed in magic, she'd swear he had cleaning fairies.

A sudden knock on the door nearly made her fall off the stool. Her heartbeat picked up as she stared at the door with apprehension.

Another knock preceded a quiet voice. "Holly?"

She let out a breath of relief. It was just Mrs. Neberkins. The woman had to be pushing ninety, but she was always popping over when she thought Marx was gone.

Holly padded quietly toward the door so she didn't wake Marx, and peered through the peephole to see the old woman standing in the hall in one of her flower-patterned housecoats.

She unbolted the door and cracked it open. "Hi, Mrs. Neberkins."

"I baked this. You should eat some." She shoved a loaf of banana bread at her. After a suspicious glance around the hallway, she leaned in and whispered, "If you need a safe place to stay . . ."

Holly bit back a sigh. Every time they spoke, Mrs. Neberkins asked her if she felt safe and then invited her to stay in her spare room. "I'm okay. Marx is my friend."

The old woman scoffed and folded her arms. "Enjoy the bread. It's a family recipe." Mrs. Neberkins disappeared back into her apartment and shut the door. She didn't even give Holly time to thank her.

Holly turned the "homemade" bread over to see a store best-by-date sticker on the bottom and bit back a laugh.

Family recipe, huh?

She was such a peculiar old woman. Something on the hallway floor caught Holly's eye as she turned to go back inside: an envelope.

It was lying just in front of Marx's apartment door. She bent down to pick it up and flipped it over to see who it was addressed to.

Her breath froze in her lungs when she read the words written across the back: *To my little bird.*

The sound of something hard and heavy hitting the floor jolted Marx out of a sound sleep, and he opened his bedroom door just in time to catch a flash of red hair as Holly retreated into her room.

The side table where he left his keys was lying on its side—no doubt the heavy thump he'd heard—and the front door was wide open.

He crossed the room to pick everything up and close the door, but an envelope drew him up short. He picked it up and read the writing on it.

Acid burned his stomach when he saw how it was addressed: *To my little bird.*

He was tempted to rip it to pieces right then—where did that psychopath get off sending her a letter?

Holly had an order of protection against her foster brother that forbade any form of communication. This letter should never have happened.

He stepped into the hall to see if the person who had left it was still there, but there was nothing but buzzing fluorescent lights and closed doors in either direction.

He closed and bolted the door before ripping open the envelope and pulling out the letter. He unfolded the ordinary sheet of paper and began to read.

Hello little bird,

I thought you should know that I have no hard feelings about the allegations you've made against me, though I find them deeply disturbing.

I have no doubt that terrible things have happened to you, things that will probably haunt you for the rest of your life, but if you truly believe I'm responsible, then I'm concerned for your mental well-being.

You've always been one to tell wild stories, but they never caused any harm, and no one ever believed them. But you've taken things too far this time.

When the jury sees these allegations for what they truly are—just more outlandish stories created by a neglected girl who craves attention—I'll be cleared and released, but there will no doubt be consequences for the decisions you've made.

I care about you, little bird, and I don't want to see you humiliated or imprisoned.

If my presence troubles you so much, you could simply have asked me to leave. I would never want you to feel threatened or unsafe, but you chose to fabricate these horrifying stories rather than speak to me.

I hope you'll reconsider pursuing this foolish path, because in the end, it will only hurt you, and there's no need for you to suffer unnecessarily.

All my love.

Fury burned through Marx's chest, and he crumpled the letter in his fist.

I don't want to see you humiliated and imprisoned. That was exactly what Collin had done to Holly.

This letter might have been delivered by someone else, but these words were Collin's—deliberately chosen to terrify her.

He wanted to throw something, but Holly was already terrified. He shoved the crumpled ball in his pocket and sent Shannon a text.

If anyone could ensure that this didn't happen again, it was her.

He walked to the spare room and tapped a knuckle on the door. "Sweetheart." He pressed an ear to the wood, listening; the sound of her gasping and sobbing in her room broke his heart.

He twisted the knob, but she had locked it. Grabbing the set of keys off the refrigerator, he unlocked the door. "It's just me, Holly. I'm comin' in, okay?"

The door knocked into something solid as it opened. She had dragged her nightstand over to barricade the door. He pushed, and the nightstand slid across the floor.

The room was dark, lit only by a nightlight in the far corner. Holly was terrified of the dark; she had been trapped in it for days, with a pale security light as her only source of hope.

She was huddled in the furthest corner between the dresser and the wall.

Riley snarled and stepped protectively in front of her when Marx approached, trying to shield her from the only possible threat in the room.

"Settle down," Marx told him as he crouched. "You know I'm not gonna hurt her."

Riley's ears lowered and a warning rumbled through his chest. He might have grown fond of Marx, but he would protect Holly from anyone he perceived as dangerous.

Marx remained still, giving Riley time to decide that he wasn't the cause of Holly's fear.

Riley chuffed at him, as if to say, "Yeah, that's what I thought," and lay down, resting his muzzle on Holly's feet.

Marx glanced at the white-knuckled grip Holly had on the knife in her hand. "Sweetheart—"

She struggled to breathe as panic constricted her airway. "He . . . h-he's h-here."

The knife shook in her hand, and he could barely understand her when she spoke again, her words strangled by tears. All he managed to catch was the word "bird."

Little Bird was the pet name her foster brother had given her, the one he used while hurting her. Those words had become synonymous with pain and terror in Holly's mind.

"He's not here, baby, I promise. You're safe."

She shook her head and curled deeper into the corner, condensing herself into as small a space as possible. He recognized this reaction; he'd seen it in many victims of violence—an instinct to make themselves smaller and less visible so that what they feared might simply pass them by.

"You're safe, sweetheart." He held out his hand for the knife. "I won't let anybody hurt you. Trust me."

She shook her head and gripped the knife tighter against her chest.

"Okay," he said, lowering his hand. "You keep the knife. I'm just gonna sit here with you, all right?"

Her eyes darted toward the open bedroom door, as if she expected her foster brother to materialize in the doorway.

"There's nobody out there. It's just you and me."

His phone vibrated in his pocket but he ignored it. Nothing—no dead body, robbery, or lecture from his superior—was more important to him than this.

"You know, I could really use your help at the precinct," he said, trying to distract her from her fear.

He told her about how he had written the details of his case on the whiteboard to help him put things in order, but that he needed her to rewrite it because no one could ever read his chicken scratch.

He told her how the coffee at the precinct tasted so bad yesterday morning that he considered putting cream and sugar in it, which of course was never the way a man should drink his coffee.

As he spoke, her grip on the knife loosened, and eventually she opened her fingers and let it clatter to the floor.

She scooted out of the corner and into his arms, burying her face against his side. His eyes burned as he wrapped his arms around her trembling frame and listened to the raw pain as it poured out of her in heavy sobs.

"You're safe, baby. You're safe."

There wasn't a strong enough word for how deeply he hated her foster brother.

God might want him to forgive and move on, but that was one of the many things they would never agree on. How could he forgive a man who had ripped apart a girl's life purely for the pleasure of it, a man who would do it again at the first opportunity?

No, that was a man he would never be able to forgive.

38

 $\mathcal{M}$ arx glanced at Holly's bedroom door with concern as he flipped the fried eggs in the skillet.

It had taken a while to calm her anxiety this morning, and when the overwhelming rush of fear and adrenaline finally dissipated, it left her exhausted.

She had lain down to rest, but that had been almost four hours ago. He had to leave for work soon— he was already several hours late—but he didn't want her to be alone today.

She had promised him she wouldn't try to hurt herself again, but he wasn't sure she was in the frame of mind to keep that promise. Not after she received that taunting letter.

Her bedroom door creaked open, and a tiny foot, wrapped in rainbow-colored toe socks, nudged the door the rest of the way open.

A mountain of laundry with a short pair of legs shuffled out of Holly's room and stumbled toward the laundry closet. He heard her bump into the wall with a thud and a squeak, and shook his head with a smile. She was clumsy enough, and the too-long jeans she was wearing were only going to make things worse.

He had bought her a few pairs of clothes after she got home from the hospital, since nearly all of hers had been stolen, but apparently petite was still too long for her.

She tripped on her way into the kitchen and let out a few indistinguishable grunts of frustration as she bent down to roll the extra material up around her ankles.

She straightened with an exaggerated sigh and blew a thick strand of red hair out of her face. She perked up when she saw that he was cooking brunch. "Ooh, can I help?"

He lifted an eyebrow at her. "Is that a serious question?"

"I haven't set off the smoke alarms in ages."

"If by ages you mean last week."

She folded her arms indignantly. "There was something wrong with that bag of popcorn."

"Yes, you cooked it for nine minutes. I think you found the secret to charcoal."

She had meant to cook the popcorn for ninety seconds, but she had gone to run her bath without realizing she had turned it on for nine minutes. It was a simple mistake. One that had unfortunately permeated the walls and furniture with the stench of burnt popcorn.

She plopped down at the counter, looking no more rested than she had when he left her room earlier this morning.

"Laundry day?" he asked.

She bit the corner of her bottom lip and lifted one boney shoulder in a shrug. She had just washed her entire wardrobe two days ago, which meant she was looking for a distraction from her thoughts.

"Well, come on then," he said. "Come butter the toast." When she hopped off the stool and walked into the kitchen, Riley tried to follow. Marx pointed a finger at him. "Uh-uh, not you."

Riley whined and sat down at the edge of the kitchen.

"He just wants to help make breakfast," Holly said.

"Look at that face." He gestured toward Riley, who was scenting the bacon in the air and licking his chops. "Does that look like a face that wants to help *cook* breakfast or help *eat* it?"

Holly let out a snicker and began buttering the toast. She tore off a corner and tossed it to Riley, who inhaled it and then thumped his tail on the floor, hoping for more.

"Don't feed him people food," Marx chided, but the moment she turned back to her task, he tossed Riley a piece of bacon.

Holly pointed the butter knife at him. "I saw that."

"You saw nothin'."

She narrowed her eyes and watched him out of the corner of her eye, trying to catch him in the act again. He waited until she went to fetch the cherry preserves from the refrigerator, then tossed Riley another piece.

Holly closed the refrigerator and noticed Riley licking the tile floor. She threw Marx a look of mock suspicion as she walked past him. He ruffled her hair, and she swatted at his hand in protest.

"Stop that."

Marx chuckled and mixed the hash browns on the stove top, crisping them to a buttery, crunchy perfection. Holly would still ruin them with ketchup. The first time he made her breakfast, she had made swirls on her plate with the ketchup bottle, dousing the eggs, hash browns, and sausage.

"Marx."

The seriousness of her tone captured his attention more than his own name. "What, sweet pea?"

She stood by the counter with the cherry-covered knife in her hand and faint thought lines between her eyebrows. She parted her lips to speak, then paused with uncertainty.

He knew the question she was wrestling with; he could see the anxiety of it in the tightness of her fingers around the knife. "You're curious about the letter."

She nodded slowly.

He expected her to ask eventually. Her foster brother might terrify her, but she had never been one to stand on the sidelines and let someone else deal with her problems.

"There's nothin' important in there," he said.

"Did . . ."—she struggled for a moment, trying to form her foster brother's name on her lips, then gave up—"did he say anything about . . ."

"No, he didn't say anythin' about what he did to you. Just that he's unhappy with his circumstances, and he would like them to change. But they're not gonna."

Holly swallowed. "That's all?"

"That's the abbreviated version, but yes, that's it."

She puffed out a breath of relief. Marx understood her unease; if there was a way that Collin could describe those days without incriminating himself, he would take pleasure in reminding all of them that he always got what he wanted, even if what he wanted was Holly.

Holly licked the cherry preserves from the knife, then distractedly stuck it back into the jar and scooped out another helping for her toast.

She did unusual things when she was on autopilot. On several occasions, he had watched her fold, unfold, and refold towels while lost in thought. And she wondered why things took her so long to finish.

"I think you have enough preserves on there," he said as she started to scoop another knife full.

She blinked down at her drowning toast and smiled sheepishly. She dropped the knife into the sink and screwed the lid back on the jar. "Do you have the day off today?"

"No, I have to go to work. I'm just gonna be a little late today."

Someone tapped a rhythm on the front door, and Holly shot Marx a quizzical look. Before she could ask if he was expecting company, a familiar female voice snapped from the hallway, "I'm her best friend, which means I get to go in first."

Holly's face brightened, and she floated over to the front door to unlock it and fling it open.

Jace, her best friend, sat in her wheelchair just outside the door with a wide grin on her face. "Morning, sunshine!" She threw her arms around Holly in an awkward hug that knocked her back a step.

Sam stood behind Jace, and Jordan stood to his left, his blue eyes twinkling when they settled on Holly.

Marx didn't like that twinkle. He knew Jordan's feelings for Holly went beyond friendship, and the only reason he hadn't felt the need to intervene was because Jordan had promised not to pressure her.

When Jace released Holly, Jordan held out a chocolate muffin on his palm and bowed his head dramatically. "I come bearing gifts, my lady."

"That is not breakfast," Marx said, taking the eggs and bacon off the stove.

"Technically it's lunch time. And it has eggs in it," Jordan replied, straightening. "And walnuts. Plenty of protein."

Holly took the muffin with a grin. "Why is everyone here?" She stepped back so they could file in.

Sam, the last one in, closed the door and locked it before exchanging a look with Marx. After recent events, Marx didn't want her spending the day alone, but they couldn't tell her that.

Sam cleared his throat and said, "There's a baseball game on at noon. We came over to watch it."

Holly paled, and Marx mouthed, "Baseball?" He saw the realization cross Sam's face. He'd forgotten that one of the tools Collin used to hurt Holly with was a baseball bat.

To Holly, Marx said, "You don't have to watch baseball, sweetheart. You guys can just watch a movie. That one about the dogs and a cat wanderin' through the wilderness is over there somewhere."

"*Homeward Bound?*" Jordan chimed in. "We watched that when we were kids."

Holly folded her arms and said with a resilience that surprised him, "No, baseball's fine. My dad used to watch it. I don't remember much about it, but . . . he seemed to really enjoy it." She cocked her head at Marx. "I didn't know you like baseball."

"Who doesn't love the Yankees?"

Jordan raised a hand. "That would be me. Kinda partial to the Kansas City Royals."

"Everybody's entitled to poor judgment every now and then," Marx replied, setting the breakfast food out on the peninsula. "I made plenty. Everybody come eat."

They gathered around to eat a late breakfast and catch up before crowding into the living room. Jordan and Sam stretched out on the floor so Holly, Marx, and Jace could share the couch.

Marx watched Holly for any signs of distress when the game started. She tensed when the camera showed a close-up of a player practice-swinging the bat, but she didn't look nauseous or desperate to leave the room.

She clearly knew nothing about the game, because she cheered for both teams and thought a foul ball was a point. When a player slid into home plate, she threw her arms up and cheered, "Touchdown!"

Marx and Jordan burst out laughing.

"It's called a home run, Holly," Sam said with a hint of amusement.

"Oh." She put her arms down, her cheeks pink with embarrassment. "But he earned a point?"

"He scored a run," Sam corrected.

Her nose wrinkled as she tried to work out all the terminology. Jace patted her leg sympathetically and said, "Don't worry, it's all basically the same thing. Men fight over a ball and try to beat each other with numbers."

Sam frowned at his girlfriend. "It's not even close to the same thing. She's using football terms for baseball."

Marx smiled and shook his head. "I gotta go to work." He kissed the top of Holly's head, and she smiled up at him with a pale glow of happiness surrounding her.

39

He sat against the wall with his head in his hands. He had so much more that he needed to do, but it felt like everything was falling apart.

He wasn't going to be able to hide for much longer. No doubt Detective Marx would get a warrant for the hospital video footage, and it would paint a perfect picture of what had happened. Going back for Blakely had been a mistake.

Yes, the man needed to pay for what he had done, but hospitals were filled with innocent people. What had he been thinking starting a fire?

He thumped his head back against the wall and rubbed at his burning eyes. "I didn't mean for things to happen this way."

He dragged his hands down his face and picked up his phone. Even though she wouldn't answer, he needed to hear her voice.

He dialed her number and listened to her voice mail, savoring every musical inflection and pause that made her voice unique. He would never grow tired of hearing it.

"I love you," he said.

He ended the call and set his phone on the floor before wiping the tears from his face. He looked at the journal lying next to him and picked it up. He was torn between regret and the overwhelming need to be understood, to connect with another soul.

He opened it and continued reading where he'd left off:

Dear Jesus,

It's storming today, and every bolt of lightning reminds me of home, of sitting on the back porch with my sister and watching the raindrops fall.

It's easy to see nothing but the mass of gray clouds and the heavy rain, and think, "Will it never end?" But the clouds always part and the sun always shines. It's just a matter of riding out the storm.

Thank you for the breaking of the storm.

He closed the journal as he pondered her words. How was he supposed to ride out a storm that had been raging for five years? There was no end in sight. There was no sun breaking through the clouds.

"Where were you when I needed you, God?" he cried out. "Where were you when I was on my knees, begging? Where were you?!" He flung the journal across the room in anger.

He would have to end this storm on his own, and he was over halfway there. Only a couple more things to put right before his clouds would break, and he needed to get back to work before time ran out.

40

*M*ichael plastered a sheet of paper against Marx's driver's side window the moment he pulled into the precinct. "We have a name and address for the guy who was seen fleeing from Lola's house the night she died."

Marx's pulse jumped, as it always did when he felt like he was getting closer to catching the killer. He nodded toward the passenger seat. "Get in."

Michael hopped in and buckled his seat belt. "His name is Rod Mosley." He opened the file in his lap and showed Marx the man's photo. "Bald with tattoos."

"How's he affiliated with Lola?"

Shannon had tried to remain detached when Marx told her about Lola's murder, but he knew the old memories of friendship and laughter had awakened in her mind too. He wanted an answer to give her.

"He was on the list of Lola's clients that Sully compiled, and he's the only one that matches the description the witness gave."

"He got a rap sheet?"

"I'm not sure there's anything this guy hasn't done, except for maybe terrorism." He skimmed over the man's rap sheet and summarized it. "Assault, assault and battery, drug possession, sexual battery, solicitation, attempted murder, some more assault. Think this guy likes to hit people?"

Marx chanced a look at the rap sheet as he slowed at a stoplight. "How's he even on the street?"

"I would guess because he had a really good lawyer. Emphasis on *had*. Lola got him off with community service, parole, time served . . ."

"Why would he kill her?"

"Probably because he got himself in trouble again, and she refused to take his case."

"What's he on the hook for this time?"

Michael scanned for the most recent charge and grimaced in disgust. "Child porn."

"That's why she didn't take his case. Lola might have been set on buildin' a reputation for herself, but it wasn't as someone who defended child pornographers."

"How do you know?"

Marx flexed his fingers on the wheel. "Because her brother was a victim of it. It's what made her wanna be a prosecutor."

"But she became a defense attorney," Michael said.

"Somewhere along the line somethin' changed, I guess, but that—her hatred of child abusers—that would never have changed."

"Yeah," Michael muttered, looking back down at the documents. "Sometimes it's hard to accept that guys like this walk free, after all the lives they've ruined."

Marx glanced at Michael as his words stirred an uneasy feeling. He decided not to let his mind wander down that path without more evidence. "So he got angry and started harassin' Lola?"

"Looks like it. She took out a restraining order against him."

Oh, Lola, Marx thought with a twinge of heartache. Why hadn't she come to Shannon or to him if she thought she was in danger? Despite her choices, they never would've turned her away.

He pulled onto a one-way street. "Where am I goin' from here?"

Michael gave him the address for a bar downtown. It was owned by a friend of Mosley's, which was probably why it had taken Sully so long to find him. Mosley wasn't listed as a resident or employee.

They walked past the tables to the counter to speak with the bartender, and Marx held up Mosley's picture. "Where is he?"

The woman flipped her cherry-red hair behind her as she eyed the picture. Lifting her gaze to them, she asked, "You cops?"

They both showed her their badges.

She puckered her shiny lips in thought, then jerked her head toward the staircase on her left. "Hasn't come down today. But sometimes he drinks himself unconscious."

"Are you the owner?" Michael asked.

She scoffed. "Honey, if I was the owner, that piece of garbage up there would be out on the street where he belongs. I'm just the bartender." She winked at him. "You can call me Cherry."

"Thank you," Marx said, heading for the stairs. He paused when he noticed a wood plank over the rear window of the bar. "Somebody break a window?"

Cherry filled a glass and slid it down the counter to a patron before joining them. She jutted her chin toward the back of the bar. "Window was fine when I closed down last night. Must've happened before we opened. Funny thing—nothing's missing."

Marx's stomach churned at her words. Something was wrong. He drew his weapon and started up the steps to the wooden door at the top. He pounded the side of his fist on the door. "Mosley!"

No one answered. He was about to call down to Cherry and ask for a key, but the doorknob twisted. He released it and let the door drift open. The room was dark, and he pulled out his flashlight, holding it flush against his gun as he crept inward, Michael close behind him.

The light bounced over a bed and dresser, a small kitchenette with a refrigerator, and landed on a man's foot.

"Found a switch," Michael said, and he pulled a string that ignited the lone bulb on the ceiling.

Marx clicked off his flashlight and lowered his gun as he stared at Mosley's body on the floor. Every time he tried to get ahead of this killer, he was still a step behind. There was no note on this body, as if Mosley had been killed as an afterthought. Or to keep him from talking.

The latter possibility worried Marx, because if Sam was right in his suspicions, then he couldn't ignore the fact that Michael had gotten Mosley's location from Sully before anyone else. It would've given him the opportunity to come here and kill Mosley before passing along the details to Marx.

Keeping his gun at his side, Marx turned toward his partner. "We have a problem, Michael."

41

"*I*f it makes you feel any better, you made the right choice," Sam said.

Marx stood beside him outside of the interrogation room, watching Michael through the one-way mirror. "It doesn't make me feel better, and it doesn't feel right."

They should never have to put one of their own into one of these rooms to have their privacy and their lives ripped apart. This wasn't how it was supposed to be.

"Maybe you'll prove that he didn't do it."

Marx shot him a sharp look. "At what cost?"

Even if he went in there and proved that Michael wasn't responsible for this string of murders, the sense of betrayal would drive a wedge between Michael and the rest of the department.

"I've never seen you this hesitant to get to the truth," Sam said. "What's really going on?"

Marx rested his hands on the frame of the mirror, leaning against it as he stared intently at the floor. There were so many reasons he didn't want to do this, but the one that kept him from opening that door was that Michael was his friend.

"I don't wanna lose another friend," he admitted.

Sam lowered his chin in silence. Marx had lost two people he loved in the past year, and apart from the partnership he was building with Michael, Sam was his only remaining friend.

But he still had to do his job, even if it hurt. He drew in a fortifying breath and walked into the interrogation room.

Michael looked at him with distrust in his eyes. "You can't really believe I killed these people."

"I don't." Marx tossed the notepad and pen on the tabletop and sat down in a chair. "But you've been implicated, and you know what that means."

Michael crossed his arms and leaned back. "This is a waste of time. Someone is out there killing people, and you wanna interrogate *me*."

"I don't like this anymore than you do, so let's just get it over with." He slid the notepad and pen toward him.

"Are you expecting me to write a confession?"

"No, I expect you to write down this sentence—I don't know why I should have to listen to politicians when I'm the one on the street, tryin' to protect and serve the innocent.'"

Michael smiled with an edge of bitterness. "Couldn't agree more, but how about I write what you really want." He picked up the pen and wrote this phrase: *I should have protected the innocent.*

It was the only note that hadn't been written by the victim, either because he refused to cooperate or because he was unconscious. That meant they had a sample of the killer's writing.

Marx figured Michael would be able to pick out the words and piece together what they were looking for. He knew how an interrogation worked.

Michael ripped off the sheet of paper and handed it to Marx. "What's next?"

The door opened, and Sam stepped in to collect the sheet of paper for handwriting analysis.

"Sully gave you Rod Mosley's name first thing this mornin', but you waited until this afternoon to follow up on it," Marx said. "Why?"

"Because I was waiting for you. That's what you do when you have a partner."

"There was plenty of time for somebody to break into the bar before it opened at eleven and kill Mosley."

"And you think I did that? Why would I do that, Marx?"

"I think Mosley was at Lola's house the night she was murdered, and I think he saw it happen. He was a witness that needed to be silenced."

"Assuming we're talking about someone else as the crazy killer, that makes sense. But I didn't kill him."

"'Sometimes it's hard to accept that guys like this walk free, after all the lives they've ruined.' That's what you said on the way to Mosley's address."

"And? Are you telling me it's never bothered you that garbage like that get to go about their lives after all the lives they've ruined?"

"It very much bothers me." And if he ever snapped and started hunting down the guilty, he knew where he would start. "But that doesn't mean we have the right to kill them."

Michael interlaced his fingers and rested his head against them, frustration rolling off him. "I didn't kill anyone."

"The victims were killed with a Glock 22, which is the type of gun you carry."

Michael shook his head, his face still hidden behind his hands. "Eighty percent of law enforcement have that gun, yourself included, and you know that." He looked up. "And you're gonna have the lab test-fire my gun to see if the striations on the bullet match the ones taken from the victim, but they won't."

"Where were you when the fire started at the hospital?"

"The first floor with my wife. She was having tests done."

Marx thought about Michael's pregnant wife, who was probably wondering where he was. "She still at the hospital?"

"No, they discharged her, and I took her home."

"How is she?"

Michael tried to blink back the tears that burned across his vision. "She's pretty upset. The doctor said, because she had a placental abruption with the last pregnancy, that it might happen again. If it does, we could lose the baby."

Marx's heart ached for him. "Is there anythin' that can be done?"

"No. Doctor put her on bed rest and told her to avoid any strain or stress."

Stress like finding out her husband was being questioned in connection with five homicides?

Marx cleared his throat and tried to focus on the matter at hand. "Were you with her all night?"

"Yes."

"She was never out of your sight and you were never out of hers?"

Michael hesitated. "She fell asleep, but I stayed with her until I heard the fire alarms."

"How'd you get the burn on your arm?"

"Trying to put out the fire. You know this."

Marx rubbed a hand over his mouth before saying, "A witness claims you started the fire."

Surprise flickered across Michael's face, swiftly followed by indignation. "Then your witness is confused."

"She also said you were responsible for stabbin' Benson and Blakely."

Michael slapped his hands on the table in frustration. "I've never killed anybody! Not even in the line of duty. Why would I suddenly start murdering people? Especially cops and doctors, who fight every day to save lives."

"Because they *failed* to save lives. Because they let greed or perversion get in the way of them savin' innocents. Because they became as bad as the criminals the law releases back into the world, the criminals you wish you could do somethin' about."

"This is insane."

Marx glanced back at the one-way mirror where Lieutenant Kipner and Sam stood. Both were convinced that Michael was involved, and as much as Marx wanted to trust the instincts telling him that he wasn't, those instincts had led him astray before.

"Let's talk about Holly for a second," he said, and Michael blinked in surprise.

"What about her? Is she okay?"

"Tell me what you think about her." When Michael frowned, Marx said, "It's a simple request, Michael. When you think of Holly, what comes to mind?"

"I don't know. She's . . . a victim of an awful crime, and she's a sweet kid . . . girl . . . woman." Michael let out a frustrated breath. "Whatever you wanna call her."

Sweet kid.

Marx's mind flashed back to the day Michael stopped by the hospital to see Holly. He had dropped into the vacant chair beside Marx, a line of concern between his eyebrows as he gazed at Holly. Most of their conversation had faded from Marx's memory over the past few months, but he remembered how Michael referred to Holly as a "cute kid," despite the fact that she was only seven years younger than him.

Something sour brushed along the back of Marx's tongue. He came into this room hoping to prove that Michael was innocent, but he was becoming less and less sure by the second.

"If you thought somebody was gonna hurt her, not physically, but emotionally, would you step in?" Marx asked.

"What, like a bully, or . . ."

"Bully, reporter, somebody who just wants to torment her. Doesn't matter."

Michael shrugged. "My parents raised me to stand up for people, so yeah, I would. What does this have to do with anything?"

Marx slid a picture of Miles, the journalist, across the table. "Saturday night, I took Holly out for ice cream. This man followed us."

Michael's brows knitted together as he picked up the photo. "Who is he? What did he want?"

"He's a journalist, and he followed us with the intention of cornerin' Holly and interrogatin' her about what she's been through."

Michael's lips tightened. Like most cops, he had a strong dislike of the media and the way they forced their way in, disrupting lives just for a story.

"But before he could get to her," Marx continued, "a man jumped him and his partner. He locked Miles's arms over his head, frisked him, and then put a knife to his throat."

Michael looked up at him in surprise. "Military?"

Marx hadn't considered that possibility, but now that Michael mentioned it, he realized that was how the military instructed suspects to stand—fingers interlaced behind their head—so that they couldn't break loose. With their fingers locked together and the soldier's hand wrapped around their fingers, it was the field equivalent of handcuffs.

"Miles is under the impression that the man is a cop," Marx said. "He warned Miles to stay away from Holly. But what concerns me is that this man referred to Holly as a 'sweet kid.'"

The color drained from Michael's face and he swallowed hard. "I'm not the only person who thinks of Holly as a kid. Anybody older or taller than her probably thinks of her as a kid."

That was true. Even Marx thought of her as a kid. "Where were you when my apartment was broken into on Saturday?"

Michael thought about it for a second. "Kat was sick. I was at home, taking care of her and Cam the whole day."

Cameron was the little boy Michael and his wife had adopted. Marx had never met him, but Michael talked about him from time to time, and he had pictures Cameron had colored pinned to his desk.

"Where were you the night Blakely was shot? Or, for that matter, Wilder two days before that?"

"I don't know!" Michael shouted. "I was either working or at home with my wife and son."

"That's the problem, Michael. When the victims were attacked, when my apartment was broken into, when Miles was jumped and Mosley was killed, you were unaccounted for. And you were at the hospital when the fire started and Blakely was murdered, and a witness painted you as the arsonist."

Michael stared at him, at a loss for words.

"If your wife can confirm that you were with her at the times of the murders, we can send somebody to pick her up so she can give a statement."

Michael shook his head as fresh tears pooled in his eyes. "No, I don't wanna stress her."

Marx leaned forward and lowered his voice so the camera recording the interview couldn't pick it up. "I understand that, Michael, but you need an alibi."

"I didn't do this."

Marx searched his eyes for the truth, but all he saw was fear and anger. "Whether you did this or not, it looks bad."

"Just check the gun. It's not gonna match."

"All that's gonna prove is that you didn't use your service weapon. Then they're gonna get a warrant, and they're gonna rip apart your home."

The tears spilled over, and Michael rubbed at his face with his hands. "Don't let them do that. You can't let them do that. It's gonna scare Kat, and—"

"Is there somebody I can call who can pick her up?"

"Um, her sister. She can take her and Cam back to her place for the evening." Michael scribbled down the number for Kat's sister and handed it to him. "I don't want her to know about this, Marx, not until it gets all sorted out."

"I'll take care of it." Marx pushed back from the table and knocked on the door. It opened from the outside, and he stepped out of the interrogation room.

Lieutenant Kipner turned to face him, his expression grim. "What do you think?"

Marx rubbed his forehead. "I think . . . we should give him the benefit of the doubt."

"We can't do that," Lieutenant Kipner replied. "This department has already been tainted by corruption, and if it gets out that one of our officers is a suspect in five homicides, and we're being lenient, it'll be a public relations disaster."

"I don't care about PR!" Marx shouted before he could think better of it. He struggled to rein in his temper before he spoke again. "Sir, Michael is a good man, and he's a good officer. And this isn't right."

"The evidence speaks for itself."

"The evidence is circumstantial!" Marx shot back.

Lieutenant Kipner pinned him with a cold, steady glare. "Don't let your emotions cloud your judgment. It didn't serve you or this department well last time."

Marx flinched at the veiled reference to his best friend's betrayal. Lieutenant Kipner left the room, and Marx fumed in silence until the pressure became too strong, and he punched the mirror.

42

$\mathcal{M}$arx stood in the doorway to the nursery as crime scene techs tore apart Michael's home, looking for anything that might connect him to the series of murders. He couldn't bring himself to participate, but he had told them to put everything that wasn't evidence back the way they found it.

He didn't want Kat coming home to a mess.

He tapped a finger against the elephant mobile that hung over the empty crib, and watched it spin. There were sheets draped over the rest of the furniture, protecting it from dust.

Two wooden plaques hung on the wall. One of them had the name Caleb engraved on it, and the second had the name Jonah. Stepping closer, he realized there were dates, something usually found on a tombstone.

"Oh, Michael."

They'd had months to love those babies and dream of their futures before they lost them. He was grateful that he would never have to experience the loss of a child, let alone two.

He stepped out of the nursery and walked to the next room. There was a coloring page taped to the outside of the door—drawn by an adult hand and colored by a child—that said, *Cam I am. Bring me green eggs and ham.*

Marx smiled at the reference to Dr. Seuss and pushed open the door to Cameron's room. It was a little boy's paradise, complete with a race-car bed and a racetrack in the center of the room.

Marx bent and picked up one of the micro machine cars, sadness threading through him. If he couldn't prove that Michael was innocent, if he *wasn't* innocent, Cameron was going to lose his dad. His perfect little world, where he had been adopted and loved, would shatter.

It was too painful to think about. Marx put the car back on the floor and left Cameron's room, finding his way into the master bedroom.

The bedcovers were turned down from where Kat had been resting, and he glanced at the jar of Prego spaghetti sauce with a spoon in it sitting on the nightstand next to a bottle of generic pain killers.

She was eating spaghetti sauce . . . out of the jar.

She needed her husband home to take care of her, to prepare nutritious meals for her when she wasn't supposed to be on her feet.

He opened the nightstand drawer and pulled out the well-worn leather Bible. Michael's name was engraved on the cover.

He flipped through pages with highlighted passages and notes in the margins, coming to rest in the book of Proverbs. A verse was underlined: "Trust in the Lord with all your heart and lean not on your own understanding; in all your ways submit to him, and he will make your paths straight."

Marx closed the Bible. He had always preferred to lean on his own understanding, because in his experience most people spouted opinions without any clue what they were talking about, but he was learning that his understanding wasn't good enough. He needed to lean on someone bigger and wiser.

"Michael's one of yours, Lord," he said, staring at the Bible. "If there's a less crooked path to lead us to the truth, feel free to shine a light on it."

A crime scene tech swung halfway into the room, her hand gripping the door frame, and called out, "We found something."

Marx set the Bible on the bed and followed her down the hall into the laundry room. One of her coworkers held up a man's shirt they had dug out of the laundry pile. Marx recognized it; it was one Michael had worn earlier that week.

Blood stained the front of the shirt, and Marx's throat tightened with dread. When his phone rang, he had to clear his throat several times before he could speak.

"Marx."

"Hey, Detective, it's Gage from the lab. The lieutenant told me to rush the forensics since it involves one of our own. I started with the note that was left on Officer Blakely's body."

Marx stepped out of the laundry room and onto the back porch for privacy. "What did you find?"

"Obviously, I'm not a forensic document examiner, but I can tell you that the writing sample Detective Everly provided in the interrogation room is not a match. That being said, I also compared it with some of his handwritten reports. They don't match either."

Marx frowned. "How's that possible?"

"If I had to guess, I would say the difference is due to the fact that he was under duress in the interrogation room."

"What are you tryin' to say, Gage?"

"That due to the inconsistency of the handwriting, I can neither prove nor disprove that Detective Everly is the person who wrote the note."

Marx rested his forehead against the blue siding of the house with a groan. That was not what he wanted to hear.

"I'm gonna ship it off to someone who specializes in handwriting analysis, and they should be able to give us a better comparison. But it could be weeks before we hear anything back," Gage explained.

"What about the gun?"

"Ballistics is not a match to Detective Everly's service weapon."

Marx knew better than to believe Michael only had one gun. He had three, which meant Michael probably had a backup weapon somewhere, and the crime scene techs would find it.

His phone beeped, letting him know he had an incoming call. When he saw that it was Sully, he said, "Gage, I'm gonna have to call you back." He clicked over to the other line. "I assume since you're callin' that you have somethin' important to tell me."

"What, a guy can't call just to say hi?"

"No."

Sully sighed theatrically. "You know, your lack of social skills really is unfortunate."

"Sully."

"All right! Becca Hart finally used one of her cards to rent a motel room. I have an address for you." He gave Marx the details and directions, and he wrote them down. "And Marx . . . once she used her credit card, she wasn't hard to find. If somebody's looking for her, she just painted a target on her back."

Marx showed his badge to the motel clerk and then held up a photo of Becca Hart. "What room is she in?"

The weasely man behind the counter scratched his chin as he stared at her picture, the angle of his face emphasizing his unclipped nose hairs. "You're not the first person to come looking for her."

Marx glanced over his shoulder at Sam, whose brows dipped with concern. "Who else came lookin' for her?"

The man's face spread into a gap-toothed smile. "Rooms are twenty-five bucks an hour."

"We don't want a room," Marx snapped impatiently. "I want you to answer my questions."

"I'm trying to run a business here."

Marx resisted the desire to grab the man by his sweat-stained T-shirt and drag him over the counter. He pulled out his wallet and smacked twenty-five dollars down. "Who came lookin' for her?"

Weasely rubbed the money between his fingers with a greedy glint in his eyes. "Another man came by about ten minutes before you. Tall, really short hair, angry eyes."

"What room is she in?"

"You know, he gave me a hundred dollars for that information." He leaned on the counter, eyeing the pocket where Marx had put his wallet.

Marx leaned on the other side of the counter, pressing his face close to the clerk's. "How well do you think your room-by-the-hour business is gonna fair when cops are stoppin' by every couple hours for the next *hundred days*?"

Weasely straightened and rubbed at his throat as he looked between them, trying to decide if they were serious about their threat. He plucked a key ring off the tack on the wall and tossed it on the counter. "Room 204."

Marx snatched the key and grumbled, "Thanks."

He and Sam walked around to the back of the motel, looking for room 204. Marx frowned when he saw the cleaning woman tidying up the room. They made their way back to the front office, and Marx slammed the key back down on the counter.

"She's not there."

"Oh, did I forget to mention that she only rented the room for two hours? Guess she just needed a nap and a shower," Weasely explained.

"When did she leave?" Marx demanded.

"About fifteen minutes before you got here. Shame too, pretty as she is. She could bring in a lot of business for me. And herself."

Marx left the motel before doing something that would get him thrown in jail. Then he scanned the streets, trying to figure out which way Becca would've gone.

The creak of a lid opening drew their attention to a dumpster behind the motel. A shadowed face peered out, and Marx nudged Sam back against the side of the building with him.

With a grunt of effort, a woman flung the lid open and scrambled out. She landed in a crouch on the pavement and swept her bag back up onto her shoulder as her eyes flicked nervously around the nearby streets.

Marx recognized her instantly. "Becca?" She jumped, startled, then pointed a pocketknife in his direction.

He held up both hands, his badge clearly visible in one. "I'm Detective Marx with the NYPD. I'm just here to help you."

She looked around, searching for an escape.

"Your friend Maria is worried about you."

That got Becca's attention. "Maria? Is she okay?"

"She'll be better if she knows you're safe," he said, moving slowly toward her.

Becca shook her head. "I can't go back there. And I can't stay here. He was just here." Her lips trembled with fear, and she stepped back.

"Who was here? Who wants to hurt you?"

"He doesn't wanna hurt me. He wants to make me pay for what I did, for what *we* did," she said, her voice cracking. "So many people died, and I can't stop seeing their faces."

"We can help you, Becca. We can protect you."

A gunshot cut through the ambient noise of the city, and Marx and Sam ducked, drawing their weapons.

Becca screamed and fell to the ground, blood pooling around her calf.

"We gotta get to her," Marx told Sam.

"Where's the shooter?"

"I don't know." Marx inched toward Becca as she was struggling to her hands and knees. "Stay down, Becca."

Sobbing in pain and fear, she gripped the edge of the dumpster to pull herself up onto her good leg and tried to hobble away.

"Are you crazy?" Sam pulled him back as another gunshot ripped through the air. The bullet ricocheted off the wall where Marx's head had just been.

He shrank back around the side of the motel and scanned the windows of the surrounding buildings. The angle of the shots was coming from above, which meant their shooter likely had a sniper rifle.

"I sent a message for backup," Sam said.

Marx didn't like the idea of sitting still and waiting for backup, but they couldn't pinpoint the shooter, and he had lost his visual on Becca.

43

 *M*arx studied the shell casings from a rifle in the officer's hand. They had been recovered from the sixth floor of the abandoned building across the street.

Marx squinted at the building in the receding light of evening. It would've given the shooter a perfect vantage point. Any person with the skill to be a sniper could've killed everyone outside the motel, but he'd chosen to wound Becca instead.

Marx, on the other hand, he had intended to kill.

By the time backup arrived to search for the shooter, he had already vanished, and so had Becca. Her blood trail ended by a parking space on the street.

She had fled in such a panic that she didn't stop to grab the bag she had dropped when she was shot. That might be the only break they caught today, and it depended on whether or not she had anything in her bag that might point them toward the shooter.

"Well, at least we know one thing," Marx said. "Michael's not the killer."

"He's not the *shooter*," Sam corrected. "Just because he's in lockup doesn't mean he didn't send someone after us to make himself look innocent of the murders."

"Why do you want him to be guilty so badly?"

"I don't, but you need to take a step back and look at the evidence. And you need to look at the mind we're dealing with. He's a cop. He knows the law, and he knows how we work. Inside and out. You honestly believe he wouldn't think of this?"

"I don't think Michael would try to have me shot in the head."

Sam crossed his arms. "I think your perception is skewed by the fact that he's your partner, and you don't wanna consider that he might have orchestrated this event to deflect suspicion away from himself."

Marx ground his teeth together. "I'm done talkin' about this. We're never gonna agree. Let's just get Becca's bag back to the precinct and see what we can find out."

Marx set Becca's shoulder bag on the conference room table, pulled on a pair of gloves, and loosened the string keeping the bag shut. He pulled the contents out one item at a time, lining them up on the table.

Becca's cell phone was in the side pocket, and a small ChapStick bottle of morphine tablets was in the other. He picked through the change of clothes, finding nothing but gum wrappers and ChapStick that was actually ChapStick.

In the very bottom of the bag was a notebook. He expected to find the woman's thoughts scribbled across the pages, but when he opened it, he found eerily realistic portraits of people—a different face sketched on every page.

Some of the faces looked normal, but others were splattered with red paint, as if they were bleeding right out of the paper.

"That's disconcerting," Sam commented from behind him.

As Marx flipped through the pages, he realized that he had seen some of these faces before. Different angles and expressions, but the same people.

"I'll be right back."

He jogged down to the evidence room to sign out the metal box he had found hidden in Becca's oven. He brought it back to the conference room with him and opened it.

He pulled out the newspaper clippings and online articles that she had tucked neatly into the box, and began searching for corresponding sketches. He found several within the first few minutes.

"She's drawin' dead people."

Sam cocked an eyebrow. "Does she see dead people too?"

"In her head." He grabbed the ChapStick bottle of morphine and held it up. "That's why she takes drugs to try to erase them."

What was it she had said just before the gun fire started? He'd barely had time to absorb it before the gunshot had scattered his focus.

"'He wants to make me pay for what I did, for what we did. So many people died, and I can't stop seeing their faces.'" He looked at Sam. "That's what she said, right?"

"Yeah." Sam folded his arms. "But what does this have to do with the other victims?"

Marx rifled through the clippings again, checking the dates to see if they supported the theory he was working out in his head. "Not one of these articles is from the past five years."

"So?"

"So five years ago she quit her job as an EMT and stopped collectin' obituaries. Before then, she was still workin' as an EMT with her partner, Terrence James."

"Victim number one," Sam recalled.

"Mmm hmm. Becca said this man wants to make her pay, to make *them* pay because so many people died. Somethin' they did"—he tapped his finger on the pile of articles—"caused these people to die."

Sam drew in a slow breath and let it out. "That's a lot of people. If we're thinking the killer is related to someone in that box, how are we gonna narrow it down?"

A knock on the door distracted Marx from answering. Gage stood there.

"Wanted you to know I'm headed home, but I sent that handwriting for analysis. And you'll be happy to know that the blood on the T-shirt recovered from Detective Everly's house belongs to Detective Everly. They found a spare gun on a shelf in the closet after you left. Also not a match. See you guys tomorrow."

The pressure of dread lifted from Marx's shoulders, only to be replaced by an even heavier weight of guilt. Michael was innocent, and they had treated him like a murderer.

He needed to talk to him, to try to set things right.

"Where are you going?" Sam asked when Marx started out of the room.

"To let Michael out."

"Are you a hundred percent certain he's not involved?"

"I am."

Before Sam could plant any more doubt with his questions and suspicions, Marx left and headed downstairs.

Michael was sitting on the holding cell cot with his head in his hands when Marx came downstairs. He stirred at the sound of approaching footsteps, then stood with concern when Marx approached the bars.

"What's the matter? Is Kat okay? Cam?"

"They're fine." Marx unlocked the cell door and swung it open. When Michael only stared at him in confusion, he explained, "We have a lead on the real killer."

The statement seemed to knock the breath out of Michael, and he dropped back onto the cot, rubbing his hands over his face. "That's it? I'm just free to go?"

"No, that's not it." Marx stepped into the cell and sat down on the cot beside him. He rested his elbows on his thighs and braided his fingers. "I can't apologize enough for what happened, for my part in it."

Michael sniffed and blinked at the ceiling. "I heard you yelling at the lieutenant outside the interrogation room. You stood up for me."

"I should've tried harder."

"Any harder and you would've been booted out of the precinct. You yelled at the lieutenant. I'm surprised he let you keep your badge."

Marx looked at him. "You're not angry."

"Oh, I'm angry," Michael said, rising from the cot. "After everything I've done for this department, the fact that anybody could think I was responsible for murdering those people . . ." He shook his head. "I can't even tell you how angry that makes me. How . . . much it bothers me that you thought for even a second that I did those things."

Marx swallowed, but the lump of regret clung to his throat. "I'm sorry, Michael."

"If we're gonna be partners, we have to trust each other. I trust you, but I'm not sure the feeling's mutual."

"It is," Marx said.

Michael didn't say anything for a long moment, then he shrugged the tightness from his shoulders and said, "Good. I'm tired of this cell, and we have a killer to catch."

44

Marx folded his piece of pepperoni pizza and took a bite as he moved through his dwindling pile of articles and sketches, looking for the thread that would lead them to the killer.

"What about this one?" Michael asked. He held up the photocopied sketch of a child so that Marx and Sam could see it. "This kid matches one of the obits in my pile. Killed during a home invasion. Only the father survived."

"I imagine he has some anger to work through. See if you can find his name in the article and write it down," Marx said.

Michael scratched the name down on his notebook and moved on. They were going to have to run background searches and social media checks on every name they recorded.

Marx was convinced the killer would be in the list of names they were building.

"Detective."

When Marx and Michael turned to see an officer in the doorway, the man clarified, "Sorry, Everly. I meant Marx." He tipped his head to the right. "There's a lady here wants to see you. Says her name's Becca Hart."

The three men at the table exchanged a surprised glance and then sprang up from the table.

A slender, young woman sat in the chair beside Marx's desk, vibrating with anxiety. Her chestnut skin was a shade paler than he remembered, and his eyes flicked down to the gunshot wound in her calf. She had wrapped it with gauze, but the wound was still seeping.

"Becca," he said, and her green eyes snapped up to his face.

She pushed herself to her feet and gasped when the pain caused her left leg to buckle. Marx caught her arm and lowered her back into the chair.

"You have my bag," she said, looking between the three men. "I went back for it, but it was gone. You took it."

Marx crouched in front of her. "We have it." He watched as she fidgeted in the chair and scratched at her wrist. This was more than typical anxiety; she was in withdrawal.

"Please, I need it back. I need . . . I need my ChapStick."

"You mean your morphine pills?"

She sucked in a shuddering breath and tears trickled from her eyes. "Please, I need them."

"Because you're addicted."

She shook her head. "No, no, I'm not. I just . . . I just need them." Her gaze moved from one man to the next, desperate for someone to give them back.

"Why do you need them?" Marx asked.

"They make it hurt less."

Marx glanced at the gunshot wound, but he doubted that's what she meant. He whispered for Sam to go grab the sketchbook, and he sprinted to the conference room and back, handing it over.

Marx showed her the sketch of a little boy. "Is this why you take them? Because it makes your memories of these people hurt less?"

One look at the boy's face, and her eyes flooded. "We killed him. We killed all of them."

Marx and Michael exchanged a confused look. Some of these people *had* been murdered, but some of them hadn't. "Becca, this little boy died in a home invasion."

She covered her face, ashamed, and shook her head. "He died in the ambulance."

"How is that your fault?"

She smeared away the tears on her face, but her eyes were so full that he probably looked like nothing more than a smudge of color in front of her. "I knew . . . TJ was taking kickbacks from certain hospitals, for when he brought patients who needed . . ."—she struggled for the word, her brain addled by withdrawal—"extensive or pricey surgery, but . . . I couldn't . . . prove it. And I couldn't make him stop."

Marx let out a quiet breath of realization. "He took them to hospitals further away that paid more."

She nodded. "They should've lived. They all should've lived."

"So you had him fired," Michael said.

"TJ never sexually harassed me. I'm not . . . proud of lying about that, but I didn't know how else to stop him."

It disgusted Marx that a person could be so greedy that they put another human being's life on the line. He tried to keep the disgust and anger from his voice as he asked, "Who's after you?"

"I noticed him following me a couple weeks ago, and then again a few nights ago. And I think . . . I think maybe he was in my apartment, because things had been moved. Not a lot, but . . ."

"Did you recognize him?"

She wiped her nose on her shirt sleeve. "I thought maybe the first time I saw him was just guilt playing with my head, but it wasn't."

"Guilt about what?" Marx pressed.

"His wife was in a car accident, and TJ and me . . ."

"You were the first responders."

"She was in really bad shape, but the nearest hospital wasn't that far. But TJ . . ." She rubbed at her face. "He took her somewhere else. Said he took a wrong turn, but he grew up on those streets. He didn't take a wrong turn."

"If TJ was callin' the shots, what were you doin'?" Marx asked.

"Trying to keep her alive. She barely made it to surgery before . . ." Tears choked her voice. "She lost too much blood. And the baby . . ."

Michael stiffened. "What about a baby?"

"Please," she pleaded, looking at Marx. "Can I have my pills now?" When he started to shake his head, she cried, "Please, I don't wanna think about this anymore. I don't wanna see them."

"What about a baby?" Michael asked.

"She was seven months pregnant," Becca choked out. "That man . . . he lost his wife and child in one night." She drew in a trembling breath and tried to fight back the tide of emotions. "I stayed at the hospital, praying that they would be okay. But when he realized I was one of the paramedics who brought her in . . ."—she shook her head—"he started screaming that it was my fault she was dead, and he tried to come after me, threatening to make me pay. I tried . . . to explain that she was alive in the ambulance, and we had to make a choice about which hospital to go to. He . . . he said I should've made a better one."

Becca folded over and began to sob, the guilt leaving her in pieces. *I should have made a better choice.* That was what was written on TJ's body. This man was their killer.

Sam shifted behind Marx, drawing his attention. "I think I read about that mother and baby. It was one of the obituaries in my pile. I'll be right back."

Marx looked at Michael, whose face was chiseled in stone. Becca and her partner were partially responsible for the death of a woman and her baby, and Michael didn't have an ounce of sympathy for her.

"I'll go get the first aid kit, but she should really see a doctor," he said, and Marx had a feeling he was using the first aid kit as an excuse to escape the room.

Sam returned with the obituary and handed it to Marx. "The woman's name was Angie Mathis, survived by her husband Thomas Mathis."

"We need to find out what Thomas Mathis looks like."

"Already did." Sam held up his phone, displaying a picture of Thomas Mathis and his deceased family.

Marx's stomach dropped when he looked at the man's face. He took Sam's phone and placed it under Becca's downcast face. "Is this the man who threatened you? The man you saw followin' you?"

She wiped at her eyes. "That's him."

Their killer was the man who had fled from Becca's apartment the day they searched it, the man they thought was mentally challenged and homeless. Davey. The killer they dropped off at a homeless shelter.

45

Thomas hadn't stayed at the shelter. According to the woman at the reception desk, he had waited for them to drive away before he waltzed back outside and went on his way.

There was no current address listed under his name, but Sully was able to track down his military record. Ten years ago, he was honorably discharged from the army, where he had been a sniper.

Thomas could've killed Becca with one well-placed shot outside the motel, but he'd aimed for her leg. A bullet wound would need to be treated, which would make her easier to find. He hadn't killed her because he wanted her to admit what she had done wrong, just like he had with the others.

"Check this out." Michael turned the computer monitor toward Marx to show him the Facebook page for Angie Mathis. "His wife's Facebook is still active."

Marx rolled his chair over to get a better look. The recent posts were from friends or distant family, expressing how much they missed her. "Are there photos?"

Michael pulled up the photo albums, his heart breaking as he clicked through pictures of ultrasounds and month-by-month snapshots of Angie's growing stomach.

There was even a picture of the nursery they had decorated with giraffes and elephants.

The burrito in Michael's stomach curdled as he thought about all the time he and Kat spent building the nursery, only to lose the baby weeks later.

"I need some air." He stood from his chair and walked out.

Marx considered following Michael when he left the squad room. After so many miscarriages, this case had to be a painful reminder of how it felt to lose a child.

Marx glanced at the picture of Holly on his desk, remembering how devastated and terrified he'd felt when he thought she wouldn't survive. Michael was in that position now, consumed by the fear and worry that he might lose this child too.

There was nothing Marx could say to console his partner, nothing that wouldn't sound like hollow reassurances. With a sigh, he returned his attention to the computer and continued clicking through the photo album.

He stopped on a picture of Angie, Thomas, and another man who might have been family. A name popped up when he scrolled the mouse over the man's face, and Marx sat up straighter.

Davey Mathis.

He clicked the man's name, and it took him to another profile page. The site was cluttered with cartoon movie posts and links to various kinds of toys— something he would've expected to find on a ten-year-old boy's page.

He quickly realized that the mentally challenged Davey they thought they had met in the alley was real.

Thomas had spent his childhood with an older brother who was mentally challenged, and he had slipped seamlessly into that familiar role when they caught him in Becca Hart's apartment.

There was no address listed on the site, but as he scrolled down to the bottom of the page, a video of Davey began to play automatically.

"H-hi friends," he said, waving at the camera as he stared at the ground. He looked to be somewhere in his thirties.

"Look up, Davey," a man said from behind the camera. "They wanna see your face."

Davey lifted his head and threw his hands in the air, his round eyes shining with the excitement of a child. "It's Davey again!"

The man behind the camera laughed. "They know it's you, buddy. Tell them why we're here today."

"Oh." Davey turned to gesture at the building behind him, and the camera panned with him. "I get . . . a new home today. There's"—his face scrunched in thought—"music and . . . and art, and I can play out-outside."

Marx squinted at the sign on the outside of the building: Havenwood Assisted Living Center. Davey was in an assisted living facility for mentally challenged adults.

Davey looked back at the camera with concern. "Tommy."

"What are you thinking about, Davey?"

"Th-they're g-gonna be . . . n-n-nice to me, right?"

"No one's gonna be mean to you ever again. I promise. And you'll be home for your birthday, every holiday, and when the baby's born."

Davey lit up and bobbed up and down on his toes. To the friends who would presumably be watching, he said, "W-we're gonna have a . . . baby."

Thomas laughed again. "Angie and I are gonna have a baby." He turned the camera to capture the pretty blonde, whose hand rested on the swell of her stomach. She smiled before he swept the camera back toward Davey. "You're gonna be an uncle."

"Does that mean I c-can n-n-name the baby?"

Marx paused the video and leaned back in his chair. Thomas had been a loving brother and devoted husband before his wife and unborn daughter were killed.

He could understand how that would make a man snap.

A possibility occurred to him as he stared at the frozen image of Davey Mathis. If Thomas was willing to impersonate his brother to escape suspicion, maybe he had rented an apartment under his name.

46

*S*ully pinpointed an address for Thomas—a studio just off Central Park—that was listed under Davey Mathis. Six officers crowded into the hall of the apartment building, with Michael and Marx in the lead.

Marx hammered the side of his fist on the door. "Police! We have a warrant to search the premises!"

When no one answered, he tested the handle—locked—then stepped aside. An officer slammed a battering ram into the door twice before it sprang open.

Officers flooded the studio apartment, clearing the small bathroom, kitchen, and sleeping corner.

A long partition divided the living room from the kitchen, thick gray curtains hanging over one side on a cord the length of the wall.

"Clear," echoed around the apartment, and Marx put away his gun. Thomas wasn't here.

"You think he knew we were coming?" Michael asked.

Marx looked at the laptop resting on the desk by the partition. "I doubt it. But my concern is, if he's not here, what's he doin'?" He frowned at the curtains. "Who hangs curtains over a wall?"

He stepped around the desk and pulled one of the drapes aside, revealing something he'd heard about in horror stories but never seen. "Get these curtains down."

One of the officers sliced through the cord with a knife, and the curtains dropped to the floor. They all stepped back to absorb the disturbing contents of the wall.

There were two pictures of every victim, one while they were alive and one while they were dead and posed— like a macabre before-and-after photo. Becca's photo was of a smiling, chestnut-skinned woman who looked little like the stressed and disheveled woman they had just interviewed. There was a blank space waiting for her "after" photo.

Marx walked down the line: Terrence James, Becca Hart, Holland Wilder, Lola Eubanks, Grant Blakely, and two more men whose bodies hadn't been found.

"Maybe they're still alive," Michael said, his thoughts following the same trail as Marx's. "Maybe he's going after them next."

"We need to find out who they are so we can get to them before he does."

Michael opened the laptop and booted it up. He let out a frustrated grunt when a lock screen popped up. "He's got a password."

"Try his wife's name. Angie."

Michael typed it in and hit enter. "No."

"Detectives," one of the officers called from the bedroom.

Marx walked around the shelf cluttered with books and clothes that gave the bedroom an illusion of privacy. "You find somethin'?"

"You could say that." The officer pointed upward, and Marx tipped his head back to look at the ceiling above the bed.

He turned to take in the expanse of photos. These were not of Thomas's victims but of the family he lost. The ceiling was a collage of ultrasound photos and pictures of his wife. She aged from one end of the collage to the other, the images capturing each stage of her adult life.

This man was in so much pain. Every night he probably lay across his bed, gazing up at the life that had been stolen from him—the child he would never hold, the woman he would never grow old with.

Empathy stirred in Marx's heart. He understood the heartache of never being able to hold the child he longed for, of losing the future he planned to spend with the love of his life. Only his loss hadn't come with a funeral; it had come with divorce papers.

Staring up at these memories every night had to be maddening. Five years had passed him by, and Thomas was still grieving at his family's graveside.

That was the connection. The reason Thomas had a wall of human targets, people he believed had wronged him. The loss of the two things he treasured most—his wife and his child—would be all that mattered to him.

I should have made a better choice. He blamed Terrence James and Becca Hart for his wife's death because they had chosen the wrong hospital.

I should have tried harder. Maybe Dr. Wilder had been the trauma surgeon who failed to save her when her life was placed in his hands. That would explain the scalpels through his hands.

He couldn't make sense of the other two: *I should have told the truth* and *I should have protected the innocent.*

Lola Eubanks had nothing to do with hospitals or medical care, and Officer Grant Blakely wasn't a traffic cop. He would've had nothing to do with the accident that claimed Angie Mathis's life.

Marx squinted at one of the sonograms. Written across the bottom was the date and a name: Christine.

Marx stepped back into the living room and told Michael, "Try Christine."

Michael's brow furrowed as he looked up from the computer keyboard. "Who's Christine?"

"His daughter."

Michael punched it in and waited. The desktop appeared, and he whispered, "Yes!" He clicked through files, looking for anything pertaining to the victims. "Got it. Second to last target is Robert Hanson, and he's . . ." He looked up. "Crap, Marx, he's a judge."

Marx swore and called it in, requesting that units be sent to Judge Hanson's house immediately.

"Last guy on the wall is Karl Blakely," Michael said.

Marx snapped his phone shut. "Blakely. As in related to Officer Grant Blakely?"

"Could be."

Marx exhaled an irritated breath through his nose. This was one enormous mess. "Okay, we'll put Sully on the family tree. We need to get to Judge Hanson."

47

*H*e plunged the sharpened end of the gavel into the judge's chest, a symbolic end for a man who should have judged more wisely, then sat back on his legs, breathing hard as adrenaline surged through his veins.

"Oh, Thomas, what have you done?"

Thomas dragged his eyes from his stained hands to the woman standing across from him.

Her blond hair flowed over her shoulders like molten gold, and her blue eyes were as clear and bright as a cloudless sky.

"Angie?"

She knelt on the floor on the other side of the body, a sleeping baby in her arms. "Why did you do this?"

He looked down at the body. "I did this for us. Because he failed us."

Pity glinted in Angie's eyes. "People make mistakes, Thomas."

"No, this wasn't a mistake. He made a choice and this is his sentence."

"Is this the kind of father you wanted Christine to have? A killer?"

Thomas winced at the brutal sharpness of the question. "I'm making the world a better place."

"Love makes the world a better place, Thomas, not hatred and death. You know that. This isn't who you are."

He stretched out a hand to touch her face. "Are you really here this time?"

Her lips curled into a sad smile. "You know I'm gone. You buried me. You buried us."

"But I can hear you. I can see you."

"No, my love, you can't."

The sound of a car door closing snapped his attention to the front door. Someone was here. *"Angie . . ."* When he looked back, she had disappeared as unexpectedly as she had appeared.

He was alone. Always alone.

He climbed to his feet and crept to the front window to peer out. Officers were approaching the front steps.

How did they know where he was going to be? It was impossible, unless . . . no, he hadn't left anything behind at the scenes that would give him away. He'd been careful.

Anger bubbled up inside him when he saw Detective Marx. He had almost succeeded in getting rid of him; if only that other cop hadn't pulled him out of the way a second before the bullet could reach him.

He backed away from the window, intending to slip out the back, but he heard the rough twisting of a door handle from the rear of the house. The enemy was all around him, and he had no escape.

Flitting across the room on soft feet, he retreated into the small "panic room" the judge had added to his living room. It was scarcely bigger than a guest closet, but it was expertly hidden behind a wall-length one-way mirror.

He huddled in the small space, his finger resting on the trigger of his gun, as he watched the police swarm the house.

I could kill him now, *he thought when Detective Marx and his partner came through the front door.*

His partner, Detective Everly, on the other hand, didn't seem much like a threat. He struck Thomas as a follower, heeding the commands of a superior.

A forgivable offense.

He held still as the officers passed by the mirror, afraid that the smallest movement would draw their attention. It was almost funny—he had never been one to hide, and yet he found himself hiding in a closet-like space twice in one week. Only this time it was a matter of self-preservation rather than a kindness to protect an innocent girl.

Detective Marx crouched beside the judge's body and checked for a pulse.

Too late, Detective, *Thomas thought with a hint of amusement. Not that he enjoyed killing people—it was an unfortunate necessity—but there was always a bit of a thrill in knowing that he'd won.*

"We must've just missed him," Michael said, looking around.

"This guy's gettin' on my last nerve," Marx grumbled, rising to stand beside his partner. "We're gonna check the surroundin' area, see if we can get a visual," he told the officer by the front door. "Call in CSU and stay with the body."

Thomas watched the two detectives leave and waited with agitation for the others to trickle out the door. The officer ordered to remain at the scene stepped outside to guard the front door.

He bit back a growl of frustration. He was going to be stuck in this closet until everyone left. That could be hours.

He could kill the cop out front and escape, but the man hadn't done anything to deserve a bullet.

I'm sure he's done something wrong, something punishable. *The moment the thought skittered across his brain, he heard his wife whisper, "Who hasn't, Thomas? There's no such thing as human perfection. We're all flawed. You, me, that man by the door."*

He looked over to see Angie folded into the small space beside him. She had always been his guiding force, so full of grace and forgiveness. Like the girl who wrote the journal in his bag, she had loved God, and that love had colored every aspect of her life.

But God didn't save her.

"Oh, my love, you know that's not true," she said.

"He took you from me."

"He didn't take me to hurt you. He took me from pain, from a body too broken to sustain my life. It isn't the end, Thomas. We can be together again, but you have to stop seeking vengeance and seek Jesus."

He covered his ears and hissed, "Enough about your Jesus, Angie."

He could never tell if she was truly there or if she was just his memory playing tricks on him. Maybe she was the manifestation of his conscience, always trying to guide him. So like Angie.

When he realized his harsh words had driven her away, grief filled his chest. "I'm sorry. Angie, please come back." He touched the wall she had been resting against a moment ago. "Please."

He looked around the small space, but she was gone. He was alone again. His anguish and regret leaked out of him in silent tears, and he curled up on the floor, weeping for all that he had lost. "Please come back."

48

*M*arx tossed his phone on his desk at the precinct, furious that they hadn't been able to save Judge Hanson. They had been minutes too late, and despite scouring the neighborhood for Thomas, they had found nothing.

He noticed his desk calendar as he went to fetch his coffee mug. Another message had been written in permanent marker across it:

Traitor.

He leaned on the edge of his desk and glared at the word. Someone was either trying to tick him off or torment him into transferring.

He glanced around the room for anyone who might be watching for his reaction, and caught the eye of Andy Greene, one of the detectives approaching retirement.

The disapproval and disdain in Greene's eyes was evident from clear across the room.

Marx was tired of this game. It was the seventh antagonistic note he'd received since Matt's death, and he'd had enough.

He ripped the page off the calendar and stormed into the break room where Greene was eating a bagel and sipping his coffee. Marx slammed the page down on the table in front of him.

"You think this is funny?"

Greene swallowed his bite of bagel and wiped the cream cheese from the corners of his lips with a napkin before answering, "I think it's truth."

"I did my job."

"You killed two cops."

"*Dirty* cops."

"Yeah, so you say. So a lot of people say. But it doesn't matter." He set his badge on the table. "This means family. We might throw a few jabs and run our mouths, but we always got each other's back. We don't throw other cops under the bus, and we definitely don't put them in the ground."

Marx leaned across the table. "I don't know what world you think you live in, but a badge doesn't exempt you from consequences. You threaten to kill an innocent person, you're no longer a cop."

Greene set his bagel down and dusted off his hands. "Danny, Barrera's partner, was just a confused kid. You could've set him straight without putting three rounds in his chest. And the captain—we both know he never would've hurt that girl."

"You weren't there."

"I didn't need to be. It's pretty clear what went down. You betrayed your own for a pretty piece of tail."

Marx's fingers clenched into fists, and he started around the table, but Michael stepped in his path.

"Might be a good idea to end this conversation now before someone gets hurt."

Greene leaned back in his chair and folded his hands over his round stomach. "Relax, Everly. I don't need you to protect me from this cop killer."

It took every ounce of Marx's willpower not to knock him out of his chair. "Keep runnin' your mouth. I'll put you into retirement early."

"Yeah?" Greene asked. "You gonna plug me too?"

Marx sent Greene's coffee and bagel flying across the room with one angry swipe of his arm, then stormed out of the break room before he did something that would get him fired.

Michael blew out a breath as he looked down at the mess. "You're lucky I had a craving for taffy, because this"—he pointed to the bagel and coffee—"could've been you on the floor. Probably you should get your facts straight before you go making accusations."

"I have my facts straight," Greene snapped back.

Michael stepped around him and popped two quarters into the vending machine. "Good to know. Need any boxes to pack up your things?"

"I have three more months."

Michael made a noise of disagreement as he fetched his taffy from the drop box. "Mmm, I'm pretty sure this is your last day. Soon as the captain hears about you calling a sexual assault victim a pretty piece of tail—a victim, who by the way, is the star witness in an upcoming trial—there's a good chance he's gonna toss you out the door. She's a heck of a lot more important to this department right now than a detective months from retirement." He walked to the door, then paused to add, "Let me know if you change your mind about the boxes."

He caught the glimmer of worry in the older man's face as he walked out of the room.

There was practically a cloud of steam rising from Marx when Michael reached his desk. "You good?"

Marx was quiet for a long moment before speaking. "Let's just focus on the case."

"All right." Michael tore off a piece of taffy with his teeth and sat down in the chair beside Marx's desk.

"Hey." Sully crossed the room to join them. He noticed Michael's taffy. "I'll trade you information for a piece of that. I'm dying for some sugar."

Michael tore off a piece and handed it to him.

Sully popped the taffy in his mouth and groaned, as if he'd just tasted heaven. "That is so good."

"You need to get out of your bat cave more often," Marx said.

"True," Sully agreed. "What I could really go for is a pretty girl sitting across from me while I'm eating a slice of key lime—"

"We can talk about your fantasies later," Marx broke in. "Get to the point."

Sully mumbled something under his breath before diving into the reason he had come out of his cave. "Got the info you wanted on Karl Blakely, the last guy pictured on the killer's wall. And you're right, he's Officer Grant Blakely's cousin. He's been in prison for four years for vehicular manslaughter."

"Kind of a light sentence for vehicular manslaughter, isn't it?" Michael asked.

"Usually between three and fifteen years, so . . . just above the minimum," Sully explained. "And get this, the person he killed was Angie Mathis."

"Thomas's wife," Marx said.

"But wasn't she pregnant?" Michael asked.

"Seven months, but it died from complications of the car accident."

"*She* died," Marx corrected. "The baby was a girl. There was a time when you were nothin' but a blip on a sonogram too, Sully, but that didn't make you any less alive. You just had a different environment."

Michael frowned in confusion. "So he killed two people but only got four years?"

Sully hesitated before explaining, "New York doesn't have a fetus homicide law, so he couldn't be prosecuted for the death of the fetus."

Michael looked between them. "Are you kidding me? So if somebody hurts my wife and we lose the baby, it's not murder?"

"It might be considered an illegal abortion, depending on how far along she is," Sully offered.

Michael's face flushed with anger. "This guy killed a baby and her mother, and he only got four years?" He shook his head. "I can understand why Thomas went off the deep end. If this were my family—"

"You wouldn't try to murder five people," Marx said as he hung the photo of Judge Hansen on the whiteboard.

"But that's what this is about, Marx," Michael said. "His family was killed, and he feels betrayed by the EMTs and doctors who were supposed to save her, and the legal system that refused to acknowledge the life and death of his child. The system that decided four years was enough for the unimaginable agony he suffered. For the pain he's gonna have for the rest of his life."

Michael stood and stepped to the whiteboard beside Marx.

"Terrence and Becca chose the wrong hospital. Dr. Wilder didn't try hard enough to save the life of his wife and daughter. And, correct me if I'm wrong, Sully, but Lola Eubanks defended the killer in court?"

"Yep," Sully said with a nod.

"He believes her lies swayed the judge, who then made an unwise decision to sentence the driver to only four years."

"What about Officer Blakely?" Marx asked.

"He testified as a character witness on behalf of his cousin, said he never drank before and didn't know his limits, and pleaded for leniency," Sully said.

"Looks like he got it," Michael grumbled, disturbed by the judge's decision.

"More bad news," Sully began. "Karl Blakely gets out of prison tomorrow."

That was the deadline. Thomas had been working his way toward the man behind the wheel of the car the night his family was killed.

49

Grant Blakely and his cousin could've been twins—down to the way they parted their hair. Marx pulled up outside the prison gate just as Karl took his first step as a free man, and held up his badge. "Get in."

Karl looked around in confusion. "Where's Grant? He's supposed to pick me up."

"We'll talk after you get in the car."

Michael stepped out and opened one of the rear car doors without a word, but the muscle flexing in his jaw told Marx he had plenty to say to the man; he was just biting his tongue for now.

"Now, Karl!" Marx snapped, and the man jerked in surprise, then scrambled into the backseat.

Karl leaned forward between the seats as Michael got back in the car. "Someone tell me why Grant's not here picking me up. He even took the day off work to make sure he could be here."

"I'm sorry," Marx said, meeting his eyes in the rearview mirror.

It took a moment for the meaning behind Marx's sympathetic tone to register, and Karl swallowed, shaking his head. "No, no, you're wrong. I just talked to Grant last week."

Marx pulled out onto the street. "Grant was murdered a few nights ago, and the man who killed him is comin' after you."

"Why?" Karl choked out through his tears. "I haven't done anything."

Michael turned a frigid glare on him. "You mean besides killing a woman and her unborn child."

"That was an accident. I spent four years in prison to make up for it."

"Exactly how did you make up for it? By doing laundry and washing walls? By having three meals a day and watching TV?" Michael twisted in his seat to meet his eyes. "You think any of that makes up for the lives you took?"

Karl tried to blink back his tears. "No, it doesn't. But I didn't mean to hurt anyone."

"You meant to get behind the wheel of that car while you were drunk. Nobody forced you to do that."

"Michael," Marx said, glancing at him. "That's enough."

Michael clenched his teeth and turned forward in his seat. To Karl, he growled, "Put your seat belt on. Wouldn't want you to die in a car accident."

A seat belt clicked into place, and Karl slumped down in his seat. Marx turned on the radio and switched the music to the back speakers only.

He looked at his partner. It had been a rough week for all of them, but Michael had been interrogated, locked up, and in and out of the hospital with his wife. This case was stressing him to the breaking point.

"I know you're angry at the injustice of this situation," Marx began, keeping his voice low enough that the music would drown their voices. "But he didn't kill *your* family."

"I know, and I don't mean to be so angry, but I just keep thinking . . ."

"Thinkin' what if it had been your pregnant wife."

Michael swallowed and looked at his lap. "Yeah. I don't know what I would do without them in my life."

That was something Marx could understand. The day Shannon walked out of his life, she had left him barely able to breathe. Life had become nothing but a monotonous cycle of work and sleep until Holly came along and added a little sparkle to his mundane existence.

"I know how that feels," Marx said. "I've lost a lot of people, and you remember the condition I was in when Holly was missin', and I was haunted by *what if* I couldn't find her. *What if* she didn't survive?"

"I remember. Didn't you toss me out of a room?"

"Your feet barely left the floor. That doesn't count."

Michael smiled.

"My point is," Marx continued, "if you live your life by the what-ifs, you're gonna rob yourself of the right-nows. Besides, isn't there somethin' about handin' worries to God or somethin' or other?"

Michael laughed. "Do you even have a Bible?"

"Mmm, I think I had one when I was ten."

Michael's laughter died on a sigh as reality settled back into place. "I know I'm supposed to hand my worries and my fears over to God. But I'm afraid that if I go to Him and I put my baby's life in His hands, He's gonna take that life back. Just like He did with Jonah and Caleb."

Marx floundered for the words he needed to comfort his partner. "Your baby's life has always been in

God's hands. So has yours, your wife's, mine, Holly's. He's got big hands."

Michael chuckled. "You know, you're really terrible at this?"

"Fine, I won't tell you the rest."

"No, go ahead. I really wanna hear it."

"I'm sayin' that you don't have to worry about puttin' your child in God's hands, because she's already there. You focus on prayin' for her health and takin' care of your wife."

Michael turned toward him in the seat. "What if I pray for God to help our baby make it to term, to be born healthy, and He says no? What then?"

Marx stared at the steering wheel. He didn't know how to have this conversation. "Then out there in the world is probably a little girl waitin' for a family, prayin' that a mom and dad walk through that door, pick her up, and tell her that she's loved."

Michael blinked at the moisture in his eyes. "Okay, maybe you're not *so* bad at this." He looked in the mirror to see Karl, and straightened in his seat. "Are we being followed?"

Marx glanced in the rearview mirror, noticing the car less than a hundred feet behind them. He took a casual right turn, and the car followed. "Call it in."

They had expected Thomas to be waiting and watching outside the prison. Karl was his endgame, and he wouldn't risk letting him slip through his fingers and disappear.

Marx followed the route he had planned ahead of time, and Sam, his only immediate source of backup, was exactly where he expected him to be.

He pulled out behind the gray car, closing him in.

Thomas might have been focused on his target, but not so much that he missed the unmarked car behind him, because after the second turn, he swerved into another lane and stomped on the gas.

Sam pulled out after him, cutting through the next traffic light a millisecond before it clicked to red. Marx caught a glimpse of Simmons, Sam's new partner, grinning in the passenger seat as they passed by.

A flashing squad car skidded around the corner in pursuit, and sirens wailed from the other direction.

Marx continued to the motel and pulled into the lot. The two officers who would be protecting Karl for the night were already waiting.

Michael hopped out and opened the rear door. "Out."

Karl scrambled out. "What now?"

Marx leaned across the seat. "Now you check into your room with these officers, and stay out of sight until we find Thomas Mathis." He nodded to the officers, and they stepped forward to take custody of Karl.

"But that could take months!"

Marx doubted it would take more than a week. Thomas wouldn't stop until he found his target, and when he came searching, they would be waiting.

50

*T*homas hissed in a breath of pain through his teeth as he wrapped the bandage around the gash in his arm. It needed stitches, but there wasn't time for a trip to the hospital.

He had almost been caught; that Latino officer and his female partner had been right on his bumper. He'd been forced to abandon his car and flee on foot like some kind of felon.

Finding a place to hide had been his only option; he knew he wasn't fast enough to outrun them.

He'd cut his arm breaking into an apartment. The man who lived there was high out of his mind, slumped in his chair with a needle still in his arm.

Thomas probably could've put his gun to the man's head and he wouldn't have even noticed.

He tore off a piece of medical tape with his teeth and fixed the bandage in place.

That'll do for now, *he decided, pulling his sleeve back down to cover it.*

He only had two more targets—Karl Blakely and Becca Hart—and then he would be finished. As he closed the medicine cabinet, he caught a reflection in the mirror.

"Angie."

His heart staggered at the sight of her. Her hair swept over one shoulder, her warm blue eyes gazing at him with love. He longed to draw her into his arms and hold her, to smell the scent of her perfume on her neck.

"I'm sorry. I tried to get to Karl Blakely before the police, but they moved him," he said. "I'll find him, I swear."

Sadness glinted in her eyes. "Don't do this, Thomas. Just walk away and let it go. Let the anger and hatred die."

He turned to face her. "I can't. I'm doing this for us. For Christine. She never even got to see the world."

"I know, but this isn't right, and some part of you knows that."

"No." He shook his head and rubbed at his temple as he began to pace the bathroom floor, anxiety and anger fueling his steps. "No, this is right. This is what needs to happen. This is justice."

"And what about the innocents?"

"I haven't hurt any innocents. Everyone I've punished has been guilty," he explained.

"Do you really believe that?" She gestured toward the gun on the counter. "That no innocents will be hurt today?"

He wanted her to understand why he had to do this. "Why are you making this harder for me?"

"I only want to protect you from doing something you'll regret."

The sound of a key sliding into a lock drew his attention, and he grabbed his gun off the bathroom counter. "Hide, Angie."

51

$\mathcal{M}$arx tossed his keys on the side table and slid his gun from the holster, setting it down next to them. "I'm home for the night if you wanna head out."

He glanced back at Jordan, who lingered in the hall. Jordan had been sitting outside of the apartment for most of the day, and his eyes were glazed with exhaustion.

Jordan nodded toward the plastic bag Marx was carrying. "What's in the bag?"

"The alarm company can't come until Friday to install the home security system, so I stopped at the hardware store to pick up a few locks for the front door."

"Are you gonna tell Holly?"

"That a man broke into the apartment and was hidin' in her closet? No. And you're not gonna tell her either."

The glimmer of disapproval in Jordan's eyes told him that he didn't agree with keeping Holly in the dark.

"Right now, this is the only place she feels safe, and if you tell her, that feelin' of safety evaporates," Marx explained. "Do you really wanna do that to her?"

Jordan sighed. "No, I don't. But she'll figure it out when she opens the door and finds me sitting in the hall. And I'm not gonna lie to her."

"We'll deal with that when the time comes. Now go home and get some rest before you pass out."

Jordan grabbed his jacket off the floor. "I'll be back tomorrow to keep watch." He paused at the top of the steps, then added, "Actually, maybe I'll take Holly to the park for the day if she wants to go."

"I think that's a good idea."

Jordan started down the steps, and Marx closed the door and flipped the deadbolt. He dropped the bag of sliding locks he had picked up from the hardware store onto the couch and went to fetch his tools from under the kitchen sink.

He wasn't savvy enough to install additional dead bolts, and chain locks were out of the question. From what Jordan had told him, the sound of chain locks sent Holly into a panic, and he seriously questioned their durability.

So he'd gotten the kind of locks found in bathroom stalls. A few of them would provide reinforcement, and no one would be able to pick them. He would just have to knock when he got home so Holly could let him in.

He was gathering his tool kit when the creak of a floorboard behind him sent a tingle of warning up his spine, and he stilled.

"Hello, Detective."

Marx turned slowly to see Thomas standing at the edge of the hallway, a gun in his hand. His gaze slid past him to Holly's door, his heart pounding harder in his chest.

"She's fine," Thomas said.

"Forgive me if I don't take your word for it."

"I don't believe in forgiveness."

"No, you just murder people when they offend you."

Thomas's eyes narrowed. "It's not murder if it's justified. But you know nothing about justice. If you did, you would be helping me instead of trying to stop me."

Marx's attention shifted back to Holly's door, fear pulsing through him. How long had she been alone with this man?

"I haven't touched her," Thomas assured him, sensing Marx's concern. "She doesn't even know I'm here."

Marx prayed that Thomas's moral code, no matter how warped it might be, wouldn't allow him to hurt her. "She's innocent."

"I know. And as long as she stays out of the way, she won't get hurt." He backed into the living room and gestured for Marx to follow. "Hands where I can see them."

Marx held his hands out to his sides as he moved stiffly away from the cupboards, his eyes glued to the gun. "How did you get in here? I had somebody watchin' the apartment."

"I saw the man by the door. I almost gave up waiting for him to leave, but then he stepped into the old lady's apartment across the hall, probably to use the bathroom. He was only gone for a minute, but that was long enough."

Marx clenched his teeth. "I won't tell you where Karl is, so if that's why you're here, you're wastin' your time."

Anger darkened Thomas's face. "You're protecting a murderer. That makes you just as guilty as he is."

"You're not God. You don't get to decide who lives and who—"

"He murdered my family!"

Marx's gaze flickered to Holly's bedroom door, afraid Thomas's raised voice was going to wake her. "Why don't we talk about this outside."

"You know they don't even consider my baby girl a person? To them, she had no more significance than a hangnail. Some inconvenient growth that can be snipped away without consequence. Do you know how long we tried for a baby?" He paused before saying, "Six years. *Six years* and two miscarriages."

Marx held out his hands in a pacifying gesture. "I'm sorry they're gone. I can't even imagine how hard that must've been for you."

Thomas inhaled a sharp breath through his nose and blew it out, fighting to control his grief. "Tell me where to find Karl Blakely, and maybe I'll let you live."

Marx wasn't that naïve. Thomas had already decided he was *guilty*, and he would deal with him the only way he knew how to deal with the *guilty*.

"We both know you're not gonna let me live."

It wasn't the thought of death that scared Marx; it was knowing what would happen to the people he loved after he was gone. His mother and sister would be devastated, and Holly . . .

He worried for her most of all.

She had spent her life running, living in shelters and abandoned buildings, scrounging up food where she could, and hiding from her foster brother. If he died today, he feared she would default to the life she knew.

If she ran, Collin would likely escape conviction, and he would hunt her down and kill her.

Lord, I can't die today, he prayed. There had to be a way out of this situation, a way to reason with Thomas.

"You were in the army," Marx said. "Honorably discharged. You saved lives."

Thomas swiped at a bead of sweat on his forehead. "What's your point?"

"That you're capable of bein' a hero, of bein' the man who saves lives instead of takin' them."

Thomas's head cocked slightly to his left, as if he were listening to someone beside him. "I was a sniper. I took lives, I didn't save them."

"I know from experience that sometimes takin' one life to save another is a necessary evil. I've done it. But what you're doin' now, Thomas . . . this is not the same thing. This is an act of revenge. You decided to go after these people, and you can decide to stop. You get to choose what kind of man you wanna be, and you don't have to be a man who takes lives."

"I do."

Marx glanced at the couch, where Thomas's attention seemed to be. There was no one there. "You could've hurt Holly the last time you were here, but you didn't. You stayed out of sight until you could slip out unnoticed. You went out of your way to avoid hurtin' her."

Thomas glanced at Holly's bedroom door. "I read about what happened to her. She's a victim, and there was no reason to hurt her."

"Or scare her. You protected her from that. There's still good in you, Thomas."

"No, Detective, I'm what's left after everything good has been taken away. Everything that ever meant anything is gone."

Marx recognized the distant gleam in Thomas's eyes—the look of a soul that had been hollowed out by too much pain and loss. He'd seen that look in Holly's eyes too many times before.

The person Thomas used to be had been fractured by grief, leaving fragments of a man who couldn't cope with the loss of his wife and daughter, and fragments of a long-ago soldier who tried to better the world by taking the lives of dangerous, evil people.

He couldn't see that what he was doing was wrong.

"Thomas, there are people who can help you." *They can put you back together*, he wanted to say. "You can be the man your wife fell in the love with again."

Thomas's eyes flickered to his left and he whispered, "No, he's wrong."

Marx tracked his gaze. "He who?"

Thomas growled under his breath, "I don't care if he saved that girl. He's trying to confuse me, to stop me. You know that means I have to get rid of him."

Marx took advantage of Thomas's distraction and reached slowly toward his ankle, where he kept his backup weapon.

"Stop moving! Why are you moving?" Thomas shouted, and Marx froze.

He could go for the gun, but Thomas would likely shoot him before he had it out of the holster.

The quiet click of a door latch from behind Marx made his stomach sink with dread. Holly shuffled into the hall in her pajamas and slippers with an empty glass in her hand.

She stiffened when she saw Thomas—an unfamiliar man in the only place she felt safe—and then she noticed the gun.

The empty glass slipped from her fingers and shattered across the floor. She stumbled back a step, her brown eyes sparkling with fear, and bumped into the wall.

"Sweetheart," Marx said, trying to redirect her attention. He could see the impending panic attack in the hastening of her breaths.

Thomas shifted his weight, unsettled by her sudden appearance, and Marx glanced back at him with concern.

"Please," he pleaded. "Just let me get her back to her room."

"You don't move," Thomas said when Marx started to inch toward Holly. "I don't trust you." He turned his attention to Holly, and his voice softened to a tone that was almost soothing. "Now that you're awake, Holly, I'd like you to stay where I can see you. Have a seat on the floor."

Her eyes widened when he said her name, and she shot Marx a frightened glance.

"There's no reason for her to be out here," Marx snapped. "You're just gonna scare her."

Riley trotted out of the bedroom, his nose scenting the air. The moment he spotted the intruder, his hackles raised, and he let out a snarl as he stepped protectively in front of Holly.

Thomas licked his lips nervously. "Put the dog in the bedroom and close the door."

Holly's gaze shifted between Marx and the intruder, and she swallowed hard. She wrapped trembling fingers around Riley's collar and pulled, but he didn't budge. She tried again, managing to move him a couple inches, but he jerked back, pulling her forward.

"I can't," she said.

"He can sense her fear," Marx explained. "He won't let anybody hurt her, which means he's gonna stay between her and the person he thinks is threatenin' her."

Thomas shifted his jaw in frustration. "Sit down on the floor and keep a hold of him. I don't wanna have to shoot your dog."

Holly shrank to the floor behind Riley, keeping both hands on his collar.

Thomas returned his focus to the matter at hand. "Now tell me where you're hiding the monster who killed my family."

"Karl Blakely is not a monster. He's a man who made a bad choice, and he spent four years behind bars for it."

"That's not good enough!" Thomas yelled, flailing the gun in anger. "I lost everything because of him!"

Holly flinched and choked back a whimper of fear, adding fuel to Marx's already-rising anger. "You're scarin' her."

Thomas's nostrils flared as he panted through his nose, and he struggled to control his temper. "Tell me where he is, or I'll shoot you right now and go get the address from your partner."

Marx's pulse sped up as he thought about Michael and his pregnant wife. He didn't have many choices. "I'll show you where he is. I'll take you to him."

Thomas ran his tongue over his teeth as he considered it. "Okay, but Holly's coming with us."

Marx took a step toward her on reflex. "No. She's not goin' anywhere with you."

Thomas's eyes narrowed. "If it's not a trap, she'll be perfectly fine."

"It's not a trap, but I'm not gonna let you drag her around in the middle of the night at gunpoint. Besides, leadin' you into a trap doesn't do me any favors. I still die."

Holly sucked in a sharp breath at his words.

"Fine," Thomas agreed reluctantly. He gestured toward the door with the gun. "Let's go."

Holly sprang to her feet. "No." She rushed into Marx's path, Riley glued to her heels. "If you go with him, he's gonna kill you. You can't go."

Marx placed his hands on her upper arms and met her eyes. "I'll be fine."

She shook her head, tears shining in her eyes. "You're lying." She turned her back on him and faced Thomas. "I won't let you take him."

Thomas's gaze flicked over her head to Marx. "Get her out of the way."

Marx grabbed her arm to pull her aside, but she wrenched free and stepped forward. "I'm sorry you lost your family. And I'm sorry you're hurting, but that doesn't make it okay to hurt other people."

"You don't know what's going on, Holly," Thomas said, and the way he spoke to her, as if they were old friends rather than strangers, made Marx uneasy.

"You said someone killed your family. That you lost everything. I know how that feels."

"Holly, you don't have to talk to him," Marx said. He didn't want her to talk to him. The man was unstable, and if she said one thing he disagreed with, he might decide she deserved to die too.

"When I was nine, a man broke into our home." Pain-filled tears from that long-ago horror crept into her voice. "I lost everything in one night. My mom, my dad, my sister, my home. My identity." She drew in a steadying breath before adding, "I understand the pain of that loss."

Thomas gazed at her with sorrow. "'Some days I barely feel anything. Like a breathing carcass surrounded by life, but no longer alive myself. My heart is still beating, but my spirit has shriveled up like a dried leaf and crumbled to dust in my chest.'"

Holly drew in a sharp breath and stepped back into Marx. "You—"

"I know you understand." He reached one hand into the bag he had draped over his body and pulled out a purple notebook. "You put into words what I can't."

Marx recognized Holly's journal, the one that had gone missing shortly after Thomas's first visit. He'd taken it. That was why he spoke to her as if he knew her—he had read her most private thoughts and feelings.

The thought of Thomas lounging in a chair while he flipped through Holly's journal infuriated Marx. Hadn't she been violated enough?

"I feel this," Thomas said. "So much of this." He set the journal down on the couch.

Holly wrapped her arms around herself. "If you read that, then you know—Marx is the closest thing I have to family. Please . . . don't take him from me."

"I have to make them pay for what they've done. All of them. For what they've stolen from me."

"I hated the man who killed my family too. He got to live while they were buried in the ground."

"You wanted him to pay," Thomas said.

Holly shook her head. "No. I wanted my family back."

A furrow of confusion appeared in Thomas's forehead. "He deserved to die for what he did."

"Maybe, but the moment he stopped breathing, the moment his cold heart stopped beating—it didn't bring my family back. It didn't erase the pain."

"Holly." Marx caught her elbow and tried to move her behind him, but she wouldn't let him.

"Taking a life will never bring you peace," she explained.

"I won't have peace until they're all dead. Then I can be with my family," Thomas said, and Marx realized that he'd been mistaken about his endgame.

Karl Blakely wasn't the last life Thomas intended to take; he was going to kill himself when he was finished.

Thomas's attention returned to Marx, and he shifted his sweaty grip on the gun. "We're leaving."

Marx tried to step around Holly, but she blocked him again. "Please don't do this."

"Move her." Thomas demanded.

Marx hooked an arm around Holly's waist and picked her up, moving her aside, but she sprang back like a rubber band and flung her arms around his waist.

"Stop it, Holly!" Marx tried to pry her loose, but she had her hands and wrists locked behind him.

Thomas looked at his watch and grumbled, "I don't have time for this. I'll get what I need from your partner. He seems more trustworthy anyway."

"Holly." Marx tried to pull her loose and out of the path of the inevitable bullet. She stretched up onto her toes in an effort to shield him with her small frame.

"Get her out of the way," Thomas demanded, searching for a good shot.

"I'm tryin'!"

"Try harder!" Thomas shouted, his temper climbing by palpable degrees.

Holly let out a whimper of pain as Marx tried to break her grip. He was hurting her, but he didn't have any other choice. "Please, Holly . . ."

She buried her face in his chest as she held on with everything she had. He felt more than heard her muffled cry as he wrenched her arms apart.

"I'm sorry," he whispered.

He scooped her up and flung her into the kitchen with all the strength he had, praying that she would land far enough away from the path of the bullets to be safe. She hit the floor with a yelp and slid into the cupboards.

Marx saw Thomas's finger on the trigger, but the force that slammed into him and took him to the floor wasn't a bullet; it was Riley.

Riley tackled him with a ferocious snarl and sank his teeth into Marx's left arm. Marx let out a curse of pain. Riley ripped into him as if he intended to rend flesh from bone.

Marx tried to fend him off while reaching for the gun in his ankle holster. If he had any hope of surviving, he had to reach it before Thomas found a shot.

He heard Holly screaming in the background as Thomas's feet drew closer.

Come on, come on, Marx pleaded, groping for a solid grip on the handle.

If he failed and Thomas killed him, what would he do to Holly? She had tried to shield someone Thomas deemed guilty, someone who protected a "monster" and disrupted his plans. Would he kill her too?

Someone pounded on the apartment door, and Mrs. Neberkins shouted, "You stop hurting that girl, you hear me?"

Thomas's attention snapped to the front door.

Marx drew his gun and fired. The bullet connected with Thomas's shoulder, knocking him back a step.

Riley yipped and retreated from the sound of the gunshot. A bullet whizzed by Marx's head and hit the cupboard. Without Riley complicating matters, Marx was able to focus his next two shots, planting them center mass.

Thomas's eyes widened with shock, and the gun dropped from his limp fingers as he sank to his knees. He teetered for a moment and then collapsed facedown on the floor.

Marx climbed to his feet and kicked Thomas's gun across the room. He pulled the cuffs from his pocket and cuffed Thomas's wrists behind his back.

He left him to check on Holly. She was huddled on the floor against the cabinets, her arms wrapped tightly around Riley's neck.

Marx set his gun on the floor as he crouched in front of her. "I'm sorry, sweetheart. I'm so sorry."

He looked her over to make sure she was all right. "I'm so sorry," he said again, praying that she wouldn't be afraid of him now. The last thing he ever wanted to do was hurt her.

She released Riley and threw her arms around his neck with a quiet sob. "I thought . . . he . . ."

"I'm fine," he assured her. "He missed." He hugged her tightly, grateful that she was safe, and kissed the top of her head.

Thank you, Jesus.

52

*H*olly sat on a stool at the peninsula, still reeling from the evening's events as she stared at the blood on the living room rug. She hadn't known the man, but his sadness had been so overwhelming that it seemed to linger in the apartment even after the paramedics took him away.

Thomas. That was what Marx had called him. Thomas had survived the bullet wounds to his chest, and she could still hear his gurgling plea: *Just . . . let me . . . die.*

She understood the kind of pain that could rob a person of their will to live, but like Marx couldn't let her take that handful of pills, she couldn't let Thomas give up and die.

Despite Marx's objections, she had knelt on the floor beside the man. He couldn't hurt her, not when he was unarmed and so close to death. She hadn't really given much thought to her words, and she didn't remember them now, but they seemed to comfort him.

"Do you think he's gonna die?"

"I don't know," Marx said. "If he doesn't, he'll spend a long time locked up for all the people he killed."

"What's gonna happen with my journal?" Holly's eyes drifted to the couch, where her journal had been before one of the crime scene people shoved it into a plastic bag and took it with them.

It made her angry that Thomas had stolen it. Maybe he needed to read the words of someone else in pain, but it made her insides queasy to think about him being inside her head.

"They'll fingerprint it, photograph it, and catalogue it, but I'll see if I can get it back."

"The part of my journal he recited," she began, looking up at Marx, but the sadness that flashed in his eyes robbed her of the rest of her words.

"I wish you had told me you feel that way."

She dropped her eyes back to her lap. She didn't want to burden him with her struggles. He had enough to deal with without the added weight of her . . . inability to function.

"I know you're hurtin', sweetheart," he said. "And that sometimes, no matter how hard you fight, it feels like you're barely keepin' your head above water. I know it's exhaustin', but your spirit is stronger than you think it is."

Her leggings blurred as tears welled in her eyes. "It's not."

He hooked a knuckle gently under her chin and lifted her head so he could see her face. "You're a survivor, and even after everythin' he did to you, you're still here. You're still fightin'."

But she was so tired of every day being a struggle, of every moment being overshadowed by what had happened. She just wanted to be . . . normal.

"It takes time to heal. You can't force it. But I promise you, someday you'll look back and realize how far you've come."

She wished she could wrap his words up in a little box and keep them with her, to listen to when she felt like giving up.

Marx held out an ice pack wrapped in a towel. "How's your head?"

She had hit the floor and slid into the cupboards headfirst when he tossed her out of the way, and the cupboard had won, leaving her with a thundering headache. "Not too bad considering I slid all the way to home field."

"It's called home plate, not home field," he said, and she could hear the tension in his voice. He was angry with himself for hurting her, even though he hadn't done it intentionally.

"Are you sure?"

"Positive."

Her eyebrows drew together in confusion as she placed the ice pack on the back of her head. "I thought it had something to do with a field."

"Home plate is part of the infield."

"Oh, so I was close."

He cracked a barely perceptible smile. "Not really. Let me see your arms."

"They're fine. I'm not the one who got used as a chew toy, remember?"

When he just stared at her, she sighed and held out an arm. There was no point in arguing; he wouldn't let the matter drop until he was sure she was okay.

His lips thinned as he inspected the marks on her arms where he had gripped too tightly, and he cast her an apologetic look. "Holly—"

"Please don't apologize again. I'm fine. Just . . . don't throw me anymore, okay?"

"Don't stubbornly stand between me and a shooter, and I won't have to." He fetched a second ice pack and a bag of beans from the freezer.

"Frozen beans?" she asked with a crinkle of her nose. "I hate beans."

"You're not gonna eat 'em." He sat down on the stool beside her. "Give me your arms."

She sighed and held out her arms one at a time to be mummy-wrapped in ice packs and bags of frozen beans. He tended to her soon-to-be bruises and then sat back with a sigh.

She nodded to his bandaged forearm. "Are you gonna need stitches?"

Riley had punctured the skin, sinking his teeth into the muscle of Marx's left arm. The paramedics had bandaged it with strict orders for him to go to the ER the moment he had time.

"Just a scratch," he said.

Men, Holly thought with a roll of her eyes. Marx could lose a leg and he would brush it off with "it's just a scratch."

"I can't believe he attacked you."

"Well, I did throw you across the kitchen." He reached a hand toward Riley, who was hunkered behind Holly's stool. Riley let out a guilty whimper and sank lower to the floor, his tail curled close to his haunches. "Come here."

Riley whimpered and inched forward, scooting across the floor, as if he expected to be reprimanded.

Marx rubbed behind his ear. "Good boy." Riley's tail thumped the floor, and he lifted his head for more love and attention. At Holly's puzzled expression, Marx explained, "He did his job. He protected you from somebody he thought was tryin' to hurt you, even if that person was me."

Holly reached over and petted his head too. Riley licked her hand affectionately, and she smiled.

"Holly . . ." Marx paused for a second, making her worry he was about to deliver bad news. "How would you like to have Christmas with my family this year?"

She cast him a cautiously interested look. "Really?"

"Yes, really."

He talked about his family on occasion, mostly his mom and his sister, and they sounded so warm and loving. "Are you sure your family would be okay with me coming?"

"I think you might have more trouble leavin', because my mama's gonna try to keep you."

She smiled, excited by the idea of a real family Christmas. Someone knocked on the door frame and her excitement gave way to wariness as a stranger stepped into the apartment.

"Hey," Michael said, taking the open door as an invitation. He nodded to Marx before his gaze trailed to the girl seated on the stool beside him.

She was watching him with guarded eyes, her posture rigid. He hadn't seen her since the hospital, and she had no idea who he was. He opened his mouth to introduce himself, but Marx spoke first.

"Holly, this is Michael. He's . . . my partner."

Michael's instinct was to politely offer his hand and tell her it was nice to meet her, but if he stepped any closer, he thought she might take off running.

He directed his chin toward the ice pack she was holding against her head. "What happened? Are you okay?"

He glanced back at the bloodstained area rug where Thomas must have been. Had he hurt Holly?

"Marx was helping me take flying lessons. It was a rough landing," Holly said.

Michael frowned at Marx in confusion, and Marx waved off his unspoken question. "It's a long story. What brings you by?"

"CSU is completely finished, and they said you can go ahead and clean up."

Holly tilted her head. "Why does your voice sound familiar?"

Michael hadn't expected that question, and he floundered for an answer. "I, uh, stopped by to visit while you were in the hospital."

"Why?"

"Well, because . . . their vending machines have taffy, and I like taffy." His attempt at levity fell flat on its face, and she narrowed distrustful eyes at him. He glanced at Marx, who gave a subtle shake of his head.

Now might not be the best time to tell her that he was the detective who worked her kidnapping and assault, but he didn't want to lie to her.

"I'm, uh, also the detective who worked your kidnapping," he finally said, and he watched as understanding settled over her.

She looked faint enough to topple off the stool, and he hoped Marx had quick reflexes. She swallowed and asked, "So you . . . you s-saw . . ."

He had watched the videos of her torment as a part of the investigation, and they had nearly made him lose his breakfast. "I'm sorry, but yeah."

Her large brown eyes, liquid with tears, could rip a guy's heart from his chest. One glance at Marx's face told him that he wasn't the only one feeling it.

Holly slid off the stool and dashed down the hall into a room, slamming the door behind her. Michael winced when he heard her throwing up.

"Sorry," he said. "I didn't mean to upset her."

"It's been a difficult week for everybody. I'll be right back." Marx knocked on the bathroom door before going inside.

Michael couldn't understand Marx's words as he spoke to Holly, but he could hear the soothing tone of his voice.

He leaned against the back of the couch and waited, his mind revisiting the events of the past week. He hated that his wife's pregnancy had shaken his faith, that he could ever think God's plans for their family would be anything less than what was best for them.

Marx had been right, and questioning and doubting God only brought fear and worry. All he needed to focus on was praying for the life of his child and planning for her future.

Marx emerged from the bathroom a few minutes later. "She needs a little time alone."

Michael shifted his grip on the wrapped package in his hand and offered it to Marx. "Brought you a little something. Thought it might come in handy."

Marx accepted the gift with a line of curiosity between his eyebrows. "I'm not sure I deserve a gift after interrogatin' you and lockin' you in a holdin' cell."

"Yeah, well," Michael began, scratching behind his ear. He understood the position Marx had been in, and he couldn't honestly say he would have done things differently if the roles had been reversed, but it still stung. "Just open it."

Marx unwrapped the tissue paper and uncovered an old leather Bible. "Are my Bible quotes that bad?"

"Oh, they're pretty bad. But . . . thank you for what you said in the car about the baby. I was . . . kinda freaking out."

"You would've done the same for me if I were freakin' out."

"True, but I would've gotten the Bible quotes right," he said with a smile. "The Bible's not new, but I had an extra, and I thought it might serve you better than my closet shelf." He glanced at his fitness band when it vibrated. "Well, I apparently gotta head to the store to pick up some Ben and Jerry's and some Prego spaghetti sauce. Kat's hungry. See you tomorrow."

Marx waited for him to leave before he flipped open the Bible. On the inside cover, Michael had drawn a line through the previous written text, and replaced it with "To a friend, from Michael."

53

*M*arx stopped to speak with the doctor outside Thomas's hospital room. "How's he doin' today?

The woman hugged her clipboard to her chest, concern creasing her face. "It's been a difficult day. The antipsychotics are helping, but . . . he's grieving."

Thomas had been involuntarily committed to a psychiatric institution after his wife's death. Her family had been concerned when he began showing up at their homes in the middle of the night, asking if Angie was there. At first, they thought it was a cruel prank—a way to punish them for not being a bigger part of Angie's life—but they quickly realized it was something more.

"He keeps begging to be taken off the antipsychotics," the doctor said. "He says they won't let him see his wife, Angie."

Marx sighed. Thomas probably stopped taking the antipsychotics the last time because it was like losing his wife all over again. "Any violent episodes?"

"Thankfully, no. You should be safe to visit."

Marx looked down at Holly. "Are you sure you wanna do this?"

She was gazing through the open doorway into Thomas's hospital room, and Marx could see the sadness in her eyes. There were no flowers, cards, or balloons. "Has anyone even come by?"

"You'll be his first visitors since he was admitted three days ago."

Holly looked up at the balloon wrapped in a bag that she had insisted on buying, and determination glinted in her eyes. "Yep, we're doing it."

When she was hospitalized, the people who cared about her had filled her room with flowers and stuffed animals, and it had meant a lot to her. She had told him on the way over that she didn't want Thomas's room to be empty. She wanted him to know that someone cared.

Marx caught her arm in a gentle grip, stopping her when she started marching toward the room. "Holly, you understand that he killed a lot of people. He's not the victim."

She met his gaze. "Just because the attack comes from the inside instead of the outside doesn't mean he's not a victim. You can fight a mugger or a killer, but how are you supposed to fight your own mind?"

"Sweetheart—"

"When I was gonna take those pills, I tried so hard to make myself put them back in the bottle. I tried to talk myself out of it. But my mind saw it as the right thing to do, as the only option. I needed help, and you were there." She gestured toward Thomas's room. "Who did he have?"

"I understand your point, but he killed five innocent people, and their families are not gonna see it that way."

She dropped her gaze. "I know. They're grieving, and they have a right to be angry and hurt. If he'd shot you, I would be too."

He smiled, knowing she had more to say. "But . . ."

"But I see a sad man, struggling against his own mind, surrounded by coldness and hatred, grieving for his wife and daughter, and for the people he hurt."

Marx peered into the room at Thomas, who lay on his back, staring at the ceiling, with both wrists handcuffed to the bed rails.

Holly had a heart twice the size of her body, and when she saw someone suffering, she felt driven to help them. He just wished she would pick someone who hadn't murdered five people while on a psychotic rampage.

"All right, but you keep your distance from him."

She offered him a comical expression that communicated how pointless his statement was, considering she kept her distance from all men except him.

"Don't you give me that smarty-pants expression."

He nodded to the officer posted outside the door before stepping into the hospital room. Although Thomas must have heard their footsteps, he didn't react to their presence.

Holly took a small step forward and said tentatively, "Hi, Thomas."

The sound of her voice snapped him out of his grief-induced paralysis, and he looked toward his unexpected visitors with eyes swollen from the relentless pressure of tears. His focus shifted from Holly to Marx. "Why did you bring her here? I'm dangerous."

Marx folded his arms across his chest. "It wasn't my decision."

Thomas's eyes rolled back toward the ceiling, and he stared at the tiles as if he hoped they might collapse on top of him and put him out of his misery. "I told you to let me die."

"That wasn't my decision either."

"We couldn't just let you die," Holly said.

"I killed people. Some of them . . . *most* of them begged for their lives, and I . . ." Thomas twisted his wrists, rattling the cuffs against the bars, then dropped his hands back to the blanket with a strangled sob. "I don't even know who I am anymore."

The antipsychotics had brought him back to reality, one that he didn't know how to handle. Holly's desire to help him suddenly made sense.

"God knows who you are," Holly said. "You should ask Him."

"God," Thomas began, his tone mocking. "He's the one who did this to me. He took my family and left me with nothing."

"My family's gone too. But God didn't take them to hurt me any more than He took yours to hurt you." She sat down in the chair a few feet from the bed. "He rescued them from a broken world, from the pain and suffering caused by other people's decisions and mistakes. But He doesn't leave us with nothing, Thomas,

He leaves us every beautiful memory and a promise of hope."

"There is no hope. Not for me."

"That's not true. Followers of Christ will be with Him in heaven, which means if your wife believed and you believe, you will be together again one day."

Thomas sat up as much as the handcuffs would allow, and leveled a look at Holly that made Marx uneasy. "The only way I will ever get to heaven is if I murder the angels at the front gate and steal the keys. Because that's what I do. I kill people."

Marx stepped closer to Holly, his attention fixed on Thomas. "Sweetheart, maybe it's time to go."

"No." Holly popped out of her chair and crossed the room with determined steps, skillfully evading Marx's attempt to catch her. "I'm not done." She stared Thomas down as she said firmly, "You're gonna listen to me."

Marx's eyebrows crept up with surprise, and inched up even further when Thomas slouched back down in the bed, defeated. His attempt to scare her off had failed. There was nothing left to do but listen.

"You broke into Marx's apartment. You stole my journal and read it. You pointed a gun at him, and you threatened to take away the closest person I have to family."

Thomas closed his eyes and turned his face away from her. "That's the kind of man I am." He tried to sound indifferent, but regret and shame haunted his voice.

"I forgive you."

He froze for just an instant, then blinked up at her, moisture clinging to his lashes, as if he thought he'd misheard. "What?"

She leaned closer, just a hairsbreadth out of his reach in case he leaned forward, and repeated, "I. Forgive. You."

Emotions flickered across Thomas's face— shock, hope, shame, and finally doubt. "I don't deserve forgiveness."

"It's not about what you deserve. None of us *deserve* forgiveness. Jesus gave His life for our sins because He loves us, and He wanted to give us the gift of grace and forgiveness."

"The things I did . . ."

"You were sick, Thomas. That doesn't make it okay, but . . . it makes it easier to understand."

Thomas dropped his head back into the pillows and stared at the ceiling, trying to work through her words.

"I've done things I regret. And I would do almost anything to go back and change them, but . . . I can't," Holly said, and Marx knew she was talking about what happened the night her family died. She felt like she had abandoned them, but she had only been a child. "I have to live with my choices and the consequences that come with them, just like you will, but even if you spend the rest of your life behind bars, you don't have to be imprisoned by the choices you've made."

"You're talking about freedom through God."
When Holly nodded, Thomas gazed at her with a strange sort of affection. "You remind me so much of Angie."

Marx shifted closer, uncomfortable with him comparing Holly to his dead wife. If he had another psychotic episode, he didn't want him fixating on her.

"She would talk about Jesus, like He was the only way."

"He is. And if you let Him, He can bring beauty from the ashes of people's flawed, selfish decisions, and He can bring peace in the middle of unimaginable pain."

"Does He bring you peace?"

Holly wrapped her arms around her stomach, hugging herself. "Sometimes, when I'm not . . . strong enough, when I can't handle it on my own, He does."

"I think I saw that, when I was in your closet. You were crying, but when you started to pray, something changed."

She looked between Marx and Thomas with a frown. "You were in my closet?"

"The day I took your journal."

"You should . . . probably not make a habit of hiding in people's closets."

"I don't think that'll be a problem where I'm going." He dropped into contemplative silence for a moment before asking, "I can understand how God can forgive someone like you, but we're very different people."

"Well, you're a little taller, and you don't have as much hair, but I don't think God will hold either of those things against you."

A hint of a smile touched Thomas's lips. "That's good to know."

"I can help you, if, um, if you want me to pray with you," she offered, then added quickly, "But I'm not gonna hold your hand while we pray."

"After what I read in your journal, I wouldn't expect you to." When Holly lowered her gaze, he said, "I'm sorry that I took it, that I read it."

"Why did you?"

"Because it helped me feel like I wasn't alone in my pain, and it made me feel connected to another human being when I felt disconnected from everything."

"I guess that makes sense." She turned and offered her hand to Marx. "Pray with me?"

Marx took her small hand in his and approached Thomas's bedside. If anyone at the precinct found out that he was visiting and praying for a man who killed a cop and a judge, he would probably find more "traitor" comments posted on his desk.

But he would deal with that when the time came.

He listened as Holly told Thomas about how she found Jesus and about the people in the Bible—murderers and prostitutes—who were forgiven. The most unlikely of people who became the hands and feet of Christ, carrying His hope and love out into the world.

And then she bowed her head to pray. Marx said a silent prayer of his own, thanking the Lord for Holly, and for all the love and light she spread, even if she didn't know it.

Thomas blinked at the flood of tears in his eyes when they said amen, then looked at Marx. "I'm sorry that I broke into your apartment, and that I almost shot you."

"Twice," Marx added. "On both counts. But given your frame of mind at the time, I'll give you a pass." The legal system wouldn't, but there was nothing he could do about that.

Holly unwrapped the purple balloon she had brought and tied it to the visitor chair. Marx had tried to tell her that men didn't like purple, but she insisted it was more blue than purple. It was about as blue as the sun was green, but he was never going to win that argument.

Now Thomas had a large purple balloon that said, "Get well soon." And as it spun with the faintest breeze, it revealed the message on the back side: "You are loved."

Epilogue

*M*arx dropped Holly off at home before taking a trip to the county jail. He stood beside a table in the visitor's room, waiting.

The walls had been painted a fresh coat of white, and the tables had been updated since the last time he was here. The man he was here to see didn't deserve clean walls and nice tables; he deserved a dark hole in the ground.

Other prisoners sat at tables with their families, chatting and trying to pretend that everything was normal. Unfortunately, children visiting their fathers in lockup was becoming all too common.

A door buzzed, and a guard escorted a prisoner into the room.

With black hair that offset his porcelain skin and chiseled features, Collin Wells was what most women would describe as handsome. No one would look at him and see the monster beneath the mask.

Unlike Thomas, whose grief had broken his mind and left him tormented and confused, Collin took pleasure in the pain and suffering of others. He had no capacity for empathy or remorse, and he spent his free time thinking up new ways to torture defenseless girls.

Collin's black brows knitted together briefly when he saw Marx, and then his face relaxed into the smug expression he typically wore. "Richard, how unexpected."

"You look like you're enjoyin' your stay," Marx said.

Collin let out a grunt of indifference as he sat down at the table. "The entertainment's lacking. Third-rate television channels, no one intelligent enough to hold a conversation with, and . . . no pretty redheads to play with."

Marx nodded toward the six-foot red-haired man to his left, whose tattoos took on a life of their own when he moved his thick arms. "Play with him. He looks friendly."

Collin smiled. "Not my type." He leaned forward and interlaced his fingers on the tabletop. "Speaking of pretty redheads, how is my sweet sister?"

"You think you can scare her into silence with this?"

He tossed the crinkled letter on the table, and Collin picked it up, looking it over. "I'm not sure I know what you mean."

Marx planted his hands on the table, meeting Collin's frigid blue gaze. "I will not let you play mind games with her. Any contact with her is a violation of the protection order she has against you."

Collin smiled, his relaxation never wavering. "If you think there's any way to prove I sent her this letter, you might want to consider a career change, because you're not a very good detective."

"You addressed it to 'my little bird.'"

"Well, someone certainly did, but I don't see Holly's name or mine on here. And unless there's a return address linking this letter to me, you've got nothing."

"You had it hand-delivered to avoid a postal trail."

"I suppose I also teleported out of my cell and dropped it at your door."

"I checked the visitor log for the day before the letter was dropped off. Your mother came by."

Collin shrugged. "She misses me. Understandable considering I'm her only son."

"I think you gave her the letter to pass along to Holly."

"Even if that's true, I have no control over what my mother does. She might not be very smart, but she has some degree of independent thought. If she delivered something to someone, that was entirely her choice."

"Since when do you give women a choice?"

Collin rolled his eyes. "Don't be barbaric, Detective. She's my mother."

"And by your own words, Holly is your sister. Obviously *family* isn't off-limits to you."

Collin's lips curled into a slow smile. "Well, if you want to paint the picture that way, I suppose Holly's the exception." He leaned forward, his face mere inches from Marx's, and lowered his voice. "You know, sometimes I can still hear her screaming. Can you?"

A muscle flexed in Marx's jaw. "That letter is the last one you write to her. And your mother . . . stays away from her."

With what Holly had told him about her time in the Wells's household, he didn't want that woman anywhere near her.

"I think about her every night," Collin continued. "Those pretty eyes filled with fear. And those plaintive little whimpers she would make when I—"

Marx slammed his fists onto the table and the visitor lounge dropped into stunned silence. "One more word . . ." And Collin's face would be hitting the table next.

Collin lifted his eyebrows. "You should really see someone about your violent temper, Detective. It makes me genuinely concerned for Holly's safety."

Marx leaned forward and whispered, "If I were you, I'd worry more about my own safety."

"And why is that?"

Marx smiled and said loudly, "Because jail can be a very difficult place for child molesters like you."

Collin stiffened fractionally and looked around the room. Everyone in the room was staring at him, and mothers were holding their children closer. "Holly isn't a child."

"Not anymore. But she was, what, about the age of that little girl right there the first time you attacked her." Marx gestured to the teenage girl sitting next to her mother at the red-haired man's table.

The other inmate's eyes bored into Collin with violent intensity, and Collin swallowed. "Are you trying to get me killed?"

"Of course not. But that phone call would make my day." Marx straightened and nodded toward the guard by the wall to signal that they were finished. "We'll see you in court."

Collin stood and stepped closer to Marx, his voice lowering to a menacing whisper. "That all depends, Detective."

"On what?"

Collin's next words made Marx's stomach clench with dread. "On whether or not our sweet little Holly makes it to the courthouse."

C.C. Warrens

The Holly Novels

Interested in seeing more with these characters?
Check out **The Holly Novels** to see where it all began.

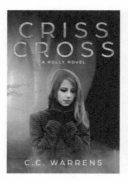  

Acknowledgments

Immeasurable amounts of prayer went into this book, so I have to thank God that it came to completion. A lot has happened that has made writing difficult, but God has seen me through it.

I want to thank my husband for supporting my dream and encouraging me even when I felt like giving up, and for going on walks with me to be my random-idea sounding board.

I want to thank my families for reading my books and eagerly awaiting more.

I want to thank every reader who takes the time to get in touch or leave me positive feedback. Your words are treasured! And a special thank-you to my beta readers (you know who you are) for being so willing to read and give me feedback to help make the story even better!

About the Author

C.C. Warrens grew up in a small town in Ohio. Never a social butterfly, she enjoyed painting, sketching, and writing, with the occasional foray into theater acting. Writing has always been a heartfelt passion, and she has learned that the best way to write a book is to go for a walk with her husband. That is where the characters—from their odd personalities to the things that make them bubble over with anger—come to life.

How to Connect

Facebook: https://www.facebook.com/ccwarrens
Website: https://www.ccwarrensbooks.com/
Email: cc@ccwarrensbooks.com

Made in United States
Troutdale, OR
02/13/2024

17656901R00213